P9-AFW-403

GRACE

Also by Elizabeth Nunez

Beyond the Limbo Silence

Bruised Hibiscus

Discretion

When Rocks Dance

GRACE

A NOVEL

ELIZABETH NUNEZ

ONE WORLD
BALLANTINE BOOKS · NEW YORK

A One World Book
Published by The Ballantine Publishing Group

Grateful acknowledgment is made for permission to reprint an excerpt from "The Nine Owned Trees" from *Voices Over Water* by D. Nurkse. Copyright © 1996 by D. Nurkse. Four Way Books, New York.

www.ballantinebooks.com/one/

Library of Congress Cataloging-in-Publication Data
Nunez, Elizabeth.
Grace / Elizabeth Nunez.—1st ed.
p. cm.
ISBN 0-345-45533-9
I. Title.
PS3564.U48 G73 2003
813'.54—dc21

2002026260

Manufactured in the United States of America

Designed by Jaime Putorti

First Edition: March 2003

10 9 8 7 6 5 4 3 2 1

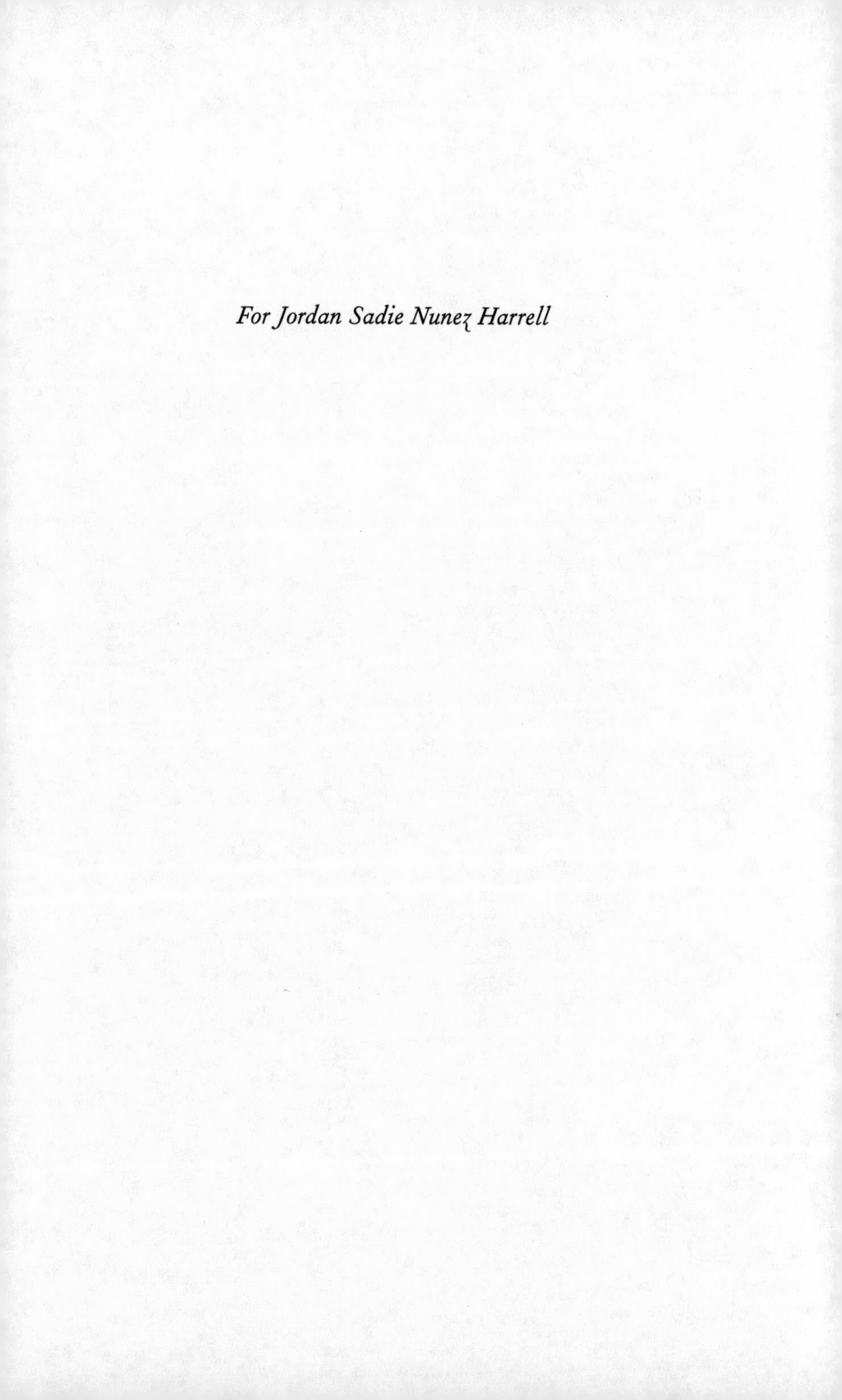

For Jordan Sadie Nunez Harrell

ACKNOWLEDGMENTS

I am grateful to the Reed Foundation for a Vera Ruben Residency Fellowship at Yaddo, where much of this novel was written. I am grateful for the critical eye of wonderful friends who read early drafts: Anne-Marie Stewart, Patricia Ramdeen Anderson, Arthur Flowers, Brenda Greene, my cousin Tony Simpson, and Jamal Greene who provided essential information. I am grateful to my agent, Ivy Fischer Stone, who stayed in my corner, Anita Diggs, my first editor, who asked insightful questions, and my final editor, Elisabeth Dyssegaard, whose guidance in the end was crucial. Mostly, I am grateful to my students at Medgar Evers College, the City University of New York, who keep me honest, and to my son, Jason Harrell, whose love bolsters me.

GRACE: 4. a. A disposition to be generous or helpful; goodwill. b. Mercy; clemency. 5. A favor rendered by one who need not do so; indulgence. 6. A temporary immunity or exemption; a reprieve. 8. *Theol.* a. Divine love and protection bestowed freely on people. b. The state of being protected or sanctified by the favor of God. c. An excellence or a power granted by God.

—*The American Heritage College Dictionary*

ONE

He wakes up one morning tracing letters in his head: the serpentine curl of the *S* in Sally, the rigid lines of the *N* in no, shimmering in capital, straight up, straight down, then up again. Capital *S*, capital *N*. Words appear before him as in a mirage and then become concrete, the letters sharp and defined. *Sally does Not love me.* Sight reaches sound and sound his tongue. He says the words aloud: Sally does Not love me.

It is a posture of indifference he affects. He does not want to lose her. He is afraid, and this fear feeds his delusion that can devalue her, make her unimportant to him. *Sally does not love me,* he repeats in his head, and then he adds, *Justin does not care.*

It is a dismal morning in March, the beginning of the month, the beginning of the first year of a new millennium, 2001, and she has come in that proverbial way, like a lion, blowing chilly winds the day before across the city that by night were leaden with snow. In the bleary light of this early dawn, Justin fixes his eyes on the oak tree outside his window, standing stoic, rigid against the wind that has long stripped it bare of leaves and threatens its branches. In the cups they form with the trunk, the snow is thick. Dense.

This tree is too big for this too-small city garden in Brooklyn, he thinks, both he and it in the wrong place: it there, he here. In the right climate for an oak tree, but not in this garden. In the right house for him, but not in this marriage.

Outside it is quiet, still like the dead. Inside, the scuttle of feet on the hardwood floor beneath him. She is up. Already in the dining room. Five steps, and in the kitchen. He closes his eyes and makes a bet with himself: He will hear the latch on the canister next, the place where she keeps her teas. Today, perhaps, Celestial Awakenings. He cannot be sure. Bounteous Sunlight, Early Sunrise, Heavenly Mornings: her panacea, her simple-minded answer to life's disturbing questions.

But the name of the tea is not part of his bet. His bet is that she will open the green canister, take out a bag of herbal tea, reach in the cupboard for a blue mug with little white flowers, fill the red kettle with water, turn on the fire, and sit with her face to the sun, planning her day while the water boils.

Primary colors: the green on the canister, the deep blues and whites on the mug, the red on the kettle, the yellow of her bathrobe. These are the colors that make Sally feel safe. A primary school teacher, she teaches these colors to the children in her class. Perhaps it is the color red she thinks of now, her lesson for the day. Perhaps the red kettle, whistling now, its shrill call piercing the silence, the signal he has been waiting for. His bet.

The herbal tea is to keep her calm, to chase away yesterday's worries: the bad news on TV last night, bills to be paid, the rash on Giselle's ankle. Giselle is their four-year-old daughter.

"Do you think she got it at the baby-sitter's?" she asked him last night.

"I don't think there's anything to be worried about."

"All the same." She rubbed calamine lotion on their daughter's tiny ankle. "You don't have to teach at the college tomorrow. Maybe she should stay home with you. If it gets any worse, you can take her to the doctor."

"It's a little rash, Sally. All children get a little rash."

"It's a rash. It does not matter if it is little or not."

"These things are normal for a child her age."

But little things like that worried Sally. Not the big things. Not that she did not love him when she married him. Not that she does not love him now. Not that he does not care.

"A rash is no reason to take her to the doctor," he said.

"Nothing bothers you, right?" Her face was tight with anger. "I wish I could be so casual."

He did not want a fight with her, not in front of their daughter. "Giselle can stay home with me," he said.

At night, in their bed, she asked, her voice soothing then: "Are you sure?"

The irritation he felt hours ago had not dissipated. "What is it you want, Sally? I said she can stay home with me tomorrow."

"Won't that be a problem for you? I mean, with your papers to grade?"

"Giselle is never a problem for me."

That was how they ended the night, his words thickening the air between them, she turning on the bed without saying good night, he closing his book, switching off the light on his night stand, and brooding: *Sally does Not love me* hovering in the dark recesses of his brain, not yet a shimmering mirage.

But he knows this morning she wants to be happy. When the little children file into her classroom, she wants the smile on her face to be bright. She wants no furrows on her forehead, no darkness around her eyes. It is to be a Heavenly Morning, a Celestial Awakening.

"Good morning, children."

She will sing out the words, her eyes trained to exude sunshine.

"Good morning, Mrs. Peters."

Mrs. Peters is happy. The children are happy. The children are happy because Mrs. Peters is happy.

This has become the essence of Sally's philosophy. Happiness is learned, she says. It is a skill like any other skill. Bad things come when they come. They cannot be stopped. I teach my children how to be happy. I show them how to forget the bad things.

She made this discovery, she told him, by accident, during a very bad time in her life. The man she loved had been murdered. She was driving home one day, tears almost blinding her, when graffiti on a wall caught her eyes. Someone had scrawled:

It takes strength to be happy. "Those words changed my life," she said.

Which is why, lying on his bed this morning, Justin Peters knows that something is very wrong with his wife. It is not working, this skill she has taught herself. For some time now he has heard the heaviness in her voice, seen the darkness under her eyes. She is hiding something. He is certain of it.

A week ago she left the house before dawn. To prepare for her class trip, she said. She would be taking the kindergarten class to the Bronx Zoo. Ten boys, nine girls. Four parents would accompany them. She wanted to be in the school early, to get everything in order. Justin agreed to take Giselle to the babysitter's and to pick her up after his classes.

Not to worry, he said. He had everything under control. He would get pizza for dinner.

When she came to say good-bye that morning, it was obvious: neither Celestial Awakenings nor Heavenly Mornings had worked its magic. The circles under her eyes were dark, the lines around her mouth stiff.

Now, as he tries to reconstruct that morning, he cannot remember if he asked about the circles, but he remembers that she offered an explanation.

"I always get so worried before a trip. It's such a responsibility. The children are so young."

"But parents will be there."

"Four children for each adult," she said. "Though not quite."

"That seems more than enough."

"I'd be worried if Giselle were on a class trip," she said.

"Giselle is not in school."

"I mean when she goes to kindergarten. I can't imagine what I would do without Giselle. She is my life."

He believes now that at that moment she was thinking of the consequences of the discovery of her secret. *She is my life.* She said it as if there were a real possibility that something could happen and Giselle could be out of her life, that she could lose her. Then, that morning, he wanted to reassure her. He kissed her and held her to his chest. "Giselle will always be with you, Sally," he said.

Now he lies in his bed and recalls that she came home late that evening. When she slid next to him on the couch, she was trembling.

"It was terrible," she said. "One of the children got sick at lunch. She was vomiting and vomiting. Something she ate. I thought she would never stop."

He put his arm around her and she curled into him.

"I took her to the hospital."

"Didn't you call her parents?"

"Her mother came."

"She couldn't get off from work, huh?" Even when he said it, he knew he was covering for her. He had already made a mental calculation. If the child got sick at lunchtime and the mother came immediately, as any mother would, Sally would not have been needed and there would have been no reason for her to be home so late.

Why had he helped her? Was it fear? Was it because he was

not yet ready to face the truth of his suspicions? For more than month she had turned away from him in bed, and when she consented, their lovemaking was passionless. She went through the motions, but she wanted to be done. "Come," she said, she urged him on. She wanted it to end.

Then there were the phone calls. Five when the caller hung up. Three times in the last month when she abruptly ended her conversation on the phone as he entered the room. All the signs were there that something, someone, was pulling her away from him. And yet that day he supplied her with an excuse.

"They're so helpless when they get sick," she said. "The little girl was so weak, she couldn't stand up. I had to lift her. They need their mothers when they are so young."

He connects that statement and the one she made earlier that morning and finds himself thinking the impossible: *If you do not love me, Sally, Giselle will not always be with you.*

She comes in the bedroom and hands him his coffee. "Are you sure you'll be okay with Giselle?"

"Haven't I always been okay with Giselle?"

"You know what I mean. You have work to do."

"I will take her to the park," he says. "When we come back, she'll be sleepy and when she sleeps, I'll correct my papers."

"I'll get her ready," she says.

"You don't have to. Let her sleep late. I'll dress her."

She hesitates. "I may come home late this evening," she says, and walks into the bathroom.

She cannot be this cunning, he thinks. It is she who suggested that Giselle remain with him today. It is he who said Giselle's rash wasn't all that bad. But in the end, it is he, not she, who is insisting that Giselle stay at home.

She wants to be free, he thinks. She does not want to be encumbered. Not by a child, not by their daughter. Not by an obligation that would have her interrupt whatever she is doing, with whomever she is doing it, in the late afternoon.

Before she leaves, she kisses the sleeping Giselle. She does not kiss him.

"Is there something you want to tell me, Sally?" He has come downstairs. She has her hands on the doorknob, but he is unable to let her leave without asking the question.

She turns. "We'll talk," she says. "When I get home."

TWO

He has it all wrong.

"I know you're seeing someone," he says.

Justin begins this accusation at breakfast. It is late in the morning. He has already taken Giselle to the baby-sitter. When he returns, Sally is in the kitchen mixing batter for pancakes.

He does not teach today. Last night he persuaded Sally to call in sick. She did not need persuasion. She had come home with a headache. It was quarter to eight when she turned the key in the front door. He had checked the clock.

"I know you are having an affair," he says. And yet he does not mean that exactly. He does not believe there has been consummation. He believes that someone is seducing her and she is weakening. That and nothing more. Machismo will not allow him consummation.

He is a big man, a man one could call a macho man, which he isn't, not in the sense that he wears his manhood as a badge of honor. But the expectations of others can be demonic. Only surrender gives reprieve. Sometimes Justin surrenders, sometimes he confuses his size with his pride, and Justin's pride will not allow him to believe that his wife is sleeping with another man.

Dressed as he is today in black jeans and a close-fitting black turtleneck sweater—his usual attire, except for the black or gray jacket he wears in his classroom—it is obvious he is sinew not fat—broad shoulders, muscular arms, a washboard torso, and long sturdy legs. He has a typical Trinidadian face, he is told by fellow Trinidadians. He knows what they mean. In his veins, as in the veins of so many from the Caribbean, runs the blood of people continents and islands apart, histories smeared with ravage and conquest. On his mother's side, African, French, and Carib Indian; on his father's side, African, English, and Arawk Indian.

He is at ease with this ancestry, confounded by the irony of the flag-wavers of cultural diversity who would have him eliminate more than half his forefathers to lump himself in that political catchall called black. We are the true originators of multiculturalism, he tells them. It is a stance that does not gain him popularity at the small public college in Brooklyn where he teaches British literature and sometimes the Classics when he is permitted.

Yet it is this bouillabaisse of cultures that has made Justin handsome. His skin is brown, the color of sapodillas, his hair darker brown and wavy, his eyes grayish green, his lips neither too thin nor too thick. Still, there is in his mannerism something not quite Caribbean. His face lacks the openness of people on the islands. He is guarded—his expressions less expansive than they were when he left Trinidad, a young man barely nineteen, to accept a scholarship at Harvard. He will not hug his friends as he used to. He will not let his arm linger on their shoulders. And this not only because of his age. It is America that has taught him wary walking.

"Perhaps you have not done anything about it yet," he says to Sally, "but even if you have not done anything physical, it is still an affair if you love him." And that, too, he does not believe nor want to believe.

She sits, puts down the batter, props up her arms by her elbows, which are bent on the table, holds her head between her hands and begins to cry uncontrollably. One or two words slip out between her sobs, but he cannot make them out.

"Is it *that* serious?" he asks her.

"No. No." It seems to him that this is what she is saying.

He is unforgiving. "Whether it is serious or not, we cannot go on this way."

"It's not an affair," she says. She is saying something else but the words are indistinct.

"Call it what you like," he says, but he is hopeful. What he wants, what he needs, is reassurance. "Infidelity is infidelity," he says.

"It's not an affair." She is looking directly at him as she repeats this. The whites of her eyes are crisscrossed with tiny squiggly red lines, and below them the skin is almost navy blue, but these eyes are large and round, and though they are sad now, they fit perfectly in a face made for them: the wide cheekbones, the nose that curves slightly at the end, the lips full and heart-shaped. She is wearing blue jeans and an off-white V neck sweater. The V exposes her skin. It is flawless. Like burnished copper. She is tall, with narrow hips and full breasts. Any man would forgive him for being jealous over her. But Justin is not jealous over her, so he tells himself. He is angry with her, a righteous anger for which he has cause. She is hiding something from him.

"I want things to change," she says.

"You want things to change?" He does not let up. His tone is almost a sneer.

"I can't keep doing this."

"I would imagine you can't. It must be difficult juggling two lives." The sneer is full-blown now, though at the edges of his lower lip a slight tremor betrays him.

"You don't understand. There is nobody else. There is no other man."

He folds his lip into his mouth and presses his upper teeth against it.

"No other man, Justin," she says.

No other man. It is all he wants to hear, but it will not do him good to have her see him cave in so quickly, to give her this advantage. "And if it is not an affair," he asks, "then what?"

"I am not happy, Justin."

"And when did you discover that?"

Last night, in spite of her headache, she gave Giselle her bath and sang nursery songs to her.

Hush little baby don't you cry,
Mama's gonna buy you a mocking bird,
and if that mocking bird don't sing,
Mama's gonna buy you a diamond ring,
and if that diamond ring is brass,
Mama's gonna buy you a . . .

It is a song for a baby and Giselle is four, but she loves it.

"What else are you going to buy me, Mama?"

"Mama may not be able to buy you everything you want, but Mama will give you all the love in the world."

"How much?" the child asked.

He imagined her opening her arms as wide as she could when she answered, "As much as this and more, much more."

Giselle makes her happy, he thinks.

"You have not been happy, either," Sally is saying to him. She has stopped crying. Her hair had fallen across her face when she bent her head. Bits of it are still stuck to her wet cheeks. She pushes them away. The natural color of her hair is dark brown, but she has lightened it and wears it in a cascade of tight curls that reach just above her shoulders.

"Don't try to weasel yourself out of this," he says. "We are talking about you."

"I am not trying to weasel myself out of anything. You, me, we have not been happy."

But we were happy once.

"Are you having some sort of midlife crisis?" She will be forty on her next birthday. It is a reasonable explanation. Perhaps that is what it is.

"No," she answers simply.

"I am happy," he says.

"Liar."

"I was happy until you started acting strangely. Coming home so late."

"I went for a long walk last night."

He has to make an effort not to say, *To read new graffiti on the walls in the street? For God's sake, how does one learn how to be happy?* He has asked her that question many, many times.

"What do you want?" he asks.

"More."

"More what?"

"More to my life."

She was already a primary school teacher when he met her, but before that she had been an assistant editor at a small press in Manhattan. She wanted to be a poet and believed that being close to literary circles would give her the courage—courage is what she said it took—to harness the thoughts that swirled in her head.

Though by chance he had seen four of her poems, he made himself accept the reasons she gave him for changing her job. Jealousy? Fear? They were love poems. Written to a lover she had not forgotten? The passion in them frightened him so he chose to believe what she told him. The big publishing companies were merging, swallowing everything in their way. Goliath struck the small press and it folded. And as if that were not enough, the poetry she was writing was no longer in vogue. Not for an African American writer, she said. She did not do performance poetry and she did not have the ear for rap. She was an anachronism at thirty.

But she was good with children. She loved them, a fact not lost on Justin when they were dating. He had been thinking it was time he had children. Then Giselle was born and she had no time for poetry. He and Giselle were enough, she said. She did not need more.

"It isn't that I don't love you," she says to him now.

The double negative that is supposed to be a positive.

"Is that the same as saying 'I love you'?" He asks the question, but not kindly. He does not feel kindly toward her.

"You know I love you."

"And how would I know that? You turn away from me in bed."

"That is not true, Justin."

"You make love as if it is some chore you have to do."

"You have not made it easy."

"*I* have not made it easy? You think it is easy to put my arms around you when I can sense you don't want me, that you are just doing your wifely duty?"

"It's sex you want, Justin. I want more than sex."

He laughs, but it is not a happy laugh. He laughs for relief for there is truth in what she says. When he heard breathing on the receiver, he was certain. Perhaps he was wrong to jump to this conclusion, but then he was convinced that someone was there, waiting, hoping it would be she who would answer. The third time he turned cold with resentment and that night he acted the part of father, the role of supporting husband. He washed the dishes after dinner, read a bedtime story to Giselle and helped tuck her in bed, asked the usual questions about Sally's day at work, offered anecdotes of his own, but all the time he guarded the wall he built around his heart, deepening his distance from her. He would not touch her when they went to bed. He would not let her humiliate him. Then familiar smells, the particular sweet odor of her skin, the scent of her soap and the lotion she smothered on afterward reminding him of the sea, the warmth of her body, the angles and curves next to him, aroused memories, habit. Desire, that traitor.

For sex? Let her call it desire for sex, but it was love, too. That is what he felt when his resolve melted away and he reached for her.

"And what more do you want?" he asks. He does not know what answer he hopes or wants to get.

"We can try," she says.

"Love is not something you try to do," he says. "Either you love me or you don't. Either you want to be with me or you don't."

"I want to be with you, Justin. I love you."

"But?" He asks the question harshly, the tone belying the hope that sprang in his heart.

"But . . ."

She sends his heart plunging again.

"I need more," she says.

"More?"

She turns her head away from him. "There is nothing you can do. *I*," she emphasizes the *I*, "I have to do it myself. *I* have to make me happy."

Her repudiation stings him. "It was only graffiti, Sally," he says. His lips curl. "Some mindless jerk's scribbling. That's all it was."

She strikes back. "I am sorry I ever told you about it. To you intellectuals, anything that doesn't come out of a book is some mindless jerk's scribbling. Mindless or not, I believe him."

"Do you hear yourself, Sally? You believe him? Some anonymous . . ." He struggles for a word. "Wall-defacer," he spits out.

"Yes, I believe him." She repeats the line she saw on the wall. "'It takes strength to be happy.' I want that strength, Justin. I want the strength to go after my happiness. I don't want to take the road of least resistance."

The word *road* stirs another memory of another conversation. "God, you fill your head with all that psychobabble."

"It was a good book. I learned a lot from it. It helped me."

"It helped you become dissatisfied with what you have. It helped to make you unhappy. We have so much, Sally."

They are locked in silence. *We have so much.* Both of them know it is true.

They are sitting in the spacious kitchen of a duplex apartment they own, in a converted brownstone in gentrified Fort Greene, Brooklyn. Trees line their street, and in the spring there will be flowers in the concrete barrels on the pavements and in the flower boxes under the windows of parlor floors of the other refurbished century-old buildings on their block. On one end of their street—comfortably distant from the squalor of Fulton Street, which in their area has already begun to change, replaced by boutiques and charming restaurants—is an old stone Methodist church, itself under renovation. At the other end is Fort Greene Park. Mothers take their children there, lovers lie in the grass in the summer. Spike Lee lived here not long ago, in one of the brownstones that border the park.

Justin had been clever enough and lucky enough to have bought this duplex before Park Slope became crowded and expensive, before young white professionals with dotcom incomes moved in and sent real estate prices soaring, displacing black families who had lived here for years never dreaming their landlords would sell. But Fort Greene was a stone's throw from Manhattan Bridge, and the Yuppies knew it was a matter of time (and enough of them willing to be pioneers), before it would go the way of Park Slope: another oasis for liberal whites, Asians who had crossed over, and a sprinkling of over-educated but harmless blacks.

It is not lost on Justin that many of his colleagues consider him one of these harmless blacks, but he chalks this down to envy. The fact is he had bought the duplex when many of his black friends thought Long Island was the place to escape the spreading urban ghettoes. With his college professor's salary, he could never have returned to Brooklyn later if he wanted to, as so many people he knows tried to do when the long commute on the Long Island Expressway taxed their aging bones and loneliness set in for the gossip at the corner store.

There are three rooms on the top floor of their duplex, a master bedroom with its own bathroom, a smaller bedroom for Giselle with a bathroom adjacent to it, a den with a huge dark-wood desk, bookshelves stacked with Justin's books, and a comfortable sofa. When they were first married, Justin invited Sally to share the den with him. She turned down his invitation. "I don't want to disturb you," she said. It was what he had hoped she would answer. The den is his alone, his own private space.

Downstairs in the kitchen where they are sitting at a round oak table, light pours through the huge windows on sunny days. Today is not a sunny day, but the kitchen is cheerful. Sally has made it cheerful. The walls are creamy, the cabinets a rich brown, the square tiles on the floor large and white. Sally hangs her orange pots on steel hooks that drop from the ceiling and puts green plants and purple and white African lilies in ceramic pots near the windows. Under the table is a colorful woolen rug. Giselle loves to sit on the rug when Sally is in the kitchen, especially when she is working at the table making pretty projects for the children in her class. Sally has made a special corner in the kitchen for Giselle's toys, but Giselle does not play in her corner. She plays near Sally's feet.

It's a comfortable kitchen. The back door leads down a concrete staircase to a tiny garden which they share with the owner of the street floor apartment. It belongs to a married man, a doctor who keeps the apartment for his afternoon trysts. The garden does not interest him and he lets Sally have total run of it. Even with the oak tree, there is space in the garden for wrought iron furniture, herbs, pink pansies in the spring and an assortment of annuals Sally plants every year.

The living room and dining room, which are in front of the kitchen, are in fact one large room with the original oak woodwork framing the ceilings, windows, and doors. The darkwood floors are covered with two large Oriental rugs, one under a mahogany dining set with an antique chandelier dropping above the table, the other between two plump couches and two matching armchairs in an assortment of red patterns. The room faces a quiet street and gets the afternoon sun.

Yes, Justin thinks, he and Sally have much to be grateful for. He wants to remind her of that.

"We have a lot," he says.

"Things," she says. "We have things."

"Things matter. On a cold day like today, things matter, Sally. It won't feel fine to be without a roof over your head on a day like today."

All he wants to do is to convey the hunter's need for recognition, for appreciation for his kill. But the millet gatherer, the bearer of children, the nurturer, does not want to feel beholden, nor believes she should.

"Are you threatening me?" Sally looks at him with steely eyes.

"You'll be forty soon, Sally," he says, his tone mollified. "A lot of people feel dissatisfied with their life at forty."

"Yes. Maybe that is it. I will be forty soon." She picks up the wooden spoon and stirs the batter. It clunks against the sides of the ceramic bowl. Kitchen sounds. Domesticity restored. A house back to normal.

There will be time to talk again tomorrow, Justin thinks.

But suddenly Sally's hand is moving faster. Muscles pop out from her forearm. Kitchen sounds become the crack of a spoon used as a weapon. "You *really* don't want to know why I am unhappy, do you, Justin?" Sally's fingers are curled tightly around the spoon; the knobs are pointed and shiny.

Justin's stomach forms a knot. "I asked you," he says. He cannot hide his exasperation.

"But you don't want to know my answer. You only want to make fun of the books I read, the things I believe. You want to take the road of least resistance."

He gets up. *A farce. I am in a farce.*

"It is space I want, Justin. Space for Sally." As suddenly as it began, her hand stops its whipping motion. She is looking directly at him. "I want to find Sally," she says.

He will not be trapped in her little farce of the road of least resistance, her psychobabble. "I think I'll go to the college after all," he says.

"Do that," she says.

But she drops the spoon and rushes out of the door before he can leave the room.

THREE

They were happy once. It was not a long time ago. Only eight months have passed since they were walking hand in hand through the park near their home, Giselle happily trailing behind them. It was Giselle's half birthday. She was three and a half. Two of her friends had already turned four. She wanted a birthday party too. Sally tried to explain: She had six more months to go. What is six months? Giselle wanted to know. Half a year, Sally told her. You have a half a year more before you are four. Half a year more? Giselle was inconsolable. Then Sally had the idea of a halfway birthday. A half birthday, Giselle called it.

They wouldn't have a party. They agreed on that. Just a celebration with Mommy and Daddy. And of course there would be a present. Justin drove to Sally's school and picked her up at her lunch hour and they bought the present together. A Barbie doll. It was what Giselle wanted.

In those days there was not much Sally and Justin didn't do together. They shopped for furniture together, they bought the weekly groceries together, they did the unpleasant chores together: the laundry, the dishes, the bathroom. When Justin needed clothes, Sally went with him to the store. When she shopped, he accompanied her. Their friends said it was a recipe for disaster. Familiarity breeds contempt. Or boredom. Too much of anything is good for nothing. You'll get tired of each other, they warned them.

But Sally and Justin could not imagine a time when they would be tired of each other.

It was a marriage that had come relatively late in life for them. He was thirty-nine when he met her, forty when they married. She was thirty-five. Both were experienced enough, smart enough, to know what they had. They treasured this marriage, safeguarded it.

They had met by accident. The heart, Sally said, will find its way, no matter the obstacles. And there were so many, it was a miracle they were together at all. Justin would have to travel almost four thousand miles to be where she was. Even with the scholarship to Harvard that took him from Port of Spain, Trinidad, to Cambridge, Massachusetts, something had to cause him to move to Brooklyn, and even then the fates had to intervene to put him on a bench in the Fort Greene Park at three o'clock, on a certain Wednesday afternoon when Sally, an American, black, born and raised in Harlem whose residents rarely, and if so, then reluctantly, journeyed across that strip of water, which to their way of thinking could be an ocean, to that peninsula that began with Brooklyn, stretched out to Queens and then to that no man's land in the Hamptons (no man's land that is, except to rich white people), would walk past that exact same park bench, at the exact same time when he was sitting there. And though it may not have been unusual for Sally to be in the park at that time, since she was a primary school teacher and her day was already over, it was unusual for him to be there, for, except for the rare occurrence of a conversion day when Wednesday became Tuesday at his college for administrative reasons, he would have been in a classroom that Wednesday afternoon.

Every pot has a cover, Justin told her. Whether he was the pot and she the cover, or the other way around, he did not say, but what he meant was clear enough to Sally. They were a match.

Indeed they were. Justin was a professor of English literature. Sally had majored in comparative literature at Spelman. Justin liked to read. Sally's bookshelves in her apartment were crammed with books. Justin wanted to be a novelist, Sally a poet. Justin had not succeeded in becoming a novelist, and neither had Sally become what she hoped. He believed, he convinced himself, that as he was reconciled to a career in teaching, so was she, content, since not writing poetry herself, to be helping little ones find the music in words, the image to express their feelings.

If Justin had to find a marker, a day he could point to when he was certain beyond any doubt that Sally loved him, it would have been the day he and Sally celebrated Giselle's half birthday, that day after the cake and ice cream, after the opening of the present which so delighted Giselle she would sleep with it curled into her tiny arms all night, it would have been that night, when they were in bed, in each other's arms. The memory stayed with him not only for the perfection of those hours with Sally, but because, in his mind, after that night, their life together began a seemingly inexorable slide downward to this moment, now, when his head mocks him with words he cannot silence and he soothes himself with a lie: *Justin does not care.*

They had just made love. Sex between them was always warm and comforting, passionate sometimes, but not the raw, unbridled passion Justin had known with women he hardly knew, women he never loved. What Justin had with Sally was love that was passionate. Passionate love. When they reached that point together—and more and more they had been arriving there at the same time, the climax of tension achieved and released almost simultaneously—he felt fused into her, not just his body, but his spirit also, his soul, his heart, his mind at one with her. She would say the same to him. Even the physical distance, she said, the space in which by nature humans are locked into themselves and from each other—the shell of our bodies—vanished, dissolved, when they made love to each other.

"I sometimes look in your face and I see mine," she said, her fingers tracing the contours of his face, lingering on his forehead, his nose, the curve of his lips, the sweep of his chin.

"What you see on my face is the way I see you. The way I love you," he said to her.

But that was not all she meant. "I see my real face, too," she said.

"You are far more beautiful."

She was not making a comparison. "I see *me*," she said. "When I look at you, it is *me* I see."

"Yourself?"

"I've longed to see my face."

"And don't you see it? I mean when you look in the mirror?" Justin was an academic, a man who required the specific, the concrete, who was trained to deconstruct the obscure, examine its parts until he could define it, label it, own it.

"When I look in the mirror what I see is a reflection of me, not me. I cannot touch the me I see in a reflection. *You* can touch me."

"And you can touch your face."

Was he such a clod then? Justin would ask himself this question months later. Didn't he know then she was trying to tell him how much she loved him?

"I cannot touch my face and see it at the same time," she said, breaking the whole into its parts so the academic could understand her. "I think all my life I have longed for this," she said.

"For what?" He was still puzzled.

"For this." Her fingers returned to his lips. "To touch and feel my face. I think," she said, "this is why we fall in love."

Still the clod, he asked her: "We fall in love so we can touch and see our faces?"

"If sex were the only reason why men and women seek out

each other, we would not have such feelings. I would not feel as close to you as I do now. As if I were in you and you were in me."

"I was," he said. "I don't know how it was possible for you, but I was in you." It was a male response, a natural instinct to take cover when intimacy became too intense. It was a foolish response.

"No, no," she said. "I don't mean that. I wasn't speaking only about the physical, though I mean that too. I feel as if I am actually in you. I feel so now. As if I am in your chest." She poked her finger in the place where his heart lay. "As if I am there and in your head, in your soul, in all of you. I find myself in you," she said.

He drew her to him. "And I in you," he said.

"I was so lonely and unhappy," she said. "Then I met you and saw my face in you."

"And you saw me, too?" He asked the question nervously because sometimes, in those early days, it was not the inanity of graffiti that bothered him when she recited the words she had seen on a wall; it was what came afterward: *It helped me get over Jack,* she said.

"Yes, yes, I fell in love with you." She eased away from him so she could face him. "Of course I fell in love with you."

He made himself feel satisfied.

"But," she said, "if we are truthful, we will admit that the first person we ever loved, *could ever love,* was ourselves, and that we long to see that self we love, not through a mirror, but through our own eyes. We long to know those lips, those eyes, that skin. We long to touch and see that face in the flesh." She smiled and stroked his mouth. "It is why we go searching for the cover to our pot."

He realized she was saying that he was the cover, she the pot, but it did not matter to him. He loved her. He would be her cover.

"And when we find it," she said, not yet done, "when we see ourselves in that person, it is then we know we are in love, and it is then the loneliness ends."

He wanted to be sure. He took himself out of the question he asked her. "Then is it herself the woman falls in love with or with the man?"

"I fell in love with you because I can love me through you. And I can love me because I see in your eyes how lovable I am."

"Yes," he said. "We are soul mates."

"Soul mates, but much more than that."

He could not say he understood her fully. Perhaps it was because it seemed to him she spoke in the manner of the poet, with the elliptical phrasing he sometimes found tiresome. And perhaps then and there he should have known that whatever she had told him, before they were married, about no longer having interest in writing poetry, about being an anachronism, was not quite true. Perhaps he should have guessed then that it would only be a matter of time before that person she had wanted to be, who she had buried, would gnaw her way through her heart and resurface.

But those thoughts did not cross Justin's mind. Nor did they cross his mind that morning when she said to him, *It's space I want, Justin. Space for Sally. I want to find Sally.* He would think of those times only as the last of those evenings he treasured when they talked sometimes until the early dawn. And he would think of Giselle's fourth birthday, six months later, as the day when, for the first time in their otherwise happy marriage, Sally turned away from him in their bed.

FOUR

Brooklyn turns ugly when it snows, but not immediately. Immediately it is a wonderland. Overnight a pristine carpet of white hides everything: the overstuffed garbage cans at street corners, dog excrement on pavements, broken banisters on front stoops, dirty paper and refuse caught in the cracks and crevices of broken buildings, trees bereft of leaves, moribund reminders of the passing of time, the absurdity of the busyness of cities: The rich will still die; nothing will change that. But by morning the magic the snow has woven disintegrates and the city is worse off than it was before. White monster trucks spew sand on streets to keep the snow from sticking. Buses trundle through, cars swish and slide. They pitch volleys of dirty snow onto sidewalks. Tempers flare, pedestrians scream at motorists, car wheels spin hopelessly in dirt and slush.

Justin does not want to be on these streets this morning. It is pride that forces him out. Sally beat him to the exit he had intended, but he had announced he would go to the college, so to the college he must go.

He does not have to dig too far to free his car. Last week, after the third big snowfall, he parked his car on an angle so that the front was facing the street. Twice before he had cleared out a space near his house, but each time he returned the next morning he found his car buried under mounds of snow his neighbors had dumped when they dug out their own cars. It is winner take all on the streets of this half city, so he devised this foolproof plan. By the end of the week everyone on his block was parking at an angle. Soon the street was littered with cars and small hills of filthy snow pocketed with the deep imprints of rubber boots.

It takes him less than five minutes to scrape off the front and back windshields and windows of his car and drive clear over the hump of soft snow, piled against his front wheels, out into the street, no mean accomplishment on a day like today. But this brings Justin no satisfaction, no comfort. His mood does not change. It is his research day. He should not be here.

Justin has tenure at his college. Technically, if he never publishes another article or presents another paper at a conference, he cannot be fired. *Cannot* is perhaps too extreme a word. Technically, there are rules. Technically, the administration could terminate a faculty who has ceased to participate in the scholarly life of the university, but Justin has never heard of a case where that has been done in the university system where he teaches. He has never heard of a tenured faculty either being fired or even chastised for lack of publications, except of course if that person wished to be promoted. But that is a matter of personal choice. A tenured faculty who applies for promotion exposes himself to scrutiny. Perhaps he cannot escape the gossip in the corridors, but he can escape scrutiny completely if, after he is tenured, he asks for nothing. Justin knows many more faculty than he would care to count who have taken this route, the route of least resistance.

He is using Sally's words, the very same phrase that annoyed him this morning, and it bothers him that it has wormed its way into his thoughts. *No, not the route of least resistance,* he says to himself, the route to security and more alternatives, to mortgages secured with a job that is guaranteed, to vacations in the summer without worries—more roads to travel. Again, it is Sally's phrase that pops into his head. He has trouble avoiding thoughts of her this morning and he wants to, which is why he is on the road on a nasty, gloomy morning instead of lying on his comfortable couch with his favorite book, in his comfortable den, wrapped in his comfortable quilt, or, (because he has not managed to quell his irritation, this more likely scenario comes crashing through the fantasy he is orchestrating) sloshing through the mounds of essays he must grade by Monday.

What roads does Sally want to travel? He thinks of her friend Anna Chang, a Chinese American with penetrating eyes and a placid smile that never fails to get under his skin. Anna works for his university system. She lives a few blocks from his apartment, but teaches at another college in Queens. Anna has her Ph.D., Anna is tenured, Anna is an assistant professor. Anna has no further ambitions. Tenure protects Anna, so Anna pursues her hobby: gardening. She is a member of the horticultural club, she is a volunteer at the Brooklyn Botanic Gardens, she is an expert on eliminating the mealy bug from houseplants.

Anna is an English teacher. She teaches composition and literature at her college. Anna doesn't think she needs to do research to teach composition and literature at a college where the majority of the freshmen read on a seventh-grade level and few can pass the university-wide placement exam. If Anna has any stirrings of conscience, this is the argument she presents to herself. The logic of it dissipates all doubt. Anna is happy with her life. Why not Sally?

He is on dangerous ground now for he does not approve of Anna's choice. He is thinking only of how contented she seems, always pleasant, always smiling. Sally folded her tent when she became an anachronism. So she would have him believe. Is he to blame for that? Is he to blame for her surrender? She was teaching kindergarten when he met her. She was not a poet. Yes, she had written some poetry, but that did not make her a poet. A poet in his mind is someone actively writing poetry, someone struggling to find tangible expressions for the intangible, no matter what. Sally has chosen to struggle with the tangible: the children in her classroom. Giselle.

Perhaps Anna knew all along she did not have it in her to be a scholar. The Ph.D. was as far as she could go. At least she has come to terms with her limitations. He has come to terms with his, why not Sally? He teaches literature but he does not create it. He does not have the hubris of other literature professors to think he can. *Those who can, do. Those who can't, teach.* He is one of those who can't. Sally cannot think it is easy for him to accept this. She knows the long hours he used to spend hunched over his laptop, trying. Doesn't every English teacher try at least once? Doesn't every English teacher say, I can do this too?

Sally read his manuscript. More show, less tell, she would say over and over again. But he was in the business of telling. He was an academic, a teacher, a preacher, a lecturer, a hector, a cajoler.

The rejection letters piled up. *More show, less tell.* But he didn't know how. In the end he and Sally made a party to celebrate his failure. He ripped, she cut in ribbons, and they put all five hundred pages of the manuscript that wasn't a novel, that would never be a novel, in the garbage, opened a bottle of Pouilly-Fuissé and made love on the living-room floor.

Surely she knew it hurt. Surely she knew it was not easy to surrender, to admit he did not have the talent, would never have the talent.

He pulls into the parking lot at the college. It is Friday. Faculty do not teach on Fridays. Teaching on Fridays ruins the weekend. The lot, as he expects, is empty; the snow has been cleared. He can park where he chooses. He chooses a spot close to the sidewalk, near to the main door of the college, the provost's spot.

Inside, some of the classroom doors are closed, but he is certain the teachers in these rooms are adjuncts, members of a cottage industry that has mushroomed in colleges across the country looking for ways to cut expenses on the rising cost of education in America. Adjuncts will teach a class for a fifth of the salary of a full-time faculty. They teach the same students, but they are not expected to have the same credentials as the full-time faculty. Educators sermonize on the need to limit the number of classes they teach. They cite burnout and diminishing returns, but this argument applies to them, not to adjuncts. Adjuncts can teach as many classes as they want to, or need to. There are rules, of course. In his system, an adjunct is permitted to teach a maximum of three courses and not all three at the same college. But everyone knows that adjuncts cannot live on the paltry salaries they are paid, so no one checks. There are budgets that have to be cut. There are classes to be taught on Fridays. There are adjuncts who teach as many as six courses a semester in as many as three different colleges.

It is thoughts like these that get Justin riled up. There are no such reminders of these inequities in his den at home, another reason why he prefers to work there.

Sally says she is an anachronism, but it is he who is the anachronism, he thinks. He is out of step and out of time with the modern age, the age of political correctness and Afrocentricity. The age of technology and big bucks. He is a tenured full professor and yet he does research, he publishes articles, he presents papers. He believes his students deserve the respect of a professor who is continuing to learn as much as he can about the subjects he teaches. He thinks his students should learn not only about their world, their culture, their ancestry, but about the larger world, about other cultures. He thinks British and European literature is relevant to them. He thinks race is irrelevant. He thinks only their humanity is relevant.

But the doubters tell him that the books he teaches were

written by DWMs, Dead White Men, who have nothing to tell inner-city students dodging police who use them for target practice, then ship them upstate to concrete pens.

"And even if there is meaning for them in the books you teach," a colleague once said to him, "they don't have the frame of reference to get it."

But Justin does not believe that. He is frustrated but he has not despaired. He, too, did not have a frame of reference when he was a boy growing up in Trinidad. There were no museums on his island where he could find artifacts from the eras he read about in books. No grand libraries where he could discover the works of great writers and philosophers barely mentioned in his textbooks; no theaters, no symphony halls, no art galleries, no monumental edifices boasting architectural designs that have lasted for centuries. Snow was something he had to imagine. Tulips that bloomed in the spring were a fantasy.

No, he believes the trick is finding a way to make the literature accessible to his students. He will teach DWMs and DBMs, Dead White Men and Dead Black Men, and living ones, too—and even women, the worthy ones.

He is reading an article about the convicted murderer Susan Smith when Mark Sandler knocks on his door. He lets him in. Mark is one of his best students. He is happy to see him. He needs a distraction from academic politics, and from the argument he had with Sally this morning, which continues to filter through his mind. It is thinking of Sally that set him on the road of defending himself as an anachronism. What does Sally want from him? Is he to be responsible for helping her find herself? *Her space?*

"Professor, what brings you out on this cold day?"

Justin shakes the last thoughts of Sally from his head and grasps Mark Sandler's outstretched hand. "I could ask you the same."

Under his black leather jacket, Mark Sandler's shoulders seem excessively wide, but Justin knows it is not only the padding in the jacket that make them seem so. Mark works out in the same gym that he does. He has seen him bench press two hundred pounds. He isn't tall but he gives the impression of height by the way he holds his head and back erect. His polished black skin reminds Justin of the La Brea Pitch Lake on a sunny day. He has dyed his hair blond. The incongruity of the color against his skin is not unattractive on him. He puts Justin in mind of one of those toga-clad young men one sees bringing wine to Caesar in Hollywood movies.

"Burrowing is for animals," Mark shadowboxes with him, making a swing for his jaw. Justin ducks.

He likes Mark. Generally he calls his students by their last name—again the anachronism—but he makes an exception for Mark. Mark has taken Comp 1 and 2 with him and the Great Books course. Mark is smart. He is a good writer. Not an excellent writer or an average writer. A good writer, good being an adjective that Justin has observed has lost favor these days along with the respectability of the C grade. Everything is hyperbole. A student is either exceptional or he is a failure. Going by some of the class rosters Justin sees posted on faculty doors, a third of the students in his college are exceptional, but so, he thinks sighing with resignation, are a third of all college students in America.

Mark wants to be a novelist and Justin has convinced him that first he has to become a reader. This is why Mark has signed up for independent study with him. They have agreed on a reading list, and he meets with Mark once a week to discuss an assigned book. Mark has to write a paper every three weeks based on one of these books. He is doing well, exceptionally well.

"So what's up?"

"I saw the light in your office. You aren't usually here on Fridays."

"I forgot something in the office." Justin makes a pretense of shuffling papers. His desk is cluttered. Papers stick out at all angles from untidy stacks of books. The only seemingly neat area, to the right of where he works, is the space he has cleared for two gold-framed pictures, one of Sally and the other of the three of them—he, Sally, and Giselle. A portrait of a happy family smiling.

His desk at home is not untidy. Sally makes sure of that. She has an uncanny sense of which books he has already thumbed through and which are important for the paper he is working on at the time. She stacks these books in separate piles and asks him later which she may return to his bookshelves. She puts his students' papers in folders and labels them for him. She bags his garbage but does not remove it from the room until she has asked for his permission. Sally is a good wife, a considerate wife, the right wife for a college professor.

"Is this what you were looking for?" Mark points to the article about Susan Smith. He is standing with his back to the door. Justin's desk is in front of him. Behind it are posters, mainly of conferences Justin has attended, and a narrow long window that looks out to the street. Books tumble on top of each other on the shelves that line the walls.

"Yes," Justin says. "I plan to use it in my class when we are finished with *Hamlet.*"

"You think she lost it?"

"Who?"

"Susan Smith. You think she went temporarily insane?"

Justin returns the question to him. "What do you think?"

"I think you have to be insane to kill your children."

Justin waits. He wants to see if Mark has made the connection. The story of Susan Smith, the young mother from South Carolina who released the emergency brakes on her car, stepped out of it, closed the door, and watched as the car slipped silently down the boat ramp into the lake carrying her two baby boys who were sleeping in the backseat, is part of his lesson plan for two of the books in his Great Books course.

"But then you'd have to say that Sethe was crazy, and Medea was crazy," Mark adds.

Bingo! Vindication! He has proven his point. Just make the work accessible and they will get it. Give them a way in, and they will understand the rest. He will begin with Susan Smith. Bring in clippings from the tabloids if he must. Then it will be smooth sailing to Euripedes' *Medea* and his students will have no trouble with Toni Morrison's *Beloved*, though he knows many of them will still find Morrison's work daunting.

"You should teach my class," Justin says.

Mark grins but in a second, oddly, his face changes. "You can never tell what a woman can do," he says. "I can't imagine killing my children to get even with their mother."

"And you think that is what Medea does? You think she kills her children to get even with her husband because he left her to marry another woman?"

Mark frowns. "I think men better straighten up and fly right," he says. "Women are doing crazy things these days. I see a lot of them going the lesbian way when their men don't treat them right. I mean beautiful, sexy women. Honeys."

This detour puzzles Justin, but he responds. "A man can't make a woman become a lesbian," he says. "Either she is a lesbian or she isn't. Either women turn her on or they don't. A man has nothing to do with it."

"Oh, yeah? Well, I know a lot of men whose women are sleeping with women. And they weren't that way before the men started treating them bad. If a man doesn't treat a woman right," he repeats, "she'll fly the coop."

Justin guesses that Mark is having problems with his girlfriend and he finds himself thinking again of Sally. Mark's theories about lesbians do not bother him, but he wonders if he is forcing Sally to leave the coop. Does he need to straighten up and fly right? Yet he does not know what he has done to make

Sally so dissatisfied. *What more does she want?* Eight months ago her life with him could not have been more perfect. She said so herself. In spite of her denial, could there be another man?

"Yes, that is what a woman will do," Mark says.

A friend would ask. A friend would say at this point: Did you and your girlfriend have a fight, Mark? But he is not Mark's friend. He is Mark's professor, so he takes the conversation back to the realm of professors, to the discussion of relationships that are fictitious, not to ones that are nonfictitious.

"Medea is aware of the consequences of killing the woman her husband is planning to marry," he says with authority. "She has no doubt that her children will be brutally slaughtered in revenge. She prefers to kill them herself and spare them a worse death." The newspapers reported that Susan Smith was going through a divorce. The week before, her new lover had rejected her. She was despondent. She did not want to live, one journalist wrote. She believed that if she killed her sons first and then committed suicide, her sons would suffer less, rather than if she committed suicide and left them on their own.

"No," Mark says, "Medea knows that the worst pain her husband can suffer is the death of his children." He wags his finger at Justin. "Beware of a woman scorned."

Justin tells himself he is fooling around, he is being melodramatic, but his heart lurches nonetheless. He laughs to prove to himself that he is not affected by what Mark is saying, but Mark is not finished.

"Professor," he says, "I think Sethe wanted revenge, too,

when she killed her daughter. She wanted to make her husband pay."

"Pay for what? Sethe kills Beloved because she does not want the slave catchers to take her daughter back to the slave plantation."

"But Sethe's husband let her down. He wasn't there to help her when she was trying to escape to freedom with three children and another one on the way."

"Because he was traumatized. He had seen when those boys raped her."

"Yes," Mark says. "That's the point. He saw those boys raping his wife and he did not help her. Remember how the women in the class agreed with Sethe when you read that section in class: 'He saw, He saw and he didn't do nothing?' They loved that. They're always talking about how it is different for a man and woman when a woman has a child. They have to stay with the child to breast-feed it, but we can leave them and go wherever we want."

I don't want to go anywhere, Justin thinks. It is Sally who is unhappy.

"Sethe did not forgive Halle for not helping her. I think she killed Beloved for revenge."

"Mark, aren't you taking this a little too far? Sethe didn't have time to think when she swung that ax. Halle was not on her mind."

"Still, Professor, you have to admit it is a good theory."

He has to admit no such thing, but he is pleased by how these books have engaged Mark. He tells Mark to think some more about what he said. He warns him against supporting his theories with extraneous material.

"The evidence must be in the text," he tells Mark. "When Sethe kills Beloved, she does not know that Halle saw those boys raping her. She finds that out eighteen years later."

"But before Paul D tells her that, she says Paul D is the only good man she knows," Mark says.

"Hmm," Justin says. "Why don't you write this up?"

"For extra credit?" Neither *Beloved* nor *Medea* is on Mark's reading list for independent study. He has already taken the Great Books course.

"Yes. Convince me of your theories if you can."

Mark's face breaks out in a wide smile. "Bet you hadn't thought of Sethe taking revenge on Halle."

Justin sighs.

It is late afternoon when he returns home. Before he left the office, he had called Sally to ask if she wanted him to get Giselle, but she had picked her up already. He hears them chattering when he enters the corridor that leads to the living room. He hangs his bulky black parka on the coat rack. His students wear leather, he thinks. Mark gets financial aid but he has a leather coat. It's a matter of priorities, he tells himself, looking around his living room: the rich Oriental rugs, the plush sofas, the mahogany table and crystal chandelier in the background.

Giselle has heard him and runs out of the kitchen where she has been playing near her mother. She throws her arms around him. *Yes, it is a matter of priorities.* He lifts her up. She wraps her arms and legs around him and gives him a sloppy kiss on his cheek.

"Come." Giselle points toward Sally. "Give Mommy a big kiss. Give her a big hug."

He cannot deny his daughter. He brushes his lips against Sally's cheek.

"On the mouth, Daddy. Give Mommy a kiss on the mouth."

Does she suspect a coolness between them? She was not at home when they had their fight in the morning. Does she sense a difference now?

Sally rescues him. She takes Giselle from his arms and puts her to stand on the floor. "Show Daddy the drawing you made."

Giselle runs to the table. Sally and Justin do not look at each other.

"Here, Daddy."

She has drawn a picture of a house. In the house are a man and a woman. They are holding hands.

"It's you and Mommy," Giselle says.

"And where are you?"

"I am drawing the picture. I can't be in the picture if I am drawing the picture, Daddy," she says with affected patience, as if the logic of it should be obvious.

He laughs.

"When do you want to have dinner?" Sally directs the question to him but she is not looking at him.

"Whenever," he says. He glances in her direction. Scattered across the table are ruled sheets of paper with the letters of the alphabet written on them. Each letter is carefully drawn between the lines. "I'm not particularly hungry," he tells her.

She shrugs and gathers the papers on the table. "Dinner will be ready in fifteen minutes," she says.

He turns to go upstairs. Giselle follows him.

"Tell me what you did today, Daddy," she says. It is Sally's question. This is what on happier days Sally asks him when he comes home from the college. *Mark Sandler came by.* He does not say this to her; he would have said it to Sally. But now it all comes back, Mark's preposterous statement. What a strange leap he had made! That Sethe would kill her daughter to make her husband pay for abandoning her! Halle had not abandoned her. No: A man ain't a goddamn ax. *Things get to him.* The words flit through his head: Paul D's defense of Halle. He purses his lips.

Giselle looks up at him. "Tired, Daddy?"

He reaches for her hand. "Never for my little girl." But he cannot stop the tension rising along his spine. *Sally wakes up one morning feeling depressed. Is it his job to play therapist to her, to make her happy?*

"So what did you do, Daddy?" Giselle has skipped one step ahead of him on the stairs. She is tugging his hand. "Tell me, Daddy."

He forces a smile. "I worked in my office. I corrected papers and I read books."

"Then read a book to me, Daddy, a big book."

Yes, this is what should be important to Sally: Giselle, their family. Mother, father, daughter as in the photograph, a happy family.

"A big book?" The tension recedes.

"One of your books."

When she comes to his den, Giselle wants him to read to her from his books. He knows she cannot understand what he reads, but if he stops in mid-line when he reads poetry to her, she notices. *Go on. Finish it,* she says.

"This book." She points to a thick, blue book. *The Complete Works of Shakespeare.*

"This book?" He frowns, faking astonishment. "This book is too big for you."

She laughs. It is their joke. He says this book is too big for you and she says, But I am a big girl, Daddy. She says so now and he replies, "So you are," and pats her on her head. "Okay." He reaches for the book and she curls up next to him on the couch. The stiffness in his back is gone. His troubles with Sally have eased away almost completely. He turns the page to his favorite passage, some of the most beautiful lines in all of Shakespeare's plays, he tells Giselle. She smiles and locks her fingers together in anticipation.

"Ready?" He knows she will listen carefully. She has a natural ear for the rhythms of poetry. She has not learned the term but she hears the beat, she can recognize iambic pentameter. She'll be the writer I am not, he thinks.

"Ready," she says.

He reads:

Be not afeard: the isle is full of noises,
Sounds and sweet airs that give delight and
hurt not.
Sometimes a thousand twangling instruments
Will hum about mine ears; and sometime
voices
That, if I then had wak'd after long sleep,
Will make me sleep again; and then, in dreaming,
The clouds methought would open and show
riches
Ready to drop upon me, that, when I wak'd,
I cried to dream again.

Giselle is silent. Finally, in a soft voice she says, "I like it, Daddy. Read it again."

His eyes are misty when he reads the lines a second time, and the child notices.

"You like it, too, don't you, Daddy?"

He nods. He tells her that it is Caliban who speaks these lines. He is talking about a place that is very much like the island where her daddy used to live before he came to America.

She loves these stories about the time before her daddy came to America. "Was it nice, Daddy? Was it nice where you were when you were little like me?" she asks him.

"I wasn't there only when I was little like you," he tells her. "I grew up to be a big man in Trinidad. I lived there until I was nineteen."

Nineteen makes no sense to her. She looks at him, waiting for more.

"I was older than Mark," he says. She has met Mark. "Oh," she says.

He repeats lines that he has just read to her. "'Sometimes a thousand twangling instruments / Will hum about mine ears; and sometime voices.'"

"Bangling, bangling." The child picks one word and mispronounces it. "What's bangling, Daddy?"

"Twangling," he says. "A thousand twangling instruments."

She twists her head to one side and asks, "Twangling?"

"Yes, twangling."

"Twangling like steel band?" He has told her about steel band. When the Africans were brought as slaves to this country, they could not take their instruments with them, so they made music on their bodies. He slapped his thighs. *Drumming, see?* In Trinidad, when slavery ended, they used discarded oil drums. *It is the only musical instrument invented in the twentieth century,* he told her.

But she has changed her mind. "Not like steel band, Daddy. Twangling like birds!" She claps her hands in delight.

They have talked about the birds, too, about the kiskadee in the orange tree near his bedroom window in Trinidad. He has imitated the whistle many times for her.

"Twangling like birds!" she says again.

He is overwhelmed with affection for her, this daughter, this one child he has had in middle age. His spitting image.

She has his gray-green eyes and his dark brown complexion.

Her hair, like his, is dark and thick. Her mother divides it into four sections and plaits the front plait into the back plait on either side of her head. She puts ribbons on the end. Giselle likes the ribbons, especially the red ones she has on today. She is a girlish girl. She prefers dresses to pants, and even on this cold day, she is wearing a jumper, dark navy blue, with a white turtleneck jersey. She has on navy tights, which she calls her pantyhose. "Just like Mommy's," she says. She will be taller than her mother, close to his height. At four years old, she is already three feet tall.

"Exactly," he says to her. "The birds, and the rustle of the trees, the rain on the galvanized roof of our house, the surf on the beach . . ."

But Sally is calling them to dinner and Giselle turns her attention abruptly away from him. "Coming!" She blows him a kiss and runs down the steps toward Sally.

Justin does not follow her. He sits quietly facing the window looking down on the mounds of snow piled around the foot of the oak tree. How had he been able to leave his grassy green for this? To stay, even after what ostensibly appeared to be his only reason for coming—Harvard and then graduate study to the Ph.D.—had been achieved? The question is more than twenty years old and he has yet to find an answer that will not wring him wet with nostalgia.

But the truth is that memories of Trinidad did not trouble him at Harvard. There were papers to write, books to read. Deadlines. The lie that protects the heart of new immigrants: *This is temporary. I will return.* After that, there was the busyness of teaching: lectures to prepare, papers to grade, exams, conferences. Time passed.

The cracks in his lie did not appear until he was close to forty. Then living in the present and remembering the past became more than he could bear. A familiar scent, a photograph, a fragment of a conversation, suddenly recalled, would reproach him: *You left this for that.* You left turquoise waters, sandy beaches, a sun that is always warm, people who do not stare because you find yourself in a place where the color of your skin arrests them. He wants to say *offends* them, for that is what he thinks when he catches the eye that returns a forced smile—say, at the Metropolitan Opera, the symphony at Carnegie Hall, at a Tom Stoppard play, the beach in the Hamptons—and he unmasks the unspoken questions: *How? Why? What is he doing here?*

To remember this loss is a kind of torture: he has left a place where he belonged—home—for this, an exile he has imposed on himself. But to bury the memories is to bury a part of himself. To die a little. He pulls himself away from the window and shuts the book. No, this death comes too early for him. He will remember: *Sometimes a thousand twangling instruments / Will hum about mine ears; and sometime / voices.*

Giselle is calling him. "Daddy, we're waiting for you."

He stands, puts the book back in the bookcase. He readies himself.

AT DINNER THE SILENCE between Sally and him deepens. If the child notices, she makes no mention of it. She talks nonstop, volleying questions to her mother and father which they answer with forced animation.

"How does snow come?" Justin takes that one.

"When will it end?" Sally answers this, segueing into her plans for the garden in the spring. Aunt Anna will show them how to root seeds.

How will Aunt Anna root the seeds, Mommy?

Aunt Anna will put them in glass jars in the kitchen.

Why will Aunt Anna put them in glass jars, Mommy?

Aunt Anna says so we can watch the seeds grow into plants.

And what will Aunt Anna do next?

In April Aunt Anna will help us plant the young shoots in the garden.

Aunt Anna. Aunt Anna. The name bounces from one to the other, sliding merrily off their tongues. One would think all is well around the table, but he and Sally have spoken only polite words to each other: Will you pass the bread? Do you want more salad?

"Will Aunt Anna come tomorrow?" Giselle's face lights up with the prospect.

Sally's special friend, her best friend, Giselle's godmother. Aunt Anna to Giselle. It is a friendship that predates him. It was forged in that foundry where life and death hung in the balance. Sally saved Anna. Not her life, not anything as dramatic, as melodramatic, as that, though to hear Anna speak of it one would think that that was what she had done.

"But those boys *could* have hurt her," Sally said to Justin. "Anna was terrified."

It was the first day of school for both of them. Hunter College High School, the prestigious high school of Hunter College of the City of the University of New York. Only the city's brightest were invited to enroll, indeed to sit for the rigorous entrance exam. Sally's counselor picked her and when the results of the exam came, she had scored in the ninety-eighth percentile. No one was surprised. The surprise was that Sally was willing to take the train from Harlem, where she lived with her aunt and brother, and travel sixty blocks downtown to go to school in an unfamiliar neighborhood, with unfamiliar people. For her aunt, like everyone else, believed Sally was a shy girl, a girl afraid of her shadow.

They were wrong, Sally said to Justin. She stayed in her room because she loved to read. The worlds in novels were a hundred times more interesting than the world outside her room, she said.

Anna's scores were just below the cutoff line, but it was 1974, nine short years since Malcolm X lay bleeding on the ballroom floor of the Audobon Hotel, just six years since Martin Luther King was shot to death on the balcony of a motel in Tennessee. Hunter had found itself under the microscope: a public institution in a so-called liberal city that, except for a smattering of black, brown, and yellow faces, was lily white. There was evidence of the Old Boys' Club at work, that not everyone had achieved the same level of excellence in the exam, that there was a network that favored the placement of the sons and daughters of the elite who had made substantial monetary contributions to the school. There were the accusations, too, of bias, that the exam was culturally skewed. Who in Ocean-Hill

Brownsville had been on a ski slope? Who played ice hockey? Who competed in swim meets? *Swim meets?* How many precious minutes could have been lost as a poor, black boy in Bed-Stuy or Harlem tried to shear away images that were alien to him, that made utterly no sense to him, struggling to understand the question he was asked in a reading comprehension or math exam? *If it takes six skiers twenty minutes to reach the ski lift . . .*

Anna was among the few Asians and African Americans carefully selected from the five boroughs to be admitted under the revised criteria. On that first day, terrified by the strangeness of the place, her first outing alone uptown outside of the familiarity of Chinatown, Anna got lost. By accident she found herself on the subway platform for the train heading to the Bronx by way of Harlem. Sally was on the train she boarded.

"She really thought those boys were going to hurt her," Sally said. "I think at first they were trying to be helpful. They knew she was on the wrong train. There were no Chinese families living in Harlem. But when they approached her, she screamed and held her book bag tightly to her chest. That got them angry. You know that stereotype that white people have of black boys? All of them could be potential criminals? The boys began to tease her. The more she held on to her book bag the more they taunted her. She started to cry and they laughed at her. Eventually, I left my seat and came next to her. I said she was my friend and when the train stopped at the next station, I pulled her off it. Anna never forgot that day. She said she was never so frightened in all her life and never so grateful for someone's help."

It is a story that now has the weight of myth. The details sometimes get fuzzy. Sometimes Anna says Sally put her arms around her and shouted to the boys to back off: Sally, the hero, the defender of the persecuted. Sometimes Sally says Anna did not get off at the next station. Anna rode with her all the way to Harlem and together they took the train back downtown. Anna, the brave, the loyal friend who would not run off and leave her defender alone to face the attacks of her persecutors. But the details do not matter. What matters is the unbreakable bond that was sealed between them that day. They lost contact for a while, when Anna went to Smith and then to the University of Colorado for a masters and Ph.D., but when Anna moved to Brooklyn, they renewed their friendship and the eight years they had spent apart vanished with the memory of those high school years when they were inseparable. For the past fifteen years they have been as close as sisters. When Justin speaks of Anna to Sally, he measures his words. He avoids direct criticism. He leaves it to Sally to infer that he does not approve of Anna's attitude toward her students, that he suspects that if Anna were teaching Asian students she would not so blithely claim that there was no need for her to do research because her students were reading on the seventh-grade level, that she seems to have forgotten that she needed revised criteria to get her foot in the door at Hunter, though, admittedly, she went on to succeed spectacularly at Smith.

"Yes, Aunt Anna will come tomorrow," Sally reassures Giselle.

"Goody," the child says.

Later, as if they had already discussed it, Sally and Justin decide to break from their usual routine. Though they take turns reading Giselle her bedtime story and giving her a bath, the other one is always close by, in the same room. Now, each of them has found something else to do. Giselle remarks on this change when Sally reads to her. "Where is Daddy?" she asks. "I want him to hear the story, too."

"Daddy read to you today already," Sally says. "He has to read for himself now." The child accepts her explanation.

In their bedroom, Justin tries to ease the discomfort between them. He tells Sally about Mark Sandler, what Mark said about Sethe and Halle. He does not want to open a door to a conversation about men who mistreat their women, so he says nothing about Mark's theories about women who become lesbians, though the moment the thought flashes through his mind, he is troubled again by a twinge of conscience. Perhaps he should talk to Mark. Perhaps he should find out what is truly bothering him. It is possible that his girlfriend has threatened to leave him, but surely not because of a woman. He has met Sandra, Mark's girlfriend. He would use Mark's word to describe her. Honey. Yes, Sandra is a honey. He can no more see her gay than he can Sally. Sally, he is certain, is not a lesbian. No amount of quarreling between them could make her turn to women. She shares his opinion that lesbians are not made; they are.

Like poets. If Sally were a poet, she would be poet. Nothing could stop her, not he, not Giselle. She needs space, she said. For what? Space to do what? He is conscious he is no longer thinking of Mark, that Sally is on his mind again.

"So how is Mark?" Sally asks. She knows Mark and agrees with Justin that he has promise. She has read his stories. "More than promise," she said. "He may be a writer one day."

He tells her, Confused. He says he has asked him to write a paper on his views on Sethe and Halle.

Mark's over the top with this one, Sally says. "But I suppose if Halle were alive and he found out that Sethe had killed his daughter, he would hate her for it." She is coming out of the bathroom, dabbing Oil of Olay on her face. She is wearing silk pajamas, aqua blue ones. The jacket falls softly against breasts. When she steps toward the bed, the pants outline her slim thighs. Justin turns away from her and plumps the pillow under his head.

"But that is not Morrison's point, is it?" he says carefully, beginning to fear that his effort to find safe ground may not be succeeding.

"Perhaps, yet in that scene I think she *is* talking about fathers who abandon their children," Sally says, massaging her hands with the lotion. "Seems to me she is saying that there is no excuse for them to do that, even if they found themselves in a situation like Halle's."

He hadn't intended to personalize the discussion, but suddenly he feels compelled to defend himself. "Nothing in the world would make me abandon Giselle," he says.

Sally gets into the bed and pulls the blanket to her chin. "Things cannot remain the way they are between us," she says quietly.

They have returned to the morning's conversation.

"I don't know what you mean when you say you need space, Sally. This house is more than enough for both of us."

"You know that is not what I am talking about."

"Then what is it?"

"You think I am happy just being a school teacher, teaching little children?"

"I thought that is what you love to do."

"Yes, but it's not my life's work."

The expression irritates him. "Your life's work," he says. "What is your *life's work*?"

"Something that gives meaning to my life."

"I thought our marriage and Giselle gave meaning to your life."

"But you have more, don't you?"

"You have more, too. You have teaching." He sits up in the bed. "And this," he says. "You have this house. And the garden, and your friends. Anna."

"You have the articles you write, the papers you give, the conferences you go to . . ."

"You want to come with me? Is that it, Sally?"

"You can be such a fool, Justin. I don't care about your conferences. Go whenever you want. Stay as long as you want."

"Then what is it?'

"I want to write poetry," she says. "I want to be a poet."

And he wonders if he did not get it right that morning when he woke up tracing letters in his mind: *Sally does Not love me.*

FIVE

Justin is told by his department how he must teach the Great Books course he has been assigned. He is told that works he selects must not be exclusively European. They must cross cultures, cover the big continents and the major island clusters. Justin believes that cross-cultural is a code word for nonwhite but he has no problems including nonwhite writers on his reading list. Indeed, he had already selected Walcott, Naipaul, Achebe, Soyinka, Morrison, and García-Márquez, literary giants in his opinion, he tells the curriculum committee—*And not because they are nonwhite*—when the committee delivered its edict in a letter to the chairperson, pointing him out as one of the faculty most in need of guidance. "We are concerned about the lack of diversity on Professor Peters's reading list. He needs to be sensitive to the evolving canon."

For the fact is that though Justin has included non-European writers on his reading list, he continues to insist on requiring

Homer, Euripides, and Sophocles, the Greeks he calls the Ancients even after the Afrocentrists have reminded him that the Egyptian civilization occurred long before the Greek. But to Justin, the Renaissance, which was the focus of his studies in graduate school, owed its debt to the Greeks not to the Egyptians. He could not begin without them. None of the books on his list would make sense without them.

The committee tells him that his students need to learn about their own heritage, their own culture. He is almost shouting when he responds that the Greeks are part of his students' heritage, the human heritage. That Western Civilization is his students' civilization. "Is Hector's courage when he shirks the protective walls of Troy and faces the mighty Achilles Ancient Greek courage, white European courage? Is Hector's sense of responsibility for his men white responsibility? Is the shame he feels for having endangered them because of a macho notion of masculinity white shame?"

His canon is the canon of good books, no matter who has written them, Justin says. Homer is relevant to him because Homer writes about human beings and he, Justin, is a human being, his students are human beings. He points to the long epic poem *Omeros* written by the Caribbean Nobel laureate Derek Walcott. Homer was Walcott's inspiration, he says.

The members of the committee continue to suspect him but ultimately they allow him Homer, and, eventually, Euripides' *Medea* when he makes the argument that Toni Morrison's Sethe was not the first woman to kill her child and expect sympathy, and then Sophocles's *Oedipus Rex* when he adds that an understanding of Okonkwo in Chinua Achebe's *Things Fall Apart* is impossible without a familiarity with Oedipus. But they warn him that he must diversify the rest of his course for race, gender, ethnicity, and class. He must have equal numbers of women writers on his reading list, he must cross ethnicities, historical periods, and class. And he must do all this in one semester. He gives in, for they threaten to relegate him to Comp 1 and 2 if he does not fall in line. As it is, he teaches one section of Comp 1 and 2, but also two sections of literature. If he angers them, Comp 1 and 2 are all he will teach.

And Sally, he says to himself, believes he has more. *She* wants more. *She* wants meaning. *She* wants her life's work. Is he to be responsible for helping her find her life's work? Is this the obligation of a husband? Was this included in his marriage vows?

On days like these, he thinks, I want my life's work, too. I was educated at Harvard, the premier university in the country. I am a scholar of Renaissance British Literature. I could have gone anywhere. I was in demand at prestigious institutions, but here I am, in this small public college in Brooklyn, of my own choosing, it is true; out of a sense of obligation, it is true: If not for those who believed a black boy like me from an outpost in the Caribbean could master the Masters, where would I be? I wanted to give back and I chose here, but now I am forced to submit to a political agenda, to a new-wave ideology cooked up by do-gooders operating under the misconception that racism will be eradicated when everyone comes to the table with his piece of the pie.

For, as Justin sees it, racism will be a fact of life until we acknowledge our common humanity, until we admit that we are all in this together—rich, poor, black, white, yellow, and red—the inheritors of a legacy that was forfeited in Eden. And so Justin has committed himself to showing his students that they can find themselves in ancient Greek literature, that Shakespeare can be meaningful to their lives.

The students are waiting for him when he enters the classroom. Today they will continue Hamlet. They have reached act 4. Hamlet is on a plain in Denmark. One more time Hamlet is berating himself for his lack of courage. He knows that his uncle murdered his father. He has the proof: his father's ghost returned from the dead to tell him all. He had actors stage a play about a king who was murdered as his father was murdered. He saw the guilt on his uncle's face. Why has he done nothing? Why has he not avenged his father's murder?

> Now, whether it be
> Bestial oblivion, or some craven scruple
> Of thinking too precisely on th' event—
> A thought which, quartered, hath but one part wisdom
> And ever three parts coward—

Justin reads the soliloquy aloud. Then suddenly, without warning, a thought sneaks up on him and plunges him into the dark tunnels of self-recrimination: *If Hamlet is a coward, then is he, Justin, a coward?*

He clears his throat. "Is Hamlet a coward?" He poses the

question to his students, but it is the answer to the question about himself he wants. Surely he has sufficient evidence that Sally is having an affair. She no longer enjoys sex with him; she stays out late; she hangs up the phone when he enters the room; the phone clicks off when he answers it. Why is he so ready to accept her word, her bogus explanation? What more evidence does he need?

A chair scrapes loudly across the tiled classroom floor in the back of the classroom and refocuses his attention. He pushes Sally away and leans forward on his desk. He forces himself to remember his purpose: to make Shakespeare relevant, *Hamlet* meaningful to his students. But *Hamlet* has become relevant to him, relevant to his quarrel with Sally.

"Miss Clark," he says. "You want to say what, Miss Clark?" Ordinarily, he does not address this student with such enthusiasm. Ordinarily he grits his teeth and does his best to cut her short, but now he wants a distraction. "What do you think, Miss Clark?"

He finds her intimidating, and not only because physically she is overpowering, a full-figured woman with big breasts, large thighs, and an ample backside; not only because she insists on Lycra, Lycra top and Lycra leggings (today, it is white top and black leggings that stretch over her voluptuous curves like the casing on sausage); not only because she has big hair, dark brown and auburn extensions rising above bangs across her forehead and falling in a thick mane to her shoulders; not only because she has hooked into her earlobes huge gold hoop earrings, two sets, the ones on the top larger than the others below them;

not only because she has plucked her eyebrows in thin streaks that arch menacingly above her eyes (menacingly is the way Justin sees them for he is ill at ease with women like Miriam Clark, women he senses know a world he is acquainted with only through books); not only because she has lined her full lips with a darker shade of the deep red lipstick she is wearing, but because, though she cannot be more than twenty-one, she is a no-nonsense, take-no-prisoners woman. Weeks before, after a discussion about Bernardo, the husband in García-Márquez's novel who returns his wife to her parents when he discovers she is not a virgin, he heard her say to one of the male students as she was leaving the class: "Yeah, let somebody just try to return me as if I was a bag of garbage!" Justin had no doubt then she would make chicken feed of such a man.

Now she is working her way to the front of the class.

"He a punk," she says. "Hamlet's a punk." She is punching the air with her finger, jerking her head back and forth on her neck like a duck as if to the beat of one of those rap songs that blast eternally from boom boxes and cars all over the city. Her earrings clang against each other. "A plain, ordinary, punky coward. Yeah, that's what he is. A cowardly punky punk. A punk." Not even her lilting Jamaican accent can soften the harshness of her accusation.

The class titters with nervous laughter. Justin too is affected. *Is that what he is: a cowardly punky punk?*

"A weak little man," Miriam Clark says. She is standing next to Justin's desk, facing the class.

"Preach, sister," one of the women in the class urges her on.

Justin feels a discomforting need to defend Hamlet, to defend himself, but he does not want to be chicken feed. He tells himself that that is what Miriam Clark will make of him if he speaks now. He knows a terrible rage burns in her. Mark Sandler has told him that her boyfriend was picked up by the police for delivering a bag of cocaine to a friend in Harlem. He is doing six to eight years. She was left with two small children, a boy four and a girl three. She was in her second year when her boyfriend was sent upstate. He made her promise to finish college.

"Thing is he never took drugs. Didn't even smoke weed," said Mark. "He was what the cops call a mule. He just delivered the goods."

"If he had any guts, he would off his uncle, Claudius, for killing his father," Miriam Clark is saying. "He's a weak crybaby making excuses. A mama's boy, that's what he is. Crying because his mama has a new boyfriend. A punk. I wouldn't let anyone get off killing my father. You hurt the people I love, and it's Good Night for you."

Mark said there was nothing Miriam Clark could do. She had no money for lawyers and the lawyer the court gave her thought black boys should be penned upstate anyway. Or sent back to Africa.

"Yeah, Hamlet knows what he is. He's right. He knows he has no balls. He knows he's coward. How many times is he going to say that? Punk!"

Justin decides to let her wear out her anger. All for a bag of cocaine, a delivery that is made every sixty seconds on Wall Street, Mark had said.

And then an older student raises his hand. He is close to sixty, older than Justin. Like the rest of the college, the students in his class are made up of young high school graduates, but older adults, too, returning to school, some after an absence of two and three decades.

"Mr. Blackstone?" Justin's voice strains with anxiety.

"What I want to say, what I am going to say, may not please Miriam, but I want her to listen."

"Miss Clark?" He turns to Miriam Clark.

Her chest is heaving, but she is consumed by private thoughts now.

"Can I speak, Miriam?" Mr. Blackstone asks her. A stately man with kind eyes, he is old enough to be her grandfather.

Miriam bites her bottom lip.

"Is it okay?"

She waves her hand in front of her face. She could have been brushing away a fly. Or a bad thought. Charles Blackstone takes it as a sign of consent.

"I'm a prison guard," he says. "In Rikers Island."

The students give him their full attention.

"Every day I see more and more hotheads come in the prison. Young Turks like you. No offense, Miriam. I don't say this to insult you." He glances in her direction. She is breathing normally. "I want to help you," he says. "All of you. The professor here wants us to figure out what is Hamlet's problem and if he did the right thing. I say Hamlet did the right thing to take his time to figure out what to do. If the young boys I see in jail took their time to figure out things, they wouldn't be in jail. You don't always have to do something when you get mad, when somebody don't do right by you."

Nobody moves. Nobody makes a sound.

"I know it's hard when the police treat you like you're nobody. When they snatch you from the corner and all you're doing is talking to your buddies. Or when they stop you in the street because you're wearing a good leather jacket they think you shouldn't own. But don't challenge them. They have the power. Say Yes, sir; No, sir, even if you want to kill them. Say Yes, sir; No, sir. Give them what they want. They just itching for an excuse to send you upstate, don't you know? A lot of the young men in Rikers Island wouldn't be there if they knew how to say Yes, sir; No, sir. Think out things first. Don't act when you're hot and sweaty and you want to hurt somebody. You end up hurting yourself. Take time to think, cool off. Figure out how you can do something so that you don't end up hurting yourself. Because that is all you do when you act with a hot head. You hurt yourself."

Even Miriam Clark is still. The corners of her mouth twitch as if she is about to cry. She gathers her books and stuffs them in her bag. She rushes out of the classroom.

Minutes later, the period ends. The classroom is empty but Justin remains sitting at the desk. *Yes, Hamlet is not a coward.* He has his answer. Not only should he not do anything more, he should not have done anything at all. He should not have said a word. He should have waited until he had spoken to Sally. He should have given himself time to think. He should not have jumped to conclusions. He should not have let a mirage of letters in the early dawn lead him to doubt her.

On his way home he buys a bunch of tulips. They are Sally's favorite flowers. He gets pink ones with white scalloped edges. Pink is Sally's favorite color.

The house is strangely quiet when he opens the front door. It is half past five. When it's Sally's turn to pick up Giselle, she is usually home by half past five. He calls out to her.

"Sally!" He walks into the kitchen. She is sitting quietly at the table sipping a mug of tea.

"Where's Giselle?"

"Anna has her."

"Anna?"

"She has taken her to the library."

There is a storytime program for young children at the central branch of the public library on Grand Army Plaza. Around six, the librarian or some good storyteller reads a bedtime story. Some of the children come to the library already dressed for bed, wearing pajamas under their coats. Giselle loves this storytime program. Either he or Sally takes her when they can.

"I thought we needed to talk," Sally is saying, "so I asked Anna to take her."

He does not want this. He feels foolish now standing next to her, the bunch of tulips clutched in his right hand and pressed against his chest. He lets his hand fall and the tulips point downward, toward the floor. She notices.

"Where did you get them?" she asks.

He does not want to say he bought them for her. "It's such a nasty day, I thought they would brighten up the house."

She takes them from him and reaches for a vase. While she puts water in it, he tells her about Miriam Clark and Charles Blackstone's response to her, how he turned *Hamlet* into a cautionary tale that seemed to scare the class. He is not conscious that he is telling her this because he wants her to come to his same conclusion: They need time to think. He should never have disturbed their calm that morning by asking the question: *Did you have something to tell me, Sally?* He is conscious only of filling spaces, of trying to ease the tension between them.

Sally knows about Miriam and sympathizes deeply with her. She knows where the tentacles of racism can reach. Right into your front yard, in the quiet of the morning, when you are turning in your sleep, when your father places an arm around your mother and draws her to him. Right in the bullet of a gunshot that triggers off a nightmare. Then your father is lying in a pool of blood, your mother is pulling her hair from the roots. Tufts of black balls fall softly to the ground, light as feathers. Your brother turns to stone and you try to move him. "Run, run," you shout. "Go get help." He is older than you. He should protect you. You scream, and his muscles soften, loosen. Urine rolls down his pants.

Sally used to live in Harlem, but not always in an apartment. When she was a child, she lived in an entire house, with four floors and a garden in the back, in a brownstone house on Strivers Row on 139th Street. Her father was a doctor, a graduate of an Ivy League medical school who baffled his friends by returning to Harlem to open a practice. They could not understand: He had his life in front of him, a future that promised fame and fortune. But Dr. George Henry was a man of conscience. He wanted to practice medicine where he was most needed. His sister called him a foolish man. She said so with a tenderness that brought water to her eyes.

In the summer of 1965 Dr. Henry decided to make good on a promise he had made to his wife, Ursula Henry. He rented a house for the summer on a lake in Alabama, the state where his wife had spent her childhood. His plan was not to stay there the entire summer, of course. He would come when he could, every two weeks. Word got out about the big shot doctor from the North. The big shot, uppity Nigra doctor acting like white folks.

One night, August 15, a posse of men in white hoods and robes rode into their front yard. Sally's father ran out with a shotgun. They killed him in self-defense, the Alabama police said. Her mother had a nervous breakdown from which she never recovered. Sally was four, her brother, Tony, was seven. He overdosed on heroin when he was twenty-five.

Sally told Justin this story just once, before they were married. She did not want his sympathy. She simply wanted to warn him about a major difference between them: He has not had the experience of growing up black in America. But she had read Khalil Gibran: Let there be spaces in your togetherness. Complete agreement, she said, is not a requirement for marriage.

Justin shares this view: the notion of two becoming one is

a fantasy, a myth. He married Sally because she understood this. She would give him room for his work. He did not think, when he proposed to her, that she would need room for her work. She taught primary school, little children learning primary colors.

"What Charles Blackstone says makes sense," she says, "but sometimes you have to take the bull by the horns."

Justin tries again. Perhaps he has not told it well. Mr. Blackstone had managed to quiet the class. Mr. Blackstone had calmed down the excitable Miriam.

"It does make sense, though, to keep a cool head. To think things out," he says.

"It depends," she says.

They are quiet again.

"Well, we better get along with it," she says abruptly, putting the vase with the tulips on the table. "I think the best thing for me to do is to move out, don't you think?" She sits down.

Cubes of ice slide down Justin's chest and settle in the brine at the pit of his stomach. "Wait, wait a minute, Sally," he says. He pulls out the chair opposite to her. This is not the way he wants things to go. This is not the way at all.

"After all, it is *your* house," she says.

The ice melts and the brine, cold, churns. Justin puts one hand on the back of the chair and braces himself. "Don't you feel you are carrying things a tidbit too far?" He is relieved he has managed to choose words that spare him from exposure, that camouflage how scared he feels at this moment.

"Tidbit?" she asks.

And at once he realizes his mistake. It is a quintessentially British word weighted with quintessentially British condescension. The colonial boy automatically mimicking British ways.

"'Tidbit too far?'" she repeats.

Why couldn't he have simply said *Too far, much too far?*

"Too far." He says it now. "You are taking things much too far."

But she is already angry. "Not when you are sneaking up on me to find out who I am talking to on the phone."

What should happen next is that his fear should intensify. What happens next is that he feels a load, a stack of bricks, topple off his shoulders and fall, crashing to pieces on the ground. *No more secrets.*

"Okay," he says and holds up his hands, the palms open wide. "Okay." He pulls the chair out further. *It's out in the open.* He sits.

"Don't think I didn't see you," Sally says.

"I wouldn't have been worried if each time you didn't end the conversation or put down the phone the minute I walked in the room," he says.

"You still had no right to do that."

"No right?" He will not sit passively for this one. "What do you mean, *no right*? I am your husband." But only a few weeks ago he was chastising a male student for treating his girlfriend as property. "At least tell your boyfriend to call you somewhere else," he says, flicking off that tremor of conscience that could have stopped him. "Don't have him intrude on my privacy. In my house."

"Yes," she says, "you don't have to remind me. I know it is *your* house."

Moments ago when she said *your house* he did not correct her though he had taken pains when they married to assure her that he considered the house to be both theirs. So he is not innocent now of flexing his muscles, of trying to dry up the liquid that had pooled in his stomach. "Don't change the subject," he says.

"I don't have a boyfriend. That is not the problem."

"And don't have him hanging up on me, either."

"There is no other man."

"You want space?" he jeers, but he is acting as much for her as for himself. "I know what you want space for."

She looks at him directly in his eyes. She does not waver. "Okay, Justin, okay. I will tell you. But it is not what you want to hear."

He sits up and prepares himself.

"I know what you want," she says. "You want a Sally done gone and done me wrong song. You want Justin, the Righteous; Justin, the sinned against; Sally, the sinner. But you won't get that, Justin, because Sally has not sinned." She looks down on her hands. "It was my therapist," she says.

"Therapist?" He repeats the word foolishly.

"Those calls," she says facing him again, "they were from my therapist. I didn't want to let you know I was in therapy. I didn't want to hear your scornful remarks. I didn't want you telling me about my psychobabble again. I told the therapist to hang up if you answered the phone. I lowered my voice because I didn't want you to hear what I was saying. And when I come home late, it is because I've had an appointment with the therapist. That's it, Justin. No man, no lover, no boyfriend, no husband betrayed. Just an unhappy wife trying to make herself better."

The liquid returns, the acidity in the brine burns. He stands up. "I bought the tulips for you," he says. He knows he says it too late.

"They're pretty," she says.

He walks to the kitchen door and looks through the glass panes into the darkening evening. "So what now?"

"I want to move in with Anna."

Frost encases his heart. "And what about Giselle?" he asks, quietly, softly.

"She goes with me, of course."

He does not move. He does not turn to look at her. He remains where he is, at the kitchen door, still staring into the dark. "No," he says and repeats it. "No."

She waits.

"I cannot have you do that. No, Sally."

"You cannot have me . . . ?" Her voice trembles with indignation.

He walks toward the table. "If you go, Giselle stays here," he says. "This plot you and Anna have cooked up won't work, Sally."

"Anna has nothing to do with this," she says.

He stands in front of her. "I don't want you to leave, Sally. I want you to stay, but if you leave, Giselle remains here." His voice is flat, toneless, but there is no mistaking its finality. "Understand me, Sally, I will not let you take Giselle out of this house."

SIX

Around seven o'clock it begins to snow, a light dusting of white that evaporates the second it reaches the ground, but twenty minutes later the snow comes down in fat flakes and makes its magic again on the filthy streets. A carpet of white pretties up the hills of dirty snow on the edges of pavements and covers the slush and garbage on the street corners.

Justin and Sally have not spoken to each other since he gave her his ultimatum. She is curled up on an armchair in the living room, her head bent over an open book propped up against her thighs. He is in his den grading papers, or trying to. It is not only his fight with Sally that makes it difficult for him to concentrate. He is worried. Giselle is not back and the snow is coming down harder.

He gets up and peers through the window. *What time is Anna expected to bring Giselle home?* He wishes he could ask Sally. He looks at his watch. It is eight o'clock. At twenty past eight, he puts down his pencil and looks outside again. He cannot see his street from the windows in his den but the oak tree is outlined in white and piles of snow surround the trunk.

He listens for sounds at the front door. The main roadways will be slushy. Cars will slide across them. There will be accidents. He cannot sit still, and ten minutes later he is up again. He goes down to the kitchen. Sally has left his dinner on the table. There is no place set for her or for Giselle. She must have eaten already. She must have fed Giselle before she left.

He pours a glass of water from the plastic container in the refrigerator and walks into the living room. Sally does not look up from her book. Perhaps she knows there is nothing to worry about. Then an awful thought snakes its way into his head. He is practically running when he climbs the stairs. But everything is as it was in Giselle's bedroom. Her favorite doll is there on her bed; her clothes are in the closet.

The snow comes down in fatter flakes, in thick drifts that stick to the window.

"Isn't it a little late for Giselle to be out?" He is in the living room again.

"Giselle will be fine. She's with Anna," Sally says, but she still does not lift her head from her book.

"The roads will be slippery," he says.

"Anna's a good driver."

"Maybe . . . ," he begins again.

"Anna has her cell phone. If there's a problem, she'll call."

Yes, he should have thought of that. Still, her calm annoys him.

"Since when have you two become such good buddies?" he asks.

"Anna and I have always been best friends," she says.

And he knows that, but it is different now. She is threatening to move in with Anna. "Well, you're real close now," he says spitefully.

"Giselle likes Anna, and Anna loves Giselle. They get along well." She seems unperturbed.

"Anna is lazy," he says.

She flashes him a dirty look. "To you, maybe. But the people at the Botanic Garden don't think so." She returns to her book and flips a page. "They love her," she says.

"She's supposed to be an English professor, for Chrissake." He has raised his voice, and Sally twists her body sharply toward him again. She opens her mouth to speak but the doorbell rings and the words, if she has uttered them, get lost in the flurry of Justin's race to the door.

"Giselle! At last!" Justin bends down to pick up his daughter. Sally hovers next to him and when he straightens up, Giselle reaches over to Sally and pulls their heads together with her tiny arms.

For an uncomfortable moment Justin and Sally find themselves cheek against cheek, and then Sally disentangles herself. She removes Giselle's arm from across her neck, kisses it and backs away. "Had a great time with Aunt Anna, didn't you, Giselle?"

Justin puts Giselle down. "My God, your hair is all covered with snow." He does not give her a chance to answer Sally's question.

"It's nice, Daddy. I like the snow in my hair." Giselle licks the side of her mouth where a speck of snow has melted.

"Where is your hat?" Justin looks at Anna as he asks this question. Anna glances at Sally and Sally rolls her eyes in sympathy.

"Where is her hat, Anna?" Justin is more direct.

"It's not Aunt Anna's fault," Giselle interjects. "I lost it in the park."

"She could catch a cold, Anna," Justin says tersely.

"She lost it when we were leaving. We went by car to the library so she didn't need it."

"Is that why her head is covered with snow?" Justin dusts Giselle's head though by now it is merely damp.

"Don't be mad with Aunt Anna, Daddy." Giselle clasps his hand.

"And why are you so late?"

"We stopped for ice cream, Daddy."

"Anna, you know I don't like Giselle having sweets so late at night. It stimulates her. She can't sleep if she eats sweets this late."

"It was not sweets, Daddy." Giselle tightens her grip. "Aunt Anna bought ice cream for me."

"I'm leaving," Anna says. She had not taken off her coat nor unbuttoned it. Now she flings one end of her scarf across her shoulder. "Bye, sweetie." She hugs Giselle. "See you tomorrow, Sally." She kisses Sally. "I'll be over by five."

Sally and Giselle follow her to the door. Justin does not move. He is thinking, as she says good-bye again to Sally, *Come over by five if you want to, but this is the last time I will permit Giselle to be alone with you.*

GISELLE TALKS NONSTOP through her bath. It is Justin's turn to bathe her. Sally makes an appearance at the doorway and then is gone, but it seems enough to satisfy Giselle that nothing has changed: one parent is nearby when the other gives her a bath or reads a bedtime story.

"The librarian looks like you, Daddy," Giselle tells him, lathering her doll's face. She keeps one doll in the bathroom and washes it when she bathes.

"*Like* me?" he asks her.

"Well, not like you, Daddy. You're more handsomer."

"More handsome," he corrects her.

"You are like the prince that woke up Snow White," she says. She has yet to learn about race.

"Well, not quite that handsome."

"Yes, you are. Yes, you are. Mommy thinks so. She told me so."

He feels a physical pang to his heart. Perhaps he and Sally can fix what is wrong between them. Perhaps they should talk some more. Perhaps when she told him that she sees a therapist he should have asked her why. He should have not allowed doubts to gnaw at him, to have prevented him from asking.

"Mommy loves you, Daddy. She loves you just as much as I do."

She knows something is not right. He tries to distract her. "Tell me about the story you heard at the library," he says.

"It was about Brer Rabbit," she says. "Throw me anywhere, but not in the briar patch." She covers her face with her hands and shakes her head. "Anywhere, but not in the briar patch."

Justin dumps a handful of bubbles on her head. She giggles. "You know, Daddy, Brer Rabbit was lying. He loves the briar patch." She is still laughing when he bundles her up in a towel.

Later, when Sally reads to her, he sits on the rocking chair in her room. It is long past her bedtime, and before Sally can finish the first page, her eyelids grow heavy. Justin sighs: He cannot imagine a night when he is not able to sit like this with her, watching her fall to sleep. He and Sally tuck her in and leave the room together.

"You didn't have to be so nasty to Anna," Sally says as soon as they are out of earshot. "She is kind to Giselle."

"We are Giselle's parents," he says. "We are kind to her. She does not need Anna."

"A child needs anyone who loves her."

He waits for the platitude: *It takes a village.*

She disappoints him.

"If Anna loved her like her parents do," he says, "she would not have given her ice cream so late at night. She would have known it was not good for her."

Sally walks away from him without a word.

He follows her into the bedroom. "And she would have brought her back home as soon as she saw the snow."

"I meant what I said, Justin." Sally stops him cold. "I'm moving in with Anna."

He feels he has no other choice but to save his dignity. "And I meant what I said. Giselle is not leaving this house."

That night he sleeps on the couch in his den.

THEY ARE CORDIAL to each other in the morning. Each does the usual chores so breakfast is finished at the usual time. They are cleaning up when Sally announces she is taking Giselle to Manhattan. There is an animated movie Giselle wants to see. It is Saturday.

"Are you coming, too?" Giselle asks him.

Sally does not give him time to answer. "Remember, Giselle? We're going with Aunt Anna."

"Goody," says the child and then abruptly her face darkens. "We're going with Aunt Anna because she has a car," she explains to Justin.

It begins at an early age, Justin thinks. We are making her feel guilty.

"And Mommy says you need to use your car today," Giselle adds, smiling brightly at Justin, happy she has something to offer him, too.

He shoots an angry look at Sally. "I think you should take the subway," he says. "The roads are dangerous."

She seems about to disagree but changes her mind. "I'll tell Anna," she says.

"Fine."

They are gone fifteen minutes when he decides to go out himself. She'll come back home tonight, he thinks. She'll not take Giselle without telling him and she will not leave without Giselle. He knows his wife. She adores her daughter.

IT IS NOT snowing this morning. He looks out the window, and, as he suspects, his car is buried. It is a light blue Volvo, a car he has driven for more than ten years. A matter of priorities, he reminds himself again. He pulls on his waterproof boots, puts on his bulky parka, and takes the red shovel from the vestibule. His neighbor, Jim Grant, is already outside, shoveling himself out.

This is how old men get heart attacks, Justin thinks. He calls out to him.

"Let me get that for you, Jim."

"Think I'm gonna drop down dead, young pup." They laugh.

"Have it your way," he says.

"'Preciate the thought, but I'm almost done. Next time."

And this is all it takes, this simple light banter between Jim Grant and himself, to spark thoughts of mortality that press upon Justin as he drives down Eastern Parkway on his way to his mother's. *Think I'm gonna drop down dead, young pup.* Suppose it is *he* who's gonna drop down dead with a heart attack?

He turns on Rochester Avenue and makes a right on Atlantic. He is forty-five, only a mere fifteen years younger than Jim Grant. He has read the reports. Cholesterol builds, the arteries harden after forty. He should have had Giselle when he was younger. He'll be fifty when she is in fourth grade, sixty-three when she graduates from college. Other thoughts begin to fill his head and he struggles hard to block them.

He works out, he goes to the gym, he eats sensibly, he reminds himself. It is not enough. It does not work, this effort he makes to stay in the present. He is on the Belt Parkway. He is heading toward Long Island.

Maybe he won't be alive to dance at Giselle's wedding.

And then there it is. The memory surfaces: His father was not alive to dance at his wedding. His father had a heart attack at fifty. But is not fear Justin feels (in only five more years he will be the age his father was) or sadness. It is resentment. He resents his father for dying. He resents his father for dying before his father was a father to him.

Not until he exits off the Southern State Parkway does this feeling dissipate, and then only because it is replaced by a deeper resentment, a greater anger. For he is now in a black residential area, an American kinder, gentler, more compassionate segregated residential area, the kind of area one finds everywhere on Long Island, where those who fought to free the world from oppression, to stop the likes of Hitler in his tracks, to put a halt to racist policies that had taken the lives of so many, bought homes with funds from the GI bill and boasted of family values.

His mother said that when his father bought here, they set off a stampede of whites to the shore. But everything has remained the same: the houses with aprons of green lawns, the park, the school on Grand Avenue, except now garbage men throw half empty garbage cans on sidewalks, flowers don't seem able to grow in the park, and overnight teachers have forgotten how to teach children to read.

Justin makes two right turns onto Jones Street and pulls up at number 25. He is in front of his mother's house, a small Cape Cod with a neat garden, a white picket fence, and a sidewalk that is spotless, because each time the garbage truck leaves his mother comes out to sweep. Five summers ago Justin took off the wooden shingles he hated to paint and put up light blue aluminum ones on the bottom half of the house, white ones on the top and on the dormers. His gift to his mother, though she jokingly said to him it was also a gift to himself. He grins now remembering. A sharp lady, his mother. Perceptive.

He rings the bell. She answers.

"Good Lord Almighty, what has brought you out on a day like today?" Her thin arms encircle his neck. She is a tall woman and her hand reaches easily to the back of his head. She presses his face into her shoulder and Justin breathes in the light scent of eau de cologne on her neck. It is a quick embrace. It is over in seconds; then she is standing apart from him, momentarily embarrassed. For she is a middle-class West Indian woman who has been taught the English ways. Stiff upper lip. Air kisses, not hugs.

"Haven't seen this much snow in years," she says, looking tenderly at him, one hand across her chest clutching her waist, the other stroking her neck.

"That's March for you," he says, unzipping his coat.

She practically leaps to help him, and he slips out his arm while she holds up his coat. "Must be that global warming they're talking about so much. Or is it the Nina and the Pinta?"

He knows she knows better, but she likes to play this game. "El Niño," he says.

"Niño, Niña, what difference does it make?"

Even when there are just the two of them to witness, she wants to be reminded: her son, flesh of her flesh, went to the best of the best with the best. He is a genius. He knows everything. It doesn't matter that he tells her his major was literature, British literature.

"And where's Sally? Giselle?"

He rarely visits her without Sally and Giselle, at first for Sally's sake, when Sally worried that his mom did not like her. She is not demonstrative, he explained. But she had told him that of all his girlfriends, she liked Sally best. "Not as a wife for you," Sally said. It was not true. His mother said it was time he married, which, admittedly, was not the same as saying, "You should marry Sally." So he made a point of taking Sally with him on his visits to her. He wanted her to know he was not only a son; he was a husband, too. And then there was the birthday card she sent Sally one year after they were married. She signed it *Mother* and put in parenthesis, *I want to be one to you.*

"A son can't come to visit his mother without his wife and daughter?" he asks her.

"A son usually doesn't," she says, but she does not pry. She does not ask for more.

Her hair has turned completely white. She has it cut close to her scalp, but it is thick and covers her head completely. In winter it is straight, but it curls in the humidity of summer. Giselle has inherited her thick hair. He hopes not its whiteness. He cannot remember when her hair was black. It began turning, she said, when she was thirty-four.

When she told him that—the age she was when her hair began to gray—he did not think: That was the year she left for America. For she was thirty-four when she left their island. He thought: That was the year she left *me* to come to America.

She has a fine nose and thin lips. With her coloring, she could pass for an Indian from India. She has told him the stories of the Indian men who wanted to court her, not believing she had not one drop of Indian blood. A mélange of African, French, and Carib Indian, she was fond of saying. Columbus made that mistake, but I don't have to. It's Carib Indian, not East Indian.

She is an elegant woman. Justin is proud to be her son.

"Tea?" she asks him when they are settled around the table in her kitchen. She will not drink coffee. She calls it the American tea. She drinks British tea. And yet she has no real love for England. They brought us as slaves to plant cocoa and sugar cane for them, she said, and when they found oil in Point à Pierre, they didn't want to leave.

She drops a tea bag in his mug. "I don't know how Americans can drink this without milk," she says. "They put lemon in it and they drink it cold, too." She pours hot water from the kettle. "I like my tea strong, with evaporated milk. Habits die hard, I guess. What you learn to do as a child, you still do when you get old like me. As the tree is bent, so will it grow."

As the tree is bent . . . It is the very reason he will not let Sally take Giselle from him. He is Giselle's father. She is his daughter. He wants to be her teacher.

"Is Giselle still bright like you were?" she asks him.

It is a double-edged question. She is asking about Giselle, but she wants to reminisce.

"Was I a bright child, Mother?" He stirs milk in his tea.

"The brightest of the bright."

"I read Shakespeare to Giselle. She likes it."

His mother laughs. "A prodigy," she says.

"She doesn't understand a word, but she knows how it's supposed to sound," he says. "Except *twangling*. She understands *twangling*. I read from *The Tempest* the other night. Caliban's soliloquy."

She knows it. "'Be not afeard: the isle is full of noises.' I miss it sometimes, you know, Justin."

"You could go back."

"It's too late to go back."

"It's never too late."

"I'm seventy. It's been thirty-six years."

"You still have friends there."

"People I know, not friends. People change. I've been away too long."

It is true for him, too. He had put one foot in front of the other, and when he looked back he discovered he had covered a forest. The trees had thickened: new leaves, new branches spread out in places where they hadn't. Undergrowth hid the path he had trodden.

He changes the subject. He does not like to hear this sadness in his mother's voice. "Sally does not drink black tea, you know," he says. He sips his tea.

"I thought she likes tea."

"She drinks Celestial Awakenings."

His mother gets up. "Have you had breakfast?"

"Or Glorious Mornings. Something like that."

"What do you want? Pancakes or toast?"

"Or Heavenly Paradise."

She takes the frying pan from out of the drawer under the stove. "Did you and Sally have a fight?" she asks.

"Whatever gave you that idea?"

"You haven't answered my question."

"Pancakes," he says.

"No, about you and Sally."

"I know that is what you meant. She wants more. She wants to move out."

His mother stands by the sink holding the frying pan. She looks out through the window. "It never stops, does it?" she says. "These modern women."

"She says she's unhappy."

She does not ask him why. She does not ask what Sally means by more. She says, "What does happiness have to do with anything? You don't break up a home because you're unhappy."

She is still standing by the window, her eyes fixed on the leafless trees. He knows she is not thinking of Sally. There is a deep hurt between them that has not healed.

"She wants to take Giselle with her. I will not let her do that."

She looks straight at him. Her eyes are watery. She blinks and the water is gone. "You can't do that, Justin. You can't be so cruel. A child needs its mother."

She has said words that are better left unsaid between them. They have come out of her mouth without her thinking. She walks away from the window and turns on the tap. She rinses the frying pan. It does not need rinsing.

"A child needs its father, too," he says.

"It needs its mother more."

"So you knew, Mother, that I needed you?" It is she who has opened this door.

"Oh Justin," she says.

"I was older than Giselle, but I still needed a mother."

She puts down the frying pan and comes to sit next to him. "Is this why you have come here this morning, Justin? You have come to beat me with that same old song."

"It's not a song."

"I know, I know." She touches his hand lightly. "I know. But what is past is past and cannot be undone."

"I came to tell you about Sally. I thought you'd understand my position."

"Your position?"

"That I can't let Sally take Giselle."

"A mother is different from a father," she says. "A child needs a father, but a child needs a mother more."

"I needed both of you," he says. "And both of you left me."

"We did not leave you, Justin. We came to America to make a better life for you. We didn't think it would take so long to get a green card, and then when we did . . . Well, you know what you did. You know better than me why you did it. But no matter how many times you explain it, I will never understand. I accept it. That's all. I accepted your decision a long time ago. I have come to terms with it."

It is old ground. He does not want to cover it again. He has come to her, however without premeditation, because he believes that of all the people in the world, she will understand why he cannot give up Giselle.

Yes, they came back to Trinidad nine years later when the INS agreed to give them green cards. And, yes, he refused to go back with them. But the story is not that simple and she knows it.

He was seven when she went to New York, but not, as she said, to make a better life for him. She went to be with her husband, the man she loved. Even today, there are people in Trinidad who still say dreamily of the marriage between Sophie Anderson, nurse, and James Peters, poet: Ah, there was a marriage made in heaven.

She cried for days when his father left, unable to eat, unable to drink. *Unable to take care of him.* Then a letter arrived with passage to New York, and she left him with her unmarried sister, gave him hugs and kisses and promised to come back soon. She never did. Not soon. It was the early 1960s. A revolution was brewing in America. They had sent for James Peters because James Peters was writing the poetry they needed: poems about resistance, poems about defiance.

Sophie stayed because Sophie loved James Peters. Six months went by and then a year. Their visas expired. One thing led to another. They became illegal immigrants.

"It took a long time for us to get a green card," his mother is saying to him. "You know we couldn't come to Trinidad until we got it. The Americans wouldn't let us back in."

He remembers the letter he wrote to her. "So what does it matter? Come home. You will not be illegal here."

They needed money. Poetry did not bring them money. It brought fame, notoriety, but not money. Sophie was a nurse. She could not work in the hospitals, of course. It was not simply a matter of a work permit; Sophie had been trained in Trinidad. To work in American hospitals, she needed an American diploma. So she took a sleep-away job with a rich family in Long Island who needed someone to look after a sickly grandfather. She came home on weekends, and then once a month, but James got lonely. He did not stop loving her, but in between he had an American girlfriend. What was a man to do?

They never stopped making promises to Justin. Soon. In a matter of months. Sophie's employers had agreed to sponsor her. The papers would be ready soon.

"You don't understand," she wrote back to him. "Your father is famous. The movement needs him."

They returned to Trinidad nine years later, in 1972. Justin was sixteen, at the top of his class at his father's alma mater, St. Mary's College, the Catholic high school. He had just gotten the results from his O level exams. He had made distinctions in the seven subjects he had taken. The hopes of St. Mary's were pinned on him. If he took the A level exams in two years, he could win the Island Scholarship. St. Mary's had never forgotten that the young V. S. Naipaul had won it in literature from the Protestant secondary school, Queens Royal College. Naipaul went on to Oxford and then fame as a writer. Justin Peters would make up for losing to Naipaul. But that was not the reason that Justin did not return to America when his parents came for him with the green card. With his seven O level distinctions, he could have been admitted to a university in America, perhaps even to Harvard, perhaps even with a scholarship.

His father was in Trinidad four days when he had a massive heart attack. He died on the spot. Justin never forgave him.

"It was the contradictions in his life that killed him," he told his mother. "He was a poet, not a politician. He had allowed America to turn him into a politician. His poetry became narrow and limited. All he ever wrote when he went to America were protest poems about American racism, segregation, and the Ku Klux Klan. He came back to Trinidad, and when he saw how much he had given up, his heart burst open."

He had to explain himself more carefully to Sally after she told him how her father was murdered.

"My father's first job was to be a father to his son and a husband to my mother," he said. "He failed at both."

Sally, too, had not forgiven her father for his recklessness.

He had a young wife and two little children when he stormed out to the yard with a shotgun.

No, they both agreed, being a good father and a good mother is a parent's first duty. Which is why neither can countenance a life without their daughter under their roof.

"I suppose staying in Trinidad did you some good." His mother is anxious to end the silence that has settled on her son. "I suppose you would not have won that scholarship to Harvard."

She is right. No matter how he explains it, she will never understand. He was not thinking of becoming a hero for St. Mary's when he refused to return to America with her. He was angry with her—with his father and with her, but especially with his father. His death was the ultimate abandonment. He would be all that his father was not, all that he truly wanted to be. He would become a writer, not a political writer, but an artist. He would embrace the literature his father eschewed. But Justin did not become a writer. In the end, he did not have the talent. In the end, he resented his father even more. His father had thrown away a gift neither money nor brains could secure.

"At some point you're going to have to accept that your father was a good man. He loved both of us." His mother continues to try to end this impasse between them.

He cannot tell her what everyone knows: James Peters had an American girlfriend. He cannot hurt her. She is his mother.

"I know he was, Mother." He squeezes her hand. "And you were a good mother. It was because of you I didn't go to Oxford."

She lets her hand linger in his. "Remember that priest?" A wide smile breaks across her face. "Your headmaster at St. Mary's?"

"Father Higginsmith."

"Lord, was he fit to be tied when you said Harvard! Almost had a heart attack."

"He was an Englishman. No university in the world was better than Oxford. That's the way he thought."

"I used to tell those uppity people at the hospital that my son could have gotten in anywhere: Oxford, Cambridge, Yale, MIT. I don't think they truly believed me until I brought that photograph of you at your graduation. I kept it at my station at the hospital until the day I retired."

He wants to tell her that he loves her, but the words do not come easily. They are not demonstrative. Not with each other. It is not only her Victorian self-consciousness that puts this barrier between them. It is the difficulty he has in closing the chasm that had yawned between them nine long years. He was a boy when she left him, a man when she returned.

"You were here, Mother," he says. "How could I go to England?"

She makes tiny circles with her fingers on his hand. "I know, Son. I know."

They find other things to talk about at breakfast, the weather, Giselle's latest expressions, her likes and dislikes, which his mother compares to his. "She is your daughter truly, Justin." And they talk about his peeves with the curriculum committee at the college. She agrees with him that his students need to know more than just the literature of their cultural heritage, but she brushes aside his arguments. All that stuff about common humanity is for you intellectuals in the Ivory Tower to figure out, she says. Her reasons are practical: His students need to have the keys to get in the door. You can't change anything if you are outside the room, she says. You have to get in. You have to speak their language. You have to know how the enemy thinks.

"The enemy?" Justin asks.

"I mean the ones who are trying to keep black people out of the room, from their share of the American pie."

No doubt his father's words.

They finish breakfast and Justin helps her clear the table and wash the dishes. Later, when he is ready to leave, one arm already in his jacket, she returns to their earlier conversation. "So what will you do about Giselle?" she asks.

"I don't know," he says.

"Can a mother give her son a piece of advice?" she asks him.

"Always, Mother."

"Give it time. Don't rush into anything. Don't say words you will regret. Don't poison the air. Talk to Sally. She loves you. Hear what she has to say. Work it out."

He kisses her.

SEVEN

Giselle comes home with a cold. She is sniffling when she greets him. Sally, too, is red-eyed. He wants to be on his best behavior. He wants to follow his mother's advice. He does not want to lose his family. He does not say to Sally he was right when he chastised Anna for keeping Giselle out so late at night. He does not tell her that if Giselle had lost her hat, Anna should have put her scarf over her head, and if Anna had done that, Giselle would not have the cold she has now. He hugs Giselle. He says, "Poor child, you need to go to bed right away." He pats her head when it drops to his shoulder.

Sally makes hot chocolate. Justin changes Giselle's clothes. They drink the hot chocolate together at the table in the kitchen. A family. Sally says Anna had invited them to dinner, but she thought it best to come home straight away. Justin says she did the right thing. They are having a conversation.

Giselle asks him if he wants her to tell him about the movie.

He says, later. Tell me tomorrow. Tomorrow is Sunday. If you feel better, Mommy and I will take you out to eat tomorrow.

"At McDonald's?" Giselle's face brightens up. "Aunt Anna was going to take us to McDonald's."

Sally interjects. "Not McDonald's," she says quickly. "You know Daddy and I don't like you to go to McDonald's."

"But Aunt Anna said . . ."

"I wasn't going to let Anna take her to McDonald's." Sally is speaking directly to Justin.

He senses a truce in the offing. "Did you get a chance to have anything to eat?" he asks her.

"Giselle had a sandwich at lunchtime."

"I'm not hungry," Giselle says.

"Then it's off to bed with you, young lady," says Justin. "When you wake up, I'll fix us all a huge breakfast."

Giselle falls asleep before Justin can read her a bedtime story. He comes downstairs and finds Sally still sitting at the table. She is intently tracing stencils on colored sheets of oak board.

"Aren't you tired?" he asks.

"Yes, but I have to finish this for my class on Monday."

"Don't you want something to eat?" he asks her again. "You said Giselle ate, but what about you?"

"I'm too tired to make anything. Have you eaten?"

"I was at Mother's," he says.

"Ahh."

"She made me a huge brunch. Pancakes, bacon, scrambled eggs."

"How is she?"

"She asked about you."

Sally is bent over the oak board, coloring the spaces in the pattern she has stenciled. It is a basket of fruit. She is coloring carefully, the apples red, the pears green, the grapes purple. No color runs into the other. "And you said?" she asks.

He takes a deep breath. "Sally, I want us to work out whatever it is that is bothering you," he says. "I don't want to lose my family. I don't want Giselle to come from a broken home, her mother one place, her father another."

She does not look up from the pattern she is coloring. "Neither do I," she says.

He turns and walks toward the cupboard. "I'll open a can of soup," he says.

"That would be good. I think I may be getting the same cold Giselle has."

He is opening a can of soup when he tries again. "I think we said things to each other last night that we should not have said."

"Things happen for a reason," she says. She has stopped coloring and is facing him.

He does not understand.

"I mean the snow. Giselle's cold," she says.

He is trying hard to be patient. "Things don't always happen for a reason, Sally."

"Well, last night we weren't talking to each other," she says, "and now we are. If Giselle didn't have a cold, and I didn't catch it from her, you wouldn't be feeling sorry for me and you wouldn't be making me soup right now."

His effort to exercise restraint comes to naught. He loses his temper. "For God's sake, Sally, what is the matter with you? Do you think everything in life can be reduced to some simple formula, some mindless cliché? Read Auden. You used to. Suffering happens willy nilly. It has no rhyme or reason. It happens. Shit happens." He is unaware of the irony in his choice of these last two words. For him, too, the terseness of subway graffiti expresses precisely what he wants to say. "You used to read books, complex books, dammit. Giselle has a cold. Her cold has nothing to do with what's going on between you and me."

Later, as he is brushing his teeth, she comes into the bathroom to explain.

"I know I'm losing it, Justin," she says. "You are right. I used to be able to handle complexities, but now I can't. I need things to be simple. I can't deal with grays anymore."

She is crying, but her face is unchanged. Her brow is not furrowed, her mouth is not upturned. Only tears roll down her cheeks in sad little rivers. The sadness penetrates his heart. He reaches out to her and wipes away the tears. She presses her head against his chest and he folds her into his arms.

He does not sleep in the den this night.

EIGHT

He knew her story before he married her. He had read her poems. He wanted to know if his rival still owned her. They blinded him. The passion in them was searing. Bordering on insanity, he would think later. And she would lose control of her mind when her beloved died. She fell into a depression, she said, from which she was saved by graffiti on a wall that gave her the strength to resist that downward plunge her mother had taken after her father died.

After Hunter College High School, she went to Spelman, on scholarship. She did not want to be a minority again, she said. Hunter had been more than enough for her. Which was probably why she was attracted to Jack Benson. He had no time for white people, he said. He did not care what they thought or what they said. He wore black, his favorite color. The color that contained all colors, he said. The richest of colors. He let his hair grow long, in thick dreadlocks that reached down to his waist. But the clothes, the hair, were superficial symbols. Money was Jack Benson's god, greed the ideology that spurred him on.

For five years she and Jack lived happily together, she spending her days in midtown at the publishing company where she worked, he uptown repairing used cars for sale in his friend's auto body shop. So she thought, for she did not know of his underground life, or that he had supplied her brother with his deadly heroin habit. She did not know it until he was shot, inexplicably, in front of her, outside a café in Lower Manhattan, in the ABC village, while they were drinking wine and talking of love.

They shot him gangster style, from their car, with deadly accuracy. She said the only thought that flashed through her mind when he fell across her lap was that the same thing had happened to Jacqueline Kennedy. For her life with Jack Benson had seemed to her a Camelot too.

But Jack Benson was no knight, as neither was Kennedy. The police came the next day and gave her his aliases. Jack the Ripper on the streets of Bed-Stuy, Jack the Enforcer in Harlem. When she righted herself, she put away the poems that had made Jack love her. She moved to Brooklyn. She would teach primary colors to primary school children. She would write no more.

Justin would meet her not long afterward, on that miraculous Wednesday afternoon in Fort Greene Park. By chance he had looked up and was stunned to see the most beautiful woman in the world pass him by. He thought, when she consented to go out with him, that his life could get no better.

He found the poems at the bottom of her drawer. He had asked for a photograph of her brother.

"In the second drawer," she said. "In the bureau in my bedroom."

The poems were wrapped in tissue that had yellowed. He pulled out four.

He could not believe she could have enough love left for him.

"It's gone. Vanished," she said. "He means nothing to me but a dead hoodlum." But she asked him for the poems and burned them all when he left.

If she had been a true poet, Justin had said, she would write no matter what. But the truth was, and he knew it, he was glad she had burned the poems. He wanted a normal wife, a wife who loved children, a wife who loved the domesticity of marriage, the security it provided. He did not want a return of his childhood: his mother sleeping in her employer's house, his father in the arms of his lover, their son cared for by a lonely aunt.

She said yes, that was what she wanted, so he married her. He loved her. He tried to forget that once, before him, she had been a poet.

NINE

Giselle comes to their bedroom early in the morning. Her eyes are puffy. She is clutching her doll. She wants her Mommy. Sally picks her up and puts her on the bed near to her, in the crack next to Justin. In seconds she falls asleep.

"I think she should stay in bed all day," says Justin. Sally agrees.

He notices that Sally, too, looks ill. "I'll take care of both of you today," he says. Sally leans across Giselle and kisses him.

They sleep past noon. When they wake up, he makes the same breakfast for them that his mother made for him—pancakes, scrambled eggs, and bacon.

"You should both stay home tomorrow," he says. He promises to call the principals at their schools.

JUSTIN DOES NOT get their cold. The next day he goes to the college. He sees Mark Sandler in the parking lot, speaking to

Lloyd Banks. Lloyd Banks is a colleague. He teaches in the Africana Studies department. He is a stocky man with bushy graying eyebrows and a heavy mustache. Every day he wears a dashiki to work, on cold days over a brown or black turtleneck sweater. He cuts a formidable figure, the ideological pedagogue who will not be toyed with. Until very recently, Lloyd Banks has had little to say to Justin.

"Professor," Mark Sandler calls out to him, "I was telling Professor Banks what we discussed."

Lloyd Banks smiles. "How's the family, Justin?" The mustache lifts.

"Under the weather right now. Both Sally and Giselle have colds."

"It's this infernal snow. My children are sick, too."

Lloyd Banks has seven, with two wives. At least that is what he calls them. One is a marriage recognized by American law, the other was officiated by a Yoruba priest. Justin does not dare ask which of his children are ill, or if all of them are. He will not go into that hornet's nest. Lloyd is a self-proclaimed Afrocentrist. He believes that the point of reference for all studies must be Africa. He calls Justin a Eurocentrist. Lately he says it with affection, teasingly.

They came close to blows more than once in the core curriculum committee. Banks was arguing that the required course in philosophy has to focus, must be concentrated on, he insisted, black philosophers. He wanted the works of Cheikh Anta Diop, George G. M. James, Molefe Kete Asante, Yosef A. A. ben-Jochannan, Marcus Garvey, and John Henrik Clarke to be central to the reading list. Students can study the other philosophers but only in relation to these men. Enough, he said, of the Eurocentric monopoly that has us studying our history and our intellectuals only by comparison to theirs.

Justin stood up and said that the men he had named were good thinkers but not philosophers. They could not replace Aristotle, Plato, Kant, Descartes, Hume, Locke, Nietzsche, and Wittgenstein. Yes, he could see putting Frederick Douglass and W. E. B. DuBois on the list, and the African philosophers, Kwasi Wiredu and Paulin Hountondji, even Kwame Anthony Appiah from Harvard, Howard McGary from Rutgers, and Laurence Thomas from Syracuse. Martin Luther King, too.

"And Malcolm X?"

"A great man, but I wouldn't compare his lectures to King's great sermons."

Banks was livid. "Don't you see? Don't you see? The only black men you would put on your list are the ones that the white man validates. Appiah from Harvard!" he snorted.

He called Justin an Uncle Tom, an Uncle Clarence Thomas Uncle Tom, the modern traitor to the progress of peoples of the black diaspora who wanted the inequities between blacks and whites to remain the way they were, who had vested interest in maintaining the status quo.

"For Chrissake, you are an American," Justin shouted back at him. "You want inequities? Go to Africa. There should be enough inequities for you in Rwanda or Nigeria."

Banks said he was a house nigger with a f'd up head. A bandana-wearing golliwog brainwashed by British Imperialism.

"We had empires when the English were still camped in caves, using clubs to hunt for food and women. Egypt was a thriving civilization three thousand years old before it crossed the minds of the Greeks to think up one. Who do you think taught the Greek philosophers? It was Africans. Read any book of those so-called Ancients, they'll tell you who to thank."

It was not a fight Justin could win. Passions were enflamed with the recent rounds of Giuliani's cuts in the college's budget; the mayor's silence on the sodomizing of Abner Louima by some of the city's finest; his attack on the character of Dorismond, an innocent security guard gunned down by the NYPD; his refusal to meet with the parents of the slain Amadou Diallo, forty-one bullets pumped into his body by the mayor's guards who claimed they thought it was a gun he had reached for, when it was his keys. Giuliani was no friend to black people. He wanted them out of his city. Racial pride was what was needed now, a strong dose of self-esteem in the face of this onslaught.

Justin held his tongue. His course was to be considered next, in next month's meeting of the core curriculum meeting. He had just won his battle with the Great Books committee. He could not have that victory overturned by instigating Banks to revenge.

As it happened, he need not have worried. The following week Randall Robinson came to the college to talk about *The Debt*, the new book he was working on. It was his treatise on the urgency of reparations for the children of African slaves in the African diaspora.

"So what do you have to say about that?" Lloyd Banks

taunted him when they chanced to be in the bathroom at the same time during a break in Robinson's presentation.

"As a matter of fact, I agree with Robinson," Justin told him.

Lloyd Banks was astounded.

"Perhaps I don't have his same arguments—the money is irrelevant to me—but on the matter of human dignity, we *must* demand reparations."

For Justin the reason was simple. "Racism," he said to Banks, "is essentially about the denial of another person's humanity. Reparation is made to the families of Japanese Americans and to Jews exterminated by Hitler's Nazis because we recognize that these were humans who were brutalized, not animals. Their humanity, their dignity as humans, demanded this acknowledgment, this recognition."

"Well," he said to Banks, "Africans are humans, and until America makes reparation for treating them as chattel, it will be hard to argue that this government is not racist, that it is not like the previous governments that shackled our forefathers and regarded them as property, not humans. A decision to grant reparations is no less than an acknowledgment of our humanity, a recognition that a grievous wrong had been done. It will spread its stain to all generations of white America until that acknowledgment is made. Reparation is the only language that has currency in America."

"Yes," Justin continued (they were in the hallway now), "even today we see how the world—NATO, in spite of the fact that an African heads the United Nations—treats the suffering of black people differently from the suffering of white people. Children!"

Justin had become so passionate, so incensed, that he stuttered, the word breaking into fragments when it left his mouth. "Children," he said the word clearly now, are treated differently. "Children are of dying of malaria and sleeping sickness in Africa. Just some measly contribution from the rich, just some compassion, and they would live. These are treatable diseases, for God's sake! We have the medicines to cure these diseases. These children could live."

They were calling the audience back into the auditorium but Justin could not stop and Banks did not want him to.

"And I wasn't even talking about AIDS," he said. "Children are dying by the hundreds of thousands of AIDS in Africa. By the millions. In some villages the only inhabitants are children and old people. Everyone else is dead. And the children have the virus. But one article in the newspaper about the children in Romania who are dying of AIDS opens the floodgates. Thousands send money. I read where a woman who grew up in Calcutta sent money. The suffering of white children brought her to tears. In Calcutta, goddamnit, children are dying like flies from starvation. Food, Lloyd. Just food, that's all they want. But that woman can send money to Romania! Not that I don't think she shouldn't, but she has made a value judgment about her own people. White children count more. No, Lloyd, if we are to uphold our dignity as humans, we must demand reparation. The lives of our forefathers have value. Their value is the same as that of every human being. Some of us may like to deny it, but we are the same: we come to this world from a place we can't remember and we will return no matter how great we think we are, how superior we are. Donald Trump will die just as will that child in the Congo."

Banks was impressed. "And I thought you just lived in a make-believe world with all those make-believe books you read," he said.

"Good literature gives us the big *T* truth," Justin said. "I can't say this for all writers, but the ones I admire have the courage to tell the big *T* truth about our common humanity."

They ended up that night having dinner together in a restaurant and fantasizing.

"Imagine," Banks said, "if Europeans had come to Africa to trade rather than enslave. Can you imagine where Africa could be today with the diamonds, gold, oil, and uranium it has? Or your country, Justin? Imagine if they had paid fair prices for the sugar cane and tobacco and cocoa they just took from your country."

They became friends after that night, and then better friends when they discovered that they agreed on much more, though for different reasons. Lloyd Banks supported Affirmative Action. "If some horses leave the gate ahead of others, they are sure to win the race. If he didn't get a handicap, you think Uncle Clarence Thomas Tom would have gotten into Yale?"

Justin's point was not the need for the handicap, which seemed to him to imply some intrinsic deficiency in his students, but, rather, his faith in his students' intellect. "Just give them a push and they'll fly," he said. "They already have the wings."

Now Banks is slapping him on his back. "What are those ideas you're putting in Mark's head?" he says.

"We read *Beloved*," Justin says. He does not add, "Along with *Medea*." He knows his limits with Lloyd.

"So what's that about Mark saying that if we men don't watch out and start treating our women better, they will kill our children? I thought Sethe killed that baby because the slave catchers were coming to take her children back to slavery."

Justin knows that Lloyd has not read the novel, but he has seen the movie.

"Yes," says Mark, trailing behind them. "I don't disagree, but that is not the only reason she kills her child."

Lloyd Banks stops. "So teach the teacher," he says.

Mark smiles and looks at Justin. "You remember, Professor, when Paul D tells Sethe that her husband did not leave her? Remember what she answered?"

"Tell Professor Banks," Justin says.

"She says, 'What'd he leave then if not me?'"

"She said that?" Banks looks surprised.

"More," says Mark. "She said that if Halle is alive, she will never let him set foot in her house. Sethe had it in for Halle. She was thinking of him when she swung that ax."

For a moment Lloyd Banks's face darkens. His eyebrows converge and his mustache droops over his mouth. Then the mood passes. He slaps Mark on the back. "Woman troubles, Mark?"

"Nothing I can't handle." Mark grins.

Student and teachers part where the corridor divides into two pathways, one leading to faculty offices, the other to classrooms.

"Teaching subversive literature, uh, Justin?"

"You're rubbing off on me," he answers. But when he is in his office and the door is closed and the room is quiet, his thoughts return to Sally and her tears last night. She cannot handle grays, she told him. She wants only black and white, yes or no choices, nothing in between.

"Love is or it ain't," Sethe says to Paul D when he is confounded by her terrible choice. One or the other, no compromise. What black-and-white choices, he wonders, is Sally capable of making?

TEN

When the Ku Klux Klan murdered Sally's father, her mother, Ursula Henry, shut down. It was a black-or-white choice for her: either to pick up the pieces and continue as before, or to shut down, seal her heart, and swear never, ever in this life or even in the next, to love a man the way she loved her husband. She chose to shut down. There was no halfway solution for her, no compromise.

She refused to leave Alabama. *Could not,* she said, and convinced them all when two days later she began stuffing her mouth with the bloody dirt in the front yard where her husband had fallen, his body riddled with bullet holes, three that had pierced his heart.

She was hospitalized, a mental hospital for the temporarily insane. A sister who lived in Birmingham took in the children and waited for their mother to be discharged, but it was soon clear that Ursula would remain in the hospital long past the summer. So Dr. Henry's sister brought his children home, to Harlem. She sold their brownstone house on Strivers Row to pay Ursula's bills. It was not enough. Her brother had a soft heart. There were two mortgages on the house and few records of the money his patients owed him. The little life insurance he had ran out by the time Sally was ready for high school, and so it was a blessing (though no one discounted the long hours Sally spent studying in her room) when the results of the entrance exam for Hunter College High School came out and Sally had scored in the ninety-eighth percentile. Her future was assured. Tony was not so fortunate. By the time he was fourteen, he was sticking needles in his arm.

Sally told Justin that her mother's life ended in that front yard in Alabama. When she eventually came home to her sister in Alabama, her mother slept on the left side of the bed and on that side only. It was the side she had lain a lifetime, next to her husband: eight years. She was twenty-nine when he died.

It is this black-and-white choice that Ursula made that now frightens Justin. He decides that when he gets home tonight he will have the long talk with Sally he has been avoiding. He will ask her to tell him what she discusses with her therapist because, one, he does not want her to leave him, and two—mostly it is this second question that makes sleep difficult for him sometimes—he wants to know if the reason Sally cannot see gray is the return of an old heartache, a memory of a muse, the one for whom she wrote those wild and passionate poems.

He had met Ursula Henry only once. It was before he and Sally were married. Ursula was dying of cancer in the psychiatric hospital where she had committed herself when her son OD'd. Sally had asked him if he would drive with her to Alabama. It had been two years since she had seen her mother.

Sally did not tell him that the hospital where her mother was a patient was a psychiatric hospital, but on the way there, she told him everything else: about her father, about her aunt, about her brother, about her mother's helplessness. Bouts of depression, she called it. The story did not make Justin nervous. It did not cause him to reconsider his proposal of marriage (as if anything could). It did not bother him that her mother's illness could be passed on to their children. The depression had a cause, as Sally's depression had, though it was difficult for him to define it, and her father was a brilliant man, a doctor, a graduate of an Ivy League medical school.

It shocked Justin to see how thin Sally's mother was—all skin and bones—but it shocked him more to see how much Sally resembled her. The eyes were the same, large and round, though Ursula's consumed her, and the dark circles under them were not unlike Sally's, though they were much darker. Purpled. Except for the folds that gathered around her mouth and neck, her skin was stretched taut across her wide cheekbones, paper-thin and dry, yet flawless, the color of burnished copper. Like Sally's.

"So you are Sally's intended," she said the moment she saw him. "Come," she waved him closer toward her. "Did Sally tell you I am crazy? This is a crazy hospital?"

That was when Justin knew for certain where he was.

"I committed myself," she said. "Did Sally tell you?"

Sally began to cry immediately.

"Ah, I can see she did not tell you." She shut her eyes.

Sally leaned over and kissed her. Ursula put a wiry thin arm around Sally's neck and held her. When she released her, she was crying too.

"But I am not crazy," she said to Justin, wiping her eyes. "Just dying."

Sally rubbed her hand. "Mom," she said, "Mom." The word seemed wrenched from the bottom of her heart.

"Why haven't you come before, Sally?"

"Mom, I wanted to come. It's far, you know. New York is far from Alabama."

"She was afraid." Her mother said this to no one, her eyes traveling far into the distance.

"Mom, Mom." Sally put her hand on her mother's chin and turned her face toward her. "Remember what I wrote to you about Justin?"

"Justin?" Ursula looked at him as if for the first time.

"We are going to get married," Sally said.

"Justin?" She repeated his name. "You're not the one that made my Sally crazy?"

"This is Justin," Sally said. "I wrote you, remember?"

"Sally went crazy, you know. Over a man who killed her brother."

"Mom, don't say that." Sally leaned against Justin.

"Is that why you don't visit me like you used to?" Ursula

pulled herself up in the bed. "Before Sally went crazy, she used to come every day."

"Every month, Mom."

"You're not the one who made my Sally crazy?"

"I'm Justin," Justin said.

"Ahh." She closed her eyes and leaned back on the bed.

"He's a college professor," Sally said.

"Schoolteacher," her mother said.

"He has a Ph.D. from Harvard," Sally said.

"Schoolteacher," her mother said again. "It's good my Sally is marrying a schoolteacher. You'll keep her calm. You won't get her excited. Schoolteachers don't let their children get excited."

"Justin went to Harvard," Sally said.

"My husband," Ursula said, "went to Yale. The medical school. One of the first black men."

"Sally told me," Justin said. "You must have been proud of him."

"Until he got himself shot," she said. "The Klan did it, you know."

"Mom," Sally squeezed her hand, "are they treating you well here?"

"He was too excitable, too impulsive." She was still talking about her husband. "He got us nervous, too. Sally, me, and Tony. We got too nervous when he got so excited. Those men."

"Do they feed you enough?" Sally asked.

"He should not have gone out there. I told him so. I told him so, Sally."

"Yes, Mom. I know you did."

She sighed. "But you won't get my Sally nervous, will you, young man? You'll be good to her, won't you?"

"Yes," Justin said. "I love her."

She looked at Sally. "Love is not always a good thing," she said. "Love was not always good to Sally and me."

"My love will be good to Sally," Justin said. "I promise you." And he meant every word he said.

"She took such good care of her brother. I wasn't there, but she took such good care of him. What happened to your brother, Sally?"

"You know, Mom. You know Tony died."

"Sally was so good to him. You take care of Sally the way she took care of Tony. Will you do that for me, young man?"

Justin promised.

"I can die now that Sally has a good man," she said.

Sally began to cry again.

"Everyone has to die, Sally. I'll be with your father and Tony."

Justin put his arm around Sally.

"There is no accounting for love, no accounting for how it happens and when it ends. When my love ended, there was no one else. I'm glad God gave Sally someone else. Schoolteacher? That is what Sally needs: someone strong, someone steady, someone to make her happy." She left them again, her eyes taking her to a place they could not see. When they refocused, she crooked her finger and beckoned Sally to come nearer. "I'll tell you a secret," she said. "Come, come closer."

Sally bent toward her.

"You, too, Justin."

Justin bent toward her, too.

"I prayed for grace," she said. "If God had given me His grace, I would not have suffered so."

"Oh, Mom," Sally said, "God loves you."

"I know. I know. But God does not give His grace to everyone He loves. He did not give it to me. It is a gift, Sally, and it is His to give to whomever He wants. You can't earn it; you can't make Him give it to you. But God gave it to you, Sally. After that man, after your trial with that bad man, He gave you Justin." She smiled weakly at Justin. "It's God's sprinkling of stardust on you, on both of you. His grace. Don't throw His gift back in His face. And, you, Justin," she said and held his eyes. "God will make you responsible for my Sally's happiness."

Ursula Henry died the next day. Justin helped Sally bury her, and they married four months later, in the same tiny church in Alabama, where the minister said it was good her end had come at last. No one should have suffered as much as she had suffered.

It is the promise he made to Ursula Henry that Justin remembers now as he turns the key in the lock on his front door.

THEY DO NOT hear when he enters the parlor, or if they do, they are so preoccupied with what they are doing that they do not call out. Justin is in the kitchen before he sees that Anna is there too. They make a perfect circle: Anna, Sally, and Giselle. They are leaning over the kitchen table. Anna and Sally are standing, Giselle is kneeling on a chair. Her hair brushes against Anna's.

"What is it?" Justin walks over to them.

Sally breaks away first. "Justin. We weren't expecting you. You're early."

Giselle joins him and jumps into his arms.

"Anna," he says. He hugs his daughter. "What brings you here?" Her presence is like a prickly nettle that chafes his skin. He does not want her here. He resents her intrusion. He wants to be with his family alone.

"She is showing Mommy and me how to grow seeds," Giselle says. She squirms out of his arms and goes over to Anna.

Justin moves closer to the table. Anna is picking up a thick layer of damp paper towels. There are tiny seeds on them.

"How long will they take to make roots?" Giselle asks.

Anna moves the paper towels with the seeds to the window. "I'll put them here, on the shelf, so they can get the sunlight."

"How long, Aunt Anna?"

"A couple of days. I'll be back."

"Didn't you have classes today, Anna?" Justin stands close to her.

"It's my day off," she says.

"You mean your research day?" he asks.

"Yes. My research day."

"Don't you have to do research on your research day, Anna?"

"Do you do research on your research day, Justin?"

"Always."

"Goody for you," Anna says.

"Will you stay for dinner?" Sally asks Anna.

"Did you cook?" Justin asks.

"No," Sally says. "Giselle and I just lazed around all day."

"Good. You look much better."

"I feel much better. Giselle doesn't have a temperature and her nose is not running. Anna came to keep us company. Will you stay, Anna?"

Justin frowns. "Should we order out?"

"Yes," Sally says.

"Chinese? You'd like that, won't you, Anna? I know you love Chinese." He is aware of his tone as he asks this question. He knows she could find it offensive, she could think him patronizing. It is a tone that has been directed to him more than once: *You like watermelon, don't you?* But he is angry. He wants to bait her.

She bites. "I'm American," she says. "I eat American food. My parents were eating American food when your parents were picking bananas off the trees in Trinidad."

"Whoa!" Sally says. "Peace." She holds up her hands.

"What did I say wrong?" Justin asks.

"I think you should apologize," Sally says.

"Anna, I apologize for thinking you are Chinese."

"That's it," Anna says. "I'm leaving." She walks swiftly to the parlor. Sally and Giselle follow her.

"Will you come tomorrow?" Sally asks her.

"When will you be home?" She is already in her coat.

"About four as usual. After I pick up Giselle."

"Then five," Anna says. She whispers something to Sally that Justin does not hear. Sally says, "No. It'll be okay, it'll be fine." Or did she say, Justin wonders, *"He'll be fine"*?

Anna waves to Giselle. "'Bye Giselle."

Giselle hugs her.

When Anna leaves, Sally says to Justin, "Why can't you be nice to her?"

The afternoon is ruined for him. He has come home to fix his marriage. He wants to make peace. He wants to talk to Sally; he wants to find out what's on her mind.

They play their roles perfunctorily. They are a family: he orders dinner from the Chinese restaurant, she sets the table, he cleans up afterward; she gives Giselle her bath, he reads a bedtime story to her; they sleep on the same bed, she on her side, he on his. They say Good night. They do not kiss. They do not make love.

Justin is not a religious man, but his mind has been on Ursula. Perhaps he will get God's sprinkling of stardust; he will receive the gift of grace. He can steady Sally; he can steady their marriage.

ELEVEN

Sally began watching the talk shows on TV a few days after Giselle turned four. At first it was *Oprah*, but soon, it seemed to Justin, even *Oprah* became too realistic for her—too many grays overwhelming her. In the morning, before she left for work, she would set the VCR to the earlier shows. Sometimes it was *Sally*, sometimes *Montel*. Before long she was taping both and the others, too, that came later in the day. At night, while Justin was in the den grading papers, writing or reading, she looked at them in their bedroom.

Justin would hear the laughter coming from the TV, sometimes the strident voice of a man or woman, sometimes the sounds of tears, but it never occurred to him to stop what he was doing and join her. They had made their pact with Khalil Gibran. There were spaces in their togetherness. After Giselle went to bed, each gave the other time to be alone. But one night, feeling a sudden chill, Justin came into the bedroom looking for a sweater. Their bed was at the far end of the room, near the windows, and Sally was sitting on it, her eyes glued to the TV. She didn't turn when he entered in the room, and curious about what held her attention, Justin stayed to watch.

The moderator, Justin has forgotten which one it was, was standing in front of two men seated on armchairs.

"Can you look into his eyes and say what you told me? Say that you're sorry you hurt him? Admit to him that you slept with his wife and that you are sorry?" The moderator was speaking to the older man. "Because, to tell you the truth, I don't think there is any hope for the two of you to have a relationship as father and son if you can't do that. Face him. Say what's in your heart and in your soul. Tell him you want his forgiveness. Tell him you love him."

The older man's bottom lip was trembling. The moderator tugged the younger man's chair. "Get closer. Your daddy has something to tell you. You want to hear it, right?" The younger man burst into tears. "You want to hear what he has to say, right?"

The younger man's shoulders heaved with his sobs.

"Your daddy loves you. He wants to tell you that. You want him to say it, don't you?"

"Yes." His voice was muffled.

"Your daddy can't hear you, David."

"Yes." David's eyes were bloodshot, dripping wet.

The moderator patted his back. "Everything will be all right, David. Everything will be fine. I guarantee it. When you hear what your daddy has to say to you, everything will be okay. Guaranteed. Yes, doctor? Yes?" The moderator turned to a preppy looking man in a navy blue blazer and gray slacks who was sitting in the front row of the audience. The preppy man nodded and smiled. Affirmation secured, the camera swung back to the two men. Once again the moderator urged them to pull their chairs closer together.

The older man complied.

"You're ready?" the moderator asked.

"I'm sorry," the man said.

"Look at him, not at me," the moderator admonished him. "You want to tell him, not me."

"I am sorry, David. I am sorry I slept with your wife."

"Tell him how many times. He needs to know the truth. There can be no forgiveness without the truth."

"For five years," the older man said. "I slept with Stacy for five years."

Even the moderator seemed taken aback by this confession. Perhaps his aides had not warned him. Perhaps the man had lied to them. But in seconds the moderator regained his equilibrium.

"It's not the time that matters here," he said. "It is your willingness to tell all."

The camera was back on the preppy man in the front row seats. He nodded vigorously and mouthed, "That's right."

"So ask David to forgive you. Get closer. He has to hear you."

The father took his son's hand. The moderator approved. "Good, good," he said.

"Will you forgive me, David?"

The son was crying harder now.

"So what do you say, David? What do you say to your father? He is asking your forgiveness. Do you hear him?"

"I am sorry. I am sorry I caused you so much pain. I am sorry I caused your wife to take her own life. I am sorry."

David collapsed in his father's arms. The audience erupted into cheers. The moderator strutted over to the doctor. He smiled, the doctor smiled. They slapped each other high fives.

"Jesus! What crap! What inane, stupid, ridiculous, unmitigated crap!"

Sally spun around, her fingers skating to the POWER button on the remote.

"How could you look at such crap? The father has sex with his daughter-in-law for five years and drives her to suicide, and now he looks in his son's face and asks for forgiveness? Have they no shame? Have the people who put such crap on TV no shame? Why are you looking at this, Sally?"

"It works," she said, pointing the remote at the blank screen. "I've seen it work."

"You've seen it work?"

"They come back. On another show. They talk about it."

"They come back on another show? How long have you been looking at this, Sally?"

"I like these shows."

"Is that what you've been doing every night?"

"When they come back, they talk about how they were able to heal the hurt between them."

Heal is another word Justin despises.

"Heal," he shouted at her, "nothing heals. Wounds form scabs, scabs drop off, new skin grows, but the scar remains. It does not go away. Only God creates, Sally. Only He can make new things. We just go on living, adding to the past, adding to the old, living with the pain. Accumulating. Everything in the present contains the old. The future is the past. Have the courage to face that truth. 'In my end is my beginning. In my beginning is my end.' Read the poets, Sally. 'The child is the father of the man.'"

When they first met, she was reading Eliot; they were discussing Wordsworth. They read Langston Hughes and Derek Walcott together. What had changed? What had made her begin looking for the road maps to her life in the fairy tales they told on TV?

The signs had been there for Justin to read. New books had found their way onto her nightstand: *Rebuilding Lost Moments*, *A Life Fulfilled*, *Finding the True You*. The stack grew. Every week, it seemed, there were others: *The Goddess Sleeping within You*, *Repairing the Wounds*, *Daring to Live in the Present*. Clichés slipped into her conversations, presented as truisms, as considered philosophies by which she seemed to want to guide her life.

This morning he sits with Sally at breakfast and in spite of his determination to feel otherwise, the name on the tag that hangs from the string of the tea bag dunked in the hot water she has just poured into her mug annoys him. Mystical Mornings. He thinks of these names as trite messages of hope to the weak-willed. "What does this one mean?" he asks her.

"What does what mean?"

"What's mystical about the mornings?" He flicks the tag with his little finger.

She does not answer him. When they leave for work, they are barely speaking to each other again.

But at lunchtime, he is remorseful. He calls to apologize. He wants to talk, he says. He wants to listen to what she has to say.

She is expecting Anna in the afternoon, she tells him.

Perhaps she can ask Anna to watch Giselle tonight, he says. She is silent. He had been rude to Anna. Before that he had practically accused Anna of being negligent with his daughter. "I'd like us to go out to dinner," he says. "Just you and me, only the two of us, Sally."

"The two of us?"

"A date, Sally."

She considers this. Hold on a minute, she says. He waits. When she comes back to the phone she says she will call Anna. If it's okay with her, she'll drop Giselle off at her apartment. They decide on a restaurant.

THE FIRST THING he notices when she takes off her coat is that she is lovely. The first thing he thinks is that he is a lucky man.

The man at the table next to theirs stares at her. Justin reaches over and touches Sally's hand. "Thank you for coming," he says.

"I wanted to come," she says. "We need to talk."

She is wearing taupe and pale beige, her favorite colors—a

pale beige sweater set and a narrow taupe skirt. Justin thinks she has the body of a goddess, a Nubian goddess. She has lost every ounce of fat she had put on when she was having Giselle. It has sloughed off like magic. "And jogging three miles a day," she had told him.

"Wine?" He has a sudden impulse to put it off, this to need to talk, as Sally says.

"It's much too early for wine," she says.

"What then?"

She brushes back the tight curls that crowd her head. "Fruit punch," she says.

The man next to them is wearing a burgundy sweater. He, as usual, is dressed in black. Perhaps he should have worn something brighter, something not so serious, not so morbid.

"You look lovely," he says.

Sally smiles. "You want to start first?" she says.

He clears his throat. It is why they are here. It is why he has asked her to meet him in this restaurant. "Before we begin," he says, "I want to give you my terms."

"Terms?" She raises her eyebrows.

The waiter interrupts. They place their orders.

"You were saying about terms?" she begins again.

This hardness he hears in her voice makes him uneasy. Anna has said something to her. He is sure of it, as he is sure that it is Anna who put the thought in her head that she should move in with her. Misery likes company. Anna has never been married. Anna does not have a boyfriend. He thinks the current hoopla about female bonding is simply the consequence of the unavailability of men. It is not politically correct for him to say this, of course, but he believes he is not alone in having this view. Even women seem to agree. They say that when their women friends find boyfriends, they hardly ever see them.

"Terms is a harsh word, Sally," he says, "I want to be anything but harsh, but I think it is best that we set some bottom lines. These are mine: I love you. I do not want our marriage to end. I do not want Giselle bumped from one parent to another. I do not want her in two places."

"Is this about Giselle?" Sally asks.

"No, it is about us. About you, Sally," he says quickly. "I want to know . . . I want you to tell me what is bothering you."

"And you won't criticize?" She eyes him over the rim of her glass.

"When have I . . . ?" He decides to stop there. Whatever he was going to say is a lie, and she will point that out to him. He does not want to start this way.

"You won't talk about my platitudes and clichés? Because you may not like it, Justin, but that is how I speak."

He does not say, *That is how you have begun to speak. You did not always speak this way.*

"But perhaps you are right." She puts the glass on the table and still holding it, she traces its circumference with the tip of her finger from her other hand. "Perhaps I am in a midlife crisis," Sally says. "I look down the road of my life and I don't like what I see. I am useless," she says. "I am doing nothing useful, nothing meaningful."

Giselle. What about Giselle? What about me? The children you teach? Are we not meaningful to you? But he has asked her those questions already.

"At least my father had purpose to his life. He did something meaningful. He took a stand."

He keeps his silence. She is on holy ground. She accused her father of recklessness when she told him the story of his murder. Her words were not much different from the ones her mother used when she lay dying in the hospital.

"He stood for something," she is saying now. "He drew a line in the sand. He said, This is what I am willing to die for. My mother thought he should have protected us. She thought that was his responsibility. He should have assessed that we were outnumbered. He should not have gone out there and risked his life, our lives." Her hands are still now. They are wrapped tightly around the glass.

"I thought so once, too, but now I think there are duties one has that are more important than protecting the lives of people we love. We have duties to ourselves, responsibilities to ourselves, that we must protect first." She lowers her voice. "My father's first responsibility was to guard his integrity, to live up to his convictions." She releases the glass and clasps her hands over her mouth.

Justin thinks she is about to cry and he says, "Don't, Sally."

But she is not about to cry. She removes her hands from her mouth. "My dad had courage," she says. "The courage of his convictions. He was not going to let those racist pigs make him crawl. He was not going to let them come in his yard without a fight. He would not submit to them. My mother thought that if he had done that, he would have lived. But he would have been dead to her. He would have lost his manhood, his authority in our family. He would have lost her respect. A pity she did not know that."

"She did, Sally."

"And what is worse, she blamed him for what happened to Tony. She believed, up to the day she died, that Tony went on drugs because my father let those pigs kill him. But Dad stood up to them. That is what he did. He didn't destroy Tony. Those pigs destroyed Tony. They destroyed him when they killed his father right in front of him. Tony was seven. He never forgot. It burned a hole in his head he tried fill with drugs."

Justin holds her hand.

"My mother wanted to know why I couldn't live in the same town with her. It was because of that, because she blamed my father for what happened. I couldn't face her, knowing she thought that way. But she was the guilty one. She was the one who was not there for Tony."

"I don't think she could have helped it, Sally. She was not well."

"Yes. Yes, she was not well." She says this unconvincingly.

Justin wants to comfort her. "I am glad you are telling me this. I'm beginning to understand you, Sally."

"Are you? I don't know what my convictions are. I don't know what I believe, what I would die for. That makes me useless, Justin. It makes my life meaningless."

He aches for the sadness he sees in her eyes, but at the same time he feels a surge of happiness. They have not talked like this in months.

"You have convictions, Sally," he tells her.

"What are they? Do you know what my convictions are? You ridicule me almost every day for having none."

"Sally." He tightens his hold on her hand.

"No. I had convictions once," she says. "I used to write about them. Now I have no convictions, so I have nothing to write about."

He remembers the poems that blinded him.

"I had passion then," she says.

Jealousy closes in on him. "So what are you saying, Sally?"

"Once I knew what I wanted," she says.

"And now?" He cannot believe she can be this cruel. He lets go of her hand. "And now you do not have what you want?"

She does not answer, so he presses her. "And now you have settled for a lesser life? Is that what you are saying to me, Sally?" The palms of his hands are damp with perspiration.

"It frightened me."

"What?"

"All that passion," she says.

"So you settled for me? Is that it, Sally?"

"I wanted a normal life."

He had wanted that, too, when he married her, but not this, not what she is intimating. "And am I that normal, boring life?" he asks her.

"You are not boring, Justin."

"But our marriage is. Is that it?"

"I told you I needed to find myself."

His face is a canvas of contortions.

"I've used a cliché. I've used a platitude. Okay, okay, Justin, but I cannot hide from me anymore. I want to be me."

I want to be me. The song wafts through Justin's head and the smile forms on his lips before he can control it.

"It may be funny to you, but I can't be this way anymore."

"No," he says. "There is nothing funny about what you are saying."

"I want to start writing poems again," she says.

"Then do that, Sally."

"You haven't been listening, Justin. I can't. I'm afraid."

What he feels most of all at this moment is simply exhaustion. She has had him on a roller coaster and he has expended all his patience. "You want to be you. You want space. You want your life's work," he says, rattling off the list. "You want every goddamn cliché ever spoken on every goddamn soap opera. You want to write. You are afraid to write. Do I stop you from writing, Sally? No? Do I stop you from being a poet? No. But you will turn my life around. You will turn Giselle's life around."

She opens her mouth to say something, but he does not let her.

"Well, I will tell you now what I want, Sally. I will tell you specifically what my terms are." His fingers drum the table but he does not raise his voice. The man sitting next to them cannot hear him. He can speak logically, quietly, of terms and conditions even when his heart is breaking. He has had practice. In graduate school he had written about passion, he had developed logical theses on the world's greatest love affairs penned by the masters.

"I will not have Giselle live in two places," he says. "I will not have her sacrificed for her parents' selfish interests." He reaches for the glass of water in front of him and takes a long drink, buying time to slow down the thumping in his chest. "We wanted Giselle," he says. "She did not ask to be born. We owe her. Whatever your gurus may say, I believe divorce hurts children irreparably. I believe children need to live under the same roof with parents who take care of them. I believe that even if all we are to them is white light—the motion, sound, and light of TV in the background while they play with their toys or talk to their friends—they'd still prefer that than nothing. I believe children need to feel safe, and at a minimum, white light makes them feel safe. These are my convictions, Sally. I will fight for them."

Her face does not change when he stops. She stares at him with the same expression of sadness in her eyes that was there when she told him her life was meaningless.

"You may not care about me," he says, turning away from her, unable to face those eyes much longer, "but I thought you cared about Giselle."

"And what happens to Giselle when she has an unhappy mother?"

"Haven't you told me enough times, Sally? Your graffiti. Remember your graffiti?" He wants her to feel his pain. "'It takes strength to be happy.' Remember? Then find the strength to be happy, Sally."

He asked her here because he wants to try, because he wants to find out what is troubling her, what is causing her to be unhappy, but what he has gotten is a babbling about convictions, and he thinks that it is courage indeed she is struggling to find, courage to leave him. Not with Giselle, he says to himself. Not with my daughter.

They make it through dinner. In less than half an hour they are on their way to pick up Giselle at Anna's. Sally brings the sleeping child to the car. They drive home in silence.

TWELVE

Lloyd Banks calls him late in the night. Mark Sandler is in the hospital. Something terrible, he says, has happened to him.

"Terrible?"

"Worse than you can imagine," Banks says. "I didn't know he would take it so hard."

"What so hard?"

"She left him. His girlfriend left him and he tried to kill himself."

The news floors Justin. "We were talking to him just the other day. He seemed fine."

"Well, he wasn't fine."

"What did he do?"

"Turned on the gas in his oven."

"And they found him alive?"

"His neighbor smelled the gas. And just in time. He was slumped over the kitchen table. He had been reading. Poetry," he says.

Suddenly Justin remembers. "Sylvia Plath," he says. Guilt forces him to sit down.

"Yes. How did you know? His neighbor said the doctor had to pry the book out of his hands. Mark didn't want to let it go."

He had let Mark borrow it. They were sitting in his office when Mark asked, What about poetry, Professor? Does a novelist have to read poetry, too?

Justin said yes. Anyone who is serious about becoming a novelist needs to have the poet's sensitivity to the music of language.

Sylvia Plath's collected poems *Ariel* was on his desk. Carol Taylor, a member of the Great Books committee, a buxom woman with fierce brown eyes and prematurely gray hair that hung down the sides of her face like sheets of metal, had given it to him. "We don't all write about cooking and babies," she said. "Educate yourself." Her cheeks flushed red, the only betrayal of her vulnerability.

Mark reached for it and Justin tried, unsuccessfully, to stop him. "You'd prefer to read her husband, Ted Hughes," he said. "She was a feminist who gassed herself."

"Gassed herself?"

"I think she put her head in her oven. Something like that."

"For love?"

Justin had not read the poems but he answered all the same. "For what else?"

How was he to know that love had already made its perilous inroads deep into Mark's heart?

HE TELLS SALLY what has happened and goes with Banks to the hospital. Mark is lying on his back in a narrow bed in a small, darkened room in the crisis center. Encased in white sheets, his big shoulders seem shrunken, his body tiny. He turns and sees them through the glass partition that separates his room from the nurses' station. He sits up. His face breaks into a wide smile. "Hi, Profs." He extends his hand. His voice is weak, his handshake limp.

"Why'd you want to do something stupid like that?" Banks hugs him. "There are plenty of fish in the sea."

But Mark does not want to hear this. "She was the one, Prof. My soul mate."

"If she was your soul mate," Banks says, "you wouldn't have broken up."

"She was the one." He looks over at Justin. "You were right, Prof," he says. "She did it for love. Her husband was fooling around."

Justin winces. He knows Mark is speaking of Plath. "You'll find someone else," he says, forcing his voice to sound more confident than he feels.

"With a woman," Mark says.

The two men do not understand him.

"I caught her in bed with a woman. Told you, Prof, if you don't treat them right, they turn into lesbos."

JUSTIN AND BANKS stop at the coffee shop afterward. "That has to be hard," Banks says. "To find out your girlfriend turned into a lesbian." He inflects the ending so it sounds more as if he is asking a question.

"That's not possible," Justin says. "There is nothing Mark could have done to have made Sandra sleep with a woman."

"You know, I'm having women troubles of my own," Banks says.

It is late, they are tired, the coffee shop is dark. With the exception of a man in his overcoat and hat, huddled over a newspaper, and the waiter, who has gone back to his post in the corner scribbling down notes on sheets of grease-stained paper, there is no one else there. It is the setting for the unburdening of the heart, the confessional. They do not look at each other. Justin stirs sugar in his tea and watches its movements. One of them has been struck down. It was love that took him there.

"It's not easy, you know," Banks says, "satisfying two women."

"Tell me about it. I can't do it with one."

"Troubles?"

"Sally says she wants more."

"A man?"

"No. Nothing like that." He pauses. "A dead man, though."

"A dead man?"

"Old boyfriend. I think she took me on the rebound. She settled for me." *But not long ago, she said she felt fused into me. She said she loved me that much. We were soul mates.*

"Why would you say something like that?"

"I read her poems."

"Sally is a poet?"

"No. But I saw some of her poetry."

"She writes poetry?"

"Wrote," says Justin.

"Write or wrote, man, I think that makes her a poet, no?"

"What I meant to say is that before we were married she used to write poetry. She wrote them for her boyfriend."

Banks sucks in air. The intake is audible. "That's deep," he says. "Deep. And she didn't write any for you?" He does not say this to hurt Justin, and Justin does not take it as such.

"When I met her she wasn't writing poetry," Justin says.

"Deep," Banks says again.

"It was a bunch of love poetry."

"So you don't think she got over him?"

"The boyfriend?"

"That's who we're talking about," Banks says. "The boyfriend. She still has it on for him?"

Under other circumstances the expression Banks uses would have annoyed Justin. *Deep* was bad enough—he, too, has found himself mimicking his students—but *has it on for him* would have sent his pressure up. He hates when faculty—any older, responsible person for that matter—speaks in the street vernacular of the students. Nothing is more pitiful to him than this foolish attempt to regain lost youth. But there is no space in Justin's mind at this moment for Banks. He is thinking of Sally, of what Sally said to him. He is wondering if he is boring, if that man were not more exciting than he can ever possibly be.

"She says she doesn't love him," he says to Banks. "She says she no longer had feelings for him when she met me."

"Women lie," says Banks. "They lie to get what they want. We are fools, man. We get stuck in their web. What'd you do when you found the poetry?"

"What?"

"What'd you do when you read them?"

"I showed them to her. And she burned them."

"That was all? You didn't talk to her about it?"

"What was there to say? She said it was all in the past and she burned them and that was that."

"That was where you made a big mistake. A woman only burns things that mean something to her. If you told me that she threw them away or tore them up, that would be something else. But burned them? That's heavy, man."

"What are you trying to say, Lloyd?"

"Nothing. But you should have talked to her. You should have had your heart to heart right then. It was bound to come up sooner or later. You should have had your heart to heart when she burned those poems."

This is more than Justin can bear. It is thin ice he is on. He wants reassurance, not confirmation of his fears. He wants Banks to tell him Jack Benson no longer occupies a place in

Sally's heart. He wants him to say that when she burned those poems, she burned her memories of him.

"You are somebody, you know, Lloyd," he strikes out at him. "Talking to me about having a heart to heart. You've had a heart to heart with your two wives lately? You know if they like their situation?"

"Hey, don't jump on me because you can't keep things at home copacetic."

"Copacetic?"

"Yeah, copacetic," Banks says, and they both laugh. The word spares them of an argument neither wants.

"Cool," Justin says. "That's what they say these days: Keep things cool."

But they are facing each other now and have broken the rules of the confessional. Each man knows too much of the other. The confessional, when it works, depends on anonymity, or the semblance of it: a darkened coffeehouse where eyes do not meet, a curtain drawn between the one confessing and the other pardoning.

"Time for some shut-eye," Banks says. They stand up. Justin puts money on the table. They shake hands and part.

SALLY ASKS ABOUT Mark. Justin tells her he will recover. They got him in time. He does not tell her that Mark found his girlfriend in bed with a woman.

Giselle is groggy in the morning. She had a bad dream, she says. A wolf was in her room. It almost ate her up.

Sally murmurs to Justin, it was because of *Red Riding Hood.* She had read the story to Giselle last night.

Justin murmurs back, he would have read the same story. It was next in Giselle's favorite book.

They are generous with each other. Mark's attempt at suicide has put their quarrel on hiatus, their differences now, as often happens when one confronts a tragedy of such magnitude, seem petty and insignificant by comparison.

They comfort Giselle, and when she leaves the room they talk about changing the stories they will read to her. They should have known better, they say to each other.

Giselle is not ready for stories about little girls who get lost in the woods, Sally says. Little girls who can't find their grannies. Sally does not think that what she says can ever apply to her, to the plan she had to move in with Anna. She does not think that little girls who live apart from their daddies can sometimes get lost in the woods.

Giselle is too young to know wolves come in sheep's clothing, Justin says. Justin does not think that what he says can ever apply to him. He does not think that one day perhaps he will reflect on Mark's near suicide, and wonder if he were not that wolf in whom Mark had placed such trust.

"At least she found her way back home," Sally says, speaking of Red Riding Hood.

"Yes," Justin says. "She found her way."

They make breakfast together. As Justin pours coffee for Sally, she says to him, recalling their conversation in the restaurant last night, "You were wrong, Justin. I care about you." They kiss each other lightly on the mouth.

JUSTIN SEES BANKS in the cafeteria at lunchtime and joins him at his table. Banks says he cannot stop thinking of Mark. He was on his mind all night.

Justin thinks it is not Mark who is distracting Banks; it is the trouble Banks is having at home. That was obvious to him when Banks launched into a non sequitur about women lying so men could get stuck in their web. Mark is a warning of all the things that could go wrong when women are unhappy. *I think men better straighten up and fly right,* Mark said. Mark is a warning to him, too. But they are men. They do what men have learned to do. They circumvent. They hover on the periphery of their emotions; they do not move inward.

"Do you think Sandra was always a lesbian?" Lloyd asks, but Justin knows the true question on his mind: *Will my wives leave me if they get fed up with having to share me?*

And there is that other impossible, but nagging, follow-up: *Could they become lovers?*

On one of the few times they spoke of his wives, Banks told Justin that everything was going great in his home. "All that stuff about women being jealous of each other and scratching out each other's eyes over a man is misogynistic Eurocentric bullshit. My wives," he said, "get along like a house on fire."

"I think Sandra found someone else because things weren't going well between Mark and her," Justin says.

"Mark, Mark. Poor Mark. It's such a big responsibility we

take on with these students." Banks shakes his head. "We are teacher, mother, father, friend, therapist, social worker, lawyer, minister, even banker. I find myself lending my students money to pay the rent. The male students work the night shift and can barely keep their eyes open in class the next day, and the women students have babies to look after. Do you allow your students to bring their children to class, Justin?"

"Still judging me, huh, Lloyd?"

"Well, do you?"

"If the children are quiet and don't disturb the class."

"It's a big responsibility," Banks says again. "I shouldn't have been so flippant with Mark."

"When were you flippant?"

"I should have guessed there was something serious going on with him when he was so obsessed with that Morrison story. You know, *Beloved.*" His eyes are shadowed by the thickness of his eyebrows converging above them. "It was such an extreme position to take," he says. "How could he think Sethe would kill her children because she wanted to hurt Halle?"

"He didn't say that was the only reason. He said she had two motives."

"You're not agreeing with him, are you, Justin?"

"I am the one who should feel guilty. Mark has been telling me about Sandra. I should have suspected that his comments about lesbians weren't theoretical."

"*We,*" Banks says. "We should have suspected."

"I didn't stop him when he told me what he thought about Sethe. I told him to write it up."

"I dismissed him," Banks says.

"There's more," Justin says. "He borrowed that book from me, the one he was holding."

"The poetry?"

"Sylvia Plath committed suicide by turning on the gas and putting her head in the oven."

The admission silences them. Finally Banks says, "There's a big difference between life and fiction." He says this as if he is lecturing to his class.

Justin does not respond.

"Literature is all make-believe." Banks sits up straight in his chair. "These kids," he says, "take all that fiction stuff for the real thing."

"It *is* the real thing." Justin is unable to keep silent any longer. "Good literature is about truth," he says.

"You mean the big *T* truth." They have had this discussion before. "Yes," Banks concedes, "it is about the big *T* truth, but it is not about the real thing. These kids need to know that. They imitate what they see on television and in the movies. Look at what's happening in the high schools. And I don't mean high schools in the inner city. Kids are bringing in guns to school and shooting down their classmates. Did you ever think the day would come when we'd have to have metal detectors and police patrols in schools? Something's missing in this generation of young people. They are missing some essential factor, some essential element in their brains that will make them connect, make them feel the pain of others, make them have compassion. They have become inured to violence, to killing.

All they see is the glamour. The macho man with his guns. Did you ever see them at the arcade? They are pumped up, adrenaline high, testosterone to the sky. Zap! Zap! That's the thrill for them. That's what they learn to like: bombs exploding, blood and gore. They have no sense of the consequences. Their brains get so rewired that they seem to confuse a computer graphic with a human being. It's as though they think death is not final. You can shoot somebody down today, and fight him again tomorrow. And that gangster rap. It's the same thing. They seem to have lost the ability to tell the real from the make-believe and I think we may be to blame."

"We?" Justin asks carefully.

"Not you and me specifically. Our whole generation. We have been careless. We have been so concerned about our own agendas, we have let television and movies raise our children for us. The video arcade. Fiction. What did we expect?"

Justin twists uncomfortably in his chair. "Literature does not do that to them," he says.

"You want to tell me that when those young girls see those soppy movies and read those romances they don't get their heads all turned around? They think the be all and end all of their lives is to get married, to get a man. And look at poor Mark. Reading all that romantic stuff." Banks stops short of pointing his finger directly to the book Mark borrowed from Justin, but Justin knows he is accusing him all the same.

"I don't have my students read pulp literature," he says. "We read good literature in my classes. There is a difference between good literature and the junk you see on TV or in the movies, the stuff you say they read. Pulp literature does not exercise their imaginations, their minds. It tells them what to think, how to react. There are no easy answers in the books I have my students read. The writer doesn't tell them what to think. They have to discover that themselves. Reading good literature is not a passive activity. Good literature is about grays." He pauses. *It is grays Sally cannot bear. She wants blacks and whites. She wants clear-cut answers.* "That book did not cause Mark to want to take his life," he begins again. "Mark was already in trouble. He found comfort from Plath."

"Yeah, but it was the wrong comfort, wasn't it? He tried to take the easy way out." He pushes away his plate and gets up. "Like she did," he says, and walks away.

They meet again later that afternoon, after their classes.

"Man, I wasn't implying . . ." Banks has a sheepish look on his face. He is scratching the back of his neck and shaking his head, struggling to find more words.

Justin is forgiving. "It's all in the past," he says. "Don't give it another thought."

Still Banks insists. "I only meant to say these kids today are so vulnerable. It's the breakdown of the family. They look anywhere for their values."

Justin frowns and Banks tries again. "I apologize, man. I didn't mean to imply that you were to blame. That poetry book couldn't have made Mark think of suicide."

Yet that morning Banks blamed the violence on television and in the movies and the blood and gore in arcade games for the rash of killings that has flared up recently in high schools in leafy suburban communities.

Justin shrugs his shoulders and Banks slaps him on the back. "You're okay, you know. Mark likes you. It's good that he has someone like you who believes in him. If he turns out to be any kind of a writer, it will be because of you." He backs away and points his finger at Justin. "He trusts you," he says.

I accuse you. That is how Justin reads the motion Banks makes with his finger. *I accuse you.* Banks narrows his eyes and lifts his finger up and down close to Justin's face. "He trusts you, man." And the nursery story he and Sally read to Giselle the night before suddenly returns to Justin and fills him with dread. "Why didn't Red Riding Hood know the wolf was pretending to be her granny?" Giselle had asked him.

No, he is not responsible. A book of poems or the story of the author so despondent, so crushed by her husband's infidelity that she would put her head in an oven and turn on the gas, could not have led Mark to this.

THIRTEEN

Yet it is because of a book, an anthology that contained his father's poems, that he is teaching at a public college in Brooklyn. It is because he was witness to the power of his father's poetry, to the influence it had on a young boy's life, that he is there.

"How come you stay here?" Banks had asked him one day. "You could be teaching anywhere. You're a Harvard Ph.D. for Chrissake."

It began as an assignment. He was teaching at an Ivy League school, in New England, a place as far away geographically as it is temperamentally or ideologically from where he teaches now, when he was invited to join a committee that was designing a placement test for a public university system. Until that committee, he had not known there were eighteen-year-olds who graduated from high school without the ability to write a competent sentence or to decode the simplest of reading materials above the seventh-grade level. Until that committee, he had not thought of race and poverty in this way, not as causative factors prohibiting the acquisition of the most fundamental of human intellectual activities.

He volunteered to teach in a literacy program at his public library. One day he overheard a boy, about thirteen, reciting lines to his friend that he recognized as his father's. The boy was a troublemaker, the librarian had said. The class clown. He had repeated the fifth grade twice and had been threatened with having to repeat it again unless he joined the program.

He was showing off, rattling off the lines to the amazement of his friend, but he made a mistake. He left out a line. Later, as he was leaving the library, Justin stopped him and told him so.

"It's James Peters, man. I got it right."

Justin gave him the missing line.

"Says who?" the boy said. "You the authority on James Peters?"

Justin went to the stacks and brought him an anthology of poetry that included his father's poem.

"Read it. See, see. It says so right there. See the missing line."

But the boy could not see. He did not have the skills to see, to read the missing line.

Justin was astounded. The next day he volunteered to tutor the boy privately. The boy told him that if it were not for James Peters he would have been on the streets with the gangs. James Peters showed him he had more worth than to be a follower in a gang.

But how did he manage to memorize so many lines? Justin wanted to know.

Someone had taped James Peters at a reading and gave him the recording.

The following year Justin applied to teach at his college in Central Brooklyn.

JUSTIN HAD KNOWN his father's story. His aunt, saddened by his outbursts each time a letter arrived from America, and fearing he would lose all love for his father, had told it to him. James Peters was not always a revolutionary poet. Before the radicals sent for him, before he became theirs, he was James Peters, the poet. It was afterward that he became James Peters, the *black* poet. James Peters, the angry *black* poet.

But this knowledge did not bring about the effect his aunt had hoped for. It pained Justin even more to know that his father had been willing to abandon him, his own son, for mere strangers. So as he grew older, he devised a way to ease the sting of his hurt and yet stoke his anger. He thought of his father not in personal terms, as the man he loved, the man he thought had loved him, but as the poet who had betrayed his sources, who had let race so define him that all he once loved, all that once inspired him, became anathema.

When James Peters was young, Wordsworth was his idol. Later, it was also Homer. He had won a copy of Wordsworth's *Lyrical Ballads* in an essay contest. By the time he was twelve, he had memorized half the poems. At thirteen, he was writing his own imitations. He continued to write them until one day, his literature teacher (a very black man who was in a losing battle with the British colonial government over a cocoa estate he had inherited from his father—which the British had had no interest in until oil was discovered on it) read to the class a passage from the *Iliad*. It was the same passage Justin would read years later to his students in Brooklyn, with the same hope that it would stir in them, as his father's teacher had hoped it would stir in his students, an unquenchable desire for qualities that make us human: dignity, courage, integrity, compassion, conviction.

This teacher, who had the misfortune of having a last name most suited to the color of his skin and a first name that suggested it, was the butt of jokes. Black Blake, the students called him, or Blakey Black, liking the way the alliterative *bl* rolled off their tongues, but James never joined them in their taunts behind his teacher's back. Blake Black was a god to him, a man standing firm in the face of ridicule from the colonial powers.

It was not only the language of Homer, the story of Hector bravely confronting certain death at the hands of Achilles, that moved the young James Peters. It was the passion in Blake Black's voice, the tears that welled in his eyes, when he read the lines *But now my death is upon me. / Let me at least not die without a struggle, inglorious.*

The Jamaican poet Claude McKay, who immigrated to the United States, would make his fame on similar lines, though Justin is not certain he ever credited Homer. But neither did Winston Churchill credit McKay when he recited McKay's sonnet to rally his troops to victory in England's darkest hour, the

German squadrons hurling their death bombs on London: *If we must die, let it not be like hogs / Hunted and penned in an inglorious spot.*

But this was to be Justin's point: Good literature has relevance to everyone, regardless of race, ethnicity, class, or gender.

When Blake Black committed suicide after the British warden seized his lands for nonpayment of taxes and threatened him with a prison term, James Peters stopped writing nature poems altogether and began writing poems about resistance and courage. His inspiration remained Homer, the *Iliad* as well as the *Odyssey*, Hector as well as Ulysses, but the ones who sent for him from America did not know that. Someone had chanced upon James Peters's poems. The Movement wanted him.

It took a teenager to open Justin's eyes. James Peters's poems had value that transcended racial boundaries. The young man could barely read, but he had memorized ten stanzas of his father's longest poem. He was no animal, he told Justin, even if those racist pigs treated him like one. James Peters's poem reminded him he was human.

And if a poem had such power over a boy of thirteen, why not a book of poems and a comment about love tossed off carelessly by a professor who was admired and revered by a sensitive young man in the torment of love?

FOURTEEN

It is snowing again when Justin returns home, light flecks of white that dissolve the instant they land on his windshield. Parking is torturous though there is space in the street where he lives. But the trucks came early with their giant snow shovels and banks of snow are piled up in the area he had cleared that morning. Jim Grant watches him double park and take a shovel from the trunk of his car. He laughs.

"Still needing to use that brawn of yours, Peters?"

Jim Grant has a theory about clearing snow in the city: If it snows for more than two days, take public transportation. "This ain't the 'burbs. The sanitation department don't care one hill of beans if you been digging all day to clear a space for your car. When they come with their snow shovels, they will bury you deep." Jim Grant's car is locked in at the curb, under a mountain of snow.

"I'm a hardhead, Jim."

"All you young Turks are."

Anna is there. Giselle runs to him and announces her presence.

"Aunt Anna's in the kitchen. She says we can't plant the seeds until the snow goes away. When will it go away, Daddy?"

Justin takes her hand and walks into the kitchen. He greets Sally and Anna. Sally responds but she remains bent over a container that Justin can see is filled with dirt.

"So when will the snow stop, Daddy?" Giselle is tugging his sleeve.

"I told her it will be spring soon," Sally says.

"Anyway," Anna says, "we're still waiting for the seeds to root. Remember, Giselle: they sprout roots, then leaves and stem, and when they do that we'll be ready to plant."

"But what if the snow is still here?"

"What if? What if? You are full of what ifs, aren't you, Giselle?" Anna tweaks her ear.

"But what if it snows?" the child insists.

"We'll plant them in the little boxes Mommy made," Anna says.

"Look, Giselle," Sally says, pointing to the row of tiny plastic containers in bright primary colors turned over on the table. There is a red, green, yellow, blue, and white one, even a black one. "That's why Aunt Anna helped you and Mommy put holes in the bottom."

"For the water to drain out," Anna says.

"I told you that, Giselle," Sally says. "Did you forget?"

"Aunt Anna's going to bring more dirt tomorrow," Anna says. "We'll fill them up together."

A tight, self-contained triangle. This is what Justin thinks of them.

Anna kisses Sally. "I'm going to leave now," she says.

"I hope not on my account," Justin says.

She chooses to ignore him.

"Will you be okay, Sally? Will you be all right?"

They have talked. Sally has told her about their quarrel. The hiatus Mark's near suicide triggered is over.

"I'm fine," Sally says.

"Are you sure? Do you want me to call you tonight?"

"I'm fine. Really I am, Anna."

"Then tomorrow?"

They embrace again.

THAT NIGHT, AFTER he has read a bedtime story to Giselle and after he and Sally have tucked her in bed, he approaches the subject again, the one they have left hanging in the air since their talk in the restaurant.

"I suppose you think I'm being unfair," he says.

"I won't be made a prisoner, Justin."

"I'm not trying to imprison you."

"Then what do you think you are doing when you say that you will not have Giselle live in two places?"

"I did not say that to imprison you, Sally."

"Then what else? You know I cannot be without Giselle. I cannot leave her."

"Neither can I."

"It's that West Indian macho stuff of spreading your seed and counting it," she says bitterly.

"If you mean we don't abandon our children, yes."

The unspoken implication angers her. She strikes back. "And neither do African American men," she says.

They have descended into the quagmire of ethnic squabbling. They have been there before. It took days, sloshing through accusations and threats thick as mud, for them to resurface. When they did, they vowed never again.

Sally unbuttons and then re-buttons the top of her blouse. She sits down on the armchair. Justin crosses the room, recrosses it, and leans against the bathroom door. They must both cool down. They know they can be sucked again to the bottom of the quagmire by this difference between them, this cultural divide pried open by geography, by beasts not men, who dumped one ancestor here, the other there, like cargo, after that brutal crossing through the Atlantic.

It had not been their quarrel. They had not started it. One of Sally's friends, male, a frustrated admirer no doubt, drunk, but not too drunk to be cruel, had called Justin a leech. "All you West Indians who took that banana boat to America," he said, "you are leeches living off the blood of African Americans. If it wasn't for us, you'd all still be there cutting cane. We changed the quotas for you; we got them to let you in."

He was speaking of the Immigration Act of 1965 that came on the heels of the Civil Rights Bill of 1964.

Justin said his brains got him here. A scholarship to Harvard. Sally said nothing. It was that silence that hurt him more than anything her friend had said.

Days later, he and Sally reached a compromise. Yes, she agreed with him, he did it on his own. But Harvard, she said, would not have been so generous as to add a scholarship to graduate school to the undergraduate scholarship the Trinidadian government had given him if Harvard's doors had not been kicked down by black people in the Struggle.

What Justin chooses to remember most is what she said afterward. "You could have stayed in New England. They liked you there, but you came to Brooklyn to teach. I admire you for that," she said. "I love you for that."

Now he tries to soften his tone. "I won't abandon Giselle." He says this quietly, so quietly she does not hear.

"What?"

He repeats himself.

"I am not asking you to abandon her," she says.

"You're asking me to see her every other weekend, two weeks in the summer, every other Christmas and Thanksgiving. . . ." His voice has turned cold, hard as steel. "And to pay for her support," he says. His eyes sweep the room.

"It's the money. Is that it, Justin?"

"I simply won't have my child, my own flesh and blood, rationed to me."

"She's my flesh and blood, too." She folds her arms across her chest.

"Rationed to me like . . . like if she were some commodity that can be parceled out in bits and parts."

"It's yourself you're thinking of, not Giselle," Sally says.

He walks over to the bed. "I told you, Sally, I don't believe in divorce." He sits down. "Not when there are children," he says. He sounds tired, wrung dry by the need to say this again.

"And you think it is better for children to live in a house where there are unhappy parents?"

"I don't know, but I can tell you this for sure. I would have given anything to have lived in the same house with my parents, whether they were fighting or not. You can't tell me you wouldn't have wanted the same. I knew the difference when they left. You said a hole was left in your brother when your father died? Well, a hole was left in me when my parents left. And my aunt was kind to me. God knows, rest her soul, she did everything to please me, but it was not the same. I wanted my parents home, where I was living, or where they were. I wanted them with me—my mother *and* my father. You can't tell me your life was easy without your parents."

"It's not the same thing. My father was dead, my mother was ill."

"But it felt the same way, didn't it? You felt their absence, didn't you?"

"Giselle will know we aren't happy."

"Not if we hide it from her."

"Are you saying we should live a lie?"

"I am saying we should be good parents."

"I want more than that, Justin."

"Passion is an illusion, Sally."

"And this? This?"

"This banal, boring existence? Is that what you want to say, Sally? Yes, this is reality."

"If this, what we have, is reality, then I want the illusion."

He feels the heat in his head before the words reach his tongue. "It is the illusion that got you in trouble, Sally, when you believed Jack the Enforcer was a knight in shining armor."

She runs to the bathroom and bangs the door shut. Justin sleeps in the den.

FIFTEEN

They send an emissary. So Justin is led to believe. In the morning, before first period, when he is sitting in his office reviewing his class notes, she knocks on his door. He gets up to greet her. It is a woman he likes and respects. Helen Clumly. A feminist, or they say she is, but he thinks she is one so accidentally, falling into the role the way his father had when he became an icon for a movement he did not understand.

She is a historian. She has written a dissertation on an analysis of the history of women's movements in the Third World, examining their commonalties with Western feminist movements. The paper she presented at the International Women's Conference in South Africa was entitled *Are We Really so Different?* Overnight it made her the darling of feminists—white, black, Asian, Latina.

Her dissertation was published and soon journals were begging for her articles, publishers vying with each other for the rights to her next book, conventions seeking her out to be their keynote speaker. Now she breathes that heady, rarified air at the top of the Ivory Tower that Justin thinks sooner or later will become impossible for her to live without. Yet she stays at their small, public inner-city college. The attraction it holds for her baffles her agent, but it does not baffle Justin. Both he and she are members of a secret society: professors who at heart are simply scholars, content to spend their days in the dusty stacks of research libraries but find themselves thrust into the limelight by politics.

This, Justin knows, is by no means an accurate description of himself, but the fact remains that if not for that placement test committee, if not for that teenager unable to read his father's poetry, he would have remained where he was, in New England, in an Ivy League college, teaching predominantly white students and doing research on arcane subjects that nobody cares about. As it is, in two weeks, he will be delivering a paper at a national conference in Atlanta on combating illiteracy among inner-city youths with plays by Shakespeare.

But he is not in the limelight. Helen Clumly is in the limelight. She is the celebrity swept away by political forces: one that would canonize her for her research on women of color, the other because she also speaks for them, because she is one of them. Her college in Brooklyn meets their requirements: The students are overwhelmingly black and female, the politics sufficiently left wing.

"I've been asked to ask you—" she says. Her body is stiff, her voice terse. He braces himself.

"Who has asked you to ask me?" He does not let her finish.

"It does not matter."

"And whatever it is he or she wants you to ask me, why can't he or she ask it himself or herself?"

Helen repeats, "I have been asked to ask you." She pauses and looks up at him. "Will you let me finish?'

"Go on."

"Whether or not you told Mark Sandler that Sylvia Plath gassed herself over a man."

So that is it. Somehow, somebody has told her.

"Over, as in top of?" he says, trying to buy time, to diffuse the tension with a joke. She is, after all, a friend. They dated briefly when he first joined the faculty. She is a pretty woman, fine-boned, short, with Elizabeth Taylor blue eyes and a mass of blond curls that frame her tiny face.

"You know," she says, "I think I made a big mistake about you."

"Come on, Helen. You don't think I meant anything by that quip? I was being a wise-ass."

"Yes, that you are."

"If it means something to you, then I apologize. Okay, I am sorry I was insensitive."

"Then let me cut to the chase."

"This sounds serious."

"It is serious. There has been a complaint made about what you said to Mark Sandler."

"A complaint?"

"Did you say that, Justin? Did you tell Mark that Sylvia Plath gassed herself over . . . because of a man?"

"Mark is the only one who can corroborate what I said. What did Mark tell you?"

"I suppose you know he is in the hospital."

"Yes. I went to see him."

"Then you know how serious this is?"

"It's unfortunate, Helen. Sad. Poor Mark."

"Don't you feel in any way responsible?"

"For what?"

"For what you said."

"Look, Helen, I didn't give him Sylvia Plath to read. He saw it in my office and picked it up. I'd think those feminists would have thought well of me for having that book in my office."

"We know who gave it to you. That is not the issue."

"Issue? Are we now talking about issues? What issue?"

"We know Carol Taylor gave you the book."

"Then you know I am not responsible." He stands up. "Christ! What garbage are you having me say! No one is responsible. Mark has emotional problems. If anyone is responsible, it is all of us for not seeing that he needed help."

"He confides in you. He is taking an independent course with you."

"But that does not make me his counselor."

"God, you have become callous."

Justin sits down. "I am not callous. I will talk to Mark. I like him. I'll talk to him about getting help."

"The hospital has already done that. You have caused enough trouble."

"And what precisely do you mean by that?"

"Mark's girlfriend, his ex-girlfriend, said that just before Mark turned on the gas in the oven, he called her. He told her that he was reading Sylvia Plath's poems. He said 'Professor Peters said Sylvia Plath gassed herself over a man.' Those were the exact words Mark said to Sandra."

If he can say a poem changed a teenager's life, if he acknowledges that his father's poetry had this effect on a thirteen-year-old boy, then why not this, what Helen Clumly seems to be implying? No, he will not allow himself to think this way.

"And what is Sandra's professional expertise? Mind reader? Seer? Clairvoyant?" He covers up his discomfort with an accusation of his own.

"She . . . Sandra believes that Mark would never have done a thing like that had you not put that thought in his head."

"You know her? You know this Sandra?"

"That is irrelevant. What is relevant is what you have done. You don't feel badly, do you? You don't know how you have upset her. You've made her think she drove Mark to it."

"Who are we talking about now, Mark or Sandra? Am I to be responsible for her, too?"

"She is very, very upset. I had to take her to the doctor."

"So you know her well."

"She had to take tranquilizers to keep from shaking."

"She called you?"

Helen does not answer the question directly. "She filed a complaint."

"Do you know both of them?"

"Sandra was my student."

"You knew the nature of the relationship between Mark and her?"

"We talked."

"Do you know Mark suspects she has another lover? A woman. He told me that at the hospital."

Helen lowers her eyes and jabs her finger on the surface of his desk. "Look," she says, striking the desk again, " the point is that *you* put that idea in Mark's head."

"Do you know it is a woman she is having an affair with?" Justin repeats the question.

"What does it matter? What difference does it make if she is, was having an affair with a woman?"

He misses the shift in tense. "It matters a great deal to a man," he says. "To his masculinity."

"Shit," says Helen. "You can think about masculinity in a situation like this?"

"It was a big blow to Mark."

"And what about Sandra? You don't seem to realize what you have done. Sandra is a very fragile girl. She feels guilty. She feels she was responsible."

"You'd prefer me to feel responsible, is that it?"

"You are. You filled his head with all that stuff."

Justin gets up. "I think you should leave, Helen. We're

wasting each other's time. I have papers to grade, a class to teach. I think you're being absurd, and you know you are. You can't pin what happened to Mark on me. Or how what's-her-name—"

"Sandra," Helen says.

"—or on how Sandra is dealing with it, for that matter. You are smarter than that. You won't convince me of whatever it is that your department has concocted. Mark needs help, professional help."

She turns to leave and then pauses at the door. This is not the end of the matter, she tells Justin. I am going to take it seriously.

THREE THINGS STRIKE Justin when Helen leaves: one, she seems to know Sandra very well; two, she seems to be more concerned about her than she is about Mark; three, she seems reluctant to identify the person who sent her to him. Her last words to him were that she, not the chair of the department, was going to take "it" seriously.

Perhaps there has been no complaint made against him. Perhaps Helen was sent by her department to test him, to smoke him out. It is known, after all, that she is a friend. But, perhaps, though he cannot formulate a reason why, it is she, Helen, who wants to find out what he knows.

When he runs into the chair later in the day, he decides to take a chance and test his suspicions. He is clever. He does not ask about Plath. Instead he asks her a question about Hughes: Does she think he was as good as the critics say? The chair, an imposing brown-skinned woman with a graying close-cropped

Afro, chuckles. "Coming into the modern age, are you, Justin?" But she answers his question. "Yes, he was a good poet," she says, "but he became more famous when his wife died. You do know he was unkind to her, don't you?" She does not give Justin the slightest indication that she has any gripe against him.

Helen is still on Justin's mind when he calls the hospital. He cannot speak to Mark, he is told. Mark is resting. Mark should be more alert tomorrow. Justin believes that the person who tells him this is not speaking the truth. The pause between his request to speak to Mark and the answer is far too long. He thinks someone has given the hospital instructions to keep him away from Mark. He thinks that someone is Helen.

HE HAS MORE than he can handle when Anna calls. She came, as she had promised, and, as she had done the night before, she left soon after he arrived.

"I think you will do well with an early night tonight," she said to Sally as she was leaving, and Justin bristled at the proprietary tone she seemed to feel at liberty to use even in his presence.

But Sally does in fact complain of being tired and takes to her bed.

"I am worried about Sally," Anna says when she calls. Justin is grading papers in the den. Sally does not hear the phone in the bedroom. Justin has turned off the ringer. "What about?" he asks.

"We don't have to play games, Justin," she says. "I know what is going on. I know you and Sally are having problems."

"Then you understand that whatever is the matter, it concerns *only* my wife and me." He emphasizes *only*.

"I am her friend," Anna says.

"That is all you are, Anna."

"Justin, I know you don't like me," Anna begins, pauses, takes a deep breath and continues, "but Sally likes me and so does Giselle."

"Yes?"

"And Sally is unhappy."

He wants to end the conversation. Sally's happiness is not her business. "I don't want to be rude," he says, "but this has been a difficult day for me."

"I want to help."

"You've helped enough."

"What do you mean by that?"

"Those books she has." He is saying more than he wants to, but he has waited a long time for this moment. "It has taken me a while, but I figured out. It was you who gave them to her."

She does not deny this. "She finds them helpful," Anna says.

"They fill her with the illusion that life is simple, that there are easy answers."

"They are comforting to her."

"It's all that American optimistic bullshit," he says.

"It's American optimistic bullshit that has made this country great," Anna says. "You immigrants come from a world of disappointment and hardship. It's hard for you to imagine an easier way."

He cannot let this statement go unchallenged. "It is our hard work that gives you the luxury of optimism," he says.

She begins to answer and he cuts her off. He has had enough. He does not want to be drawn in further. "I need to go to bed," he says. But she has disturbed him. He wants her to pay. "You may not have to teach tomorrow," he says. "I do."

His remark has the desired effect. Her voice loses its authoritative edge. "You won't solve your problems the way you're going about it, Justin," she says.

"That's just it, Anna. They are my problems. Sally's and mine."

"And Sally is my friend."

He makes the effort to control his anger. "I really must get some sleep," he says.

"Okay," she says, "okay, but I'll be talking to Sally."

JUSTIN DREAMS OF death that night. It is not the usual dream. In the usual dream, which began when his father left for America and his mother followed soon afterward, he had hope, the promise the priest made on Sundays of life hereafter. They would be back one day, too, his parents. Days stretched to weeks, weeks to months, months to years never-ending, but he believed. No one came back from the dead to give witness, but the priest said, and the congregation agreed, so the boy hoped.

And there are the letters, said his aunt in the usual dream. And the phone calls. The dead do not write letters; the dead do not make phone calls.

Rainy seasons came and went. Nine times the earth got parched. Red petals fell from the immortelle tree and curled up in the dust. Nothing changed.

But this night, in the dream he has, Justin knows the promise of hope is a lie. He wakes with a start and remembers: It is true. It is final. His father is dead. He will not return.

He tiptoes into his daughter's room and kisses the top of her head. She stirs. Daddy? I'm here, he answers.

He walks toward the den, turns and retraces his steps and beyond. Justin? He brushes his lips across Sally's forehead. I'm here, he answers. He slides under the cover next to her in their bed.

SIXTEEN

Sally goes about her chores mechanically. She makes the bed, she dresses Giselle, she packs her lunch. She follows her chatter. The child notices nothing different in her behavior, but Justin sees a difference. It is mostly in her eyes. There is a dullness there, a lifelessness. The flesh around her jaw is slack. Her skin has a pallor that reminds him of wax.

When Giselle runs upstairs to get a dress for her doll which she wants to take with her to the baby-sitter's, Sally stands motionless by the window, staring vacantly outside, plucking her lower lip. Justin says her name and she responds vaguely: "Time to go?" At the door, just before she leaves, she gives him her cheek. He kisses her. She does not kiss him back.

TEN O'CLOCK. The Great Books class. Act 5 of *Hamlet*. Justin is having difficulty concentrating. He cannot erase the image of Sally looking not so much at him as through him, as if he were not there, reaching for Giselle's hand but only after their daughter had tugged her arm twice: "Mommy, we'll be late. Mommy!"

"'Not a whit, we defy augury,'" Justin reads. "'There is special providence in the fall of a sparrow.'"

What had he gained by his accusation that morning that brought them here, to this place now, where Sally turns dull eyes to the leafless tree beyond their kitchen window and stands frozen when he kisses her good-bye? What had he gained when it was only under the veil of sleep that Sally had murmured, *Justin,* when he kissed her forehead, *Justin,* said with such tenderness he would lie next to her and hold her?

Eight o'clock. Quarter to eight (for he knew the time exactly; he had looked at the clock when she turned her key in the door), quarter to eight, he tells himself now, was not late, not suspiciously late, not so late that he should accuse her the next morning of a lover. Why had he not accepted her explanation? A child was sick. She took the child to the hospital. She stayed to talk to the parents. Why did he have to force a quarrel? She was making pancakes, stirring the batter in the bowl for him. For his breakfast. Did he want to make her cry, to make her confess? Confess what? *I am not happy, Justin.* For in the end, that was all she confessed. And what if it had been a lover? What then? What would have been gained? More tears, the dissolution of his marriage. He did not want the dissolution of his marriage. He could not handle the dissolution of his marriage. So then why couldn't he have held his tongue? Why couldn't he have waited until Sally had righted herself? Why couldn't he have let her work out her troubles on her own time, at her own pace?

"Can anyone tell me what Hamlet means?" Justin looks up from the book to the students in his class. "What does he mean when he says, 'There is special providence in the fall of a sparrow'? "

No one speaks.

"Ms. Clark? Does what Hamlet says here change your opinion of him?"

Ms. Clark twists her ample body in her seat. Her hair swings across her shoulder and tumbles down her back.

"Ms. Clark? Does it seem to you that Hamlet has come to a decision?"

"If you tell me what augury means," she says.

"A sign, an omen. The predictions of a fortune teller."

"Well, I guess he decides not to go that route. He's tried everything else."

A young man in the back row guffaws.

"What do you think about that? Do you still think he is a coward, Ms. Clark?"

Another student raises her hand. He tries to ignore her, but she is insistent. "Ms. Jones? There is something you want to say, Ms. Jones?"

"Hamlet has a feeling things could go wrong for him. He has an uneasy feeling that something bad could happen if he accepts the challenge Laertes gives him and goes and duels with him."

"Yes," Justin reads the lines aloud. "'But thou wouldst not think how ill all's here about my heart.' Ms. Clark, does Hamlet have any reason to feel this way, to feel that things could go wrong?"

Ms. Jones answers for her. "He said he had been practicing his sword fighting and he thinks he's a better fighter than Laertes."

"So if he thinks he is better than Laertes, why does he have this feeling that something can go wrong? Ms. Clark?"

"Is there nobody else in this class except Ms. Clark?" Ms. Clark shoots back.

"I want to find out if you have come to a different conclusion about Hamlet. Do you still think he is a coward?"

Even as he asks this question, Justin is aware that the answer has become personal to him. Would it have been cowardly of him to have held back, to have exercised restraint, to have not let suspicion so control him that he would say to Sally, "I *know* you are having an affair." What had he known for sure? What evidence had he had?

But thou wouldst not think how ill all's here about my heart. He could have defied augury. For in the end that was what it was. There was no other man, no lover Sally was seeing. It would not have been cowardly for him to wait, to give her time. He would not have been less of a man.

"Ms. Clark," he says, "Hamlet has this strange feeling that something bad could happen to him. Was it not brave of him not to give in to this feeling?"

"I never said he was superstitious. I said he was a punk. He's a coward."

"He's a coward even though it looks as though he will duel

with Laertes in spite of this feeling he has that something bad could happen to him?"

"Didn't she just say he had been practicing his sword fighting? It doesn't take courage to fight if you know you're better than the person you're fighting."

"Good. Good point, Ms. Clark. Now we come to the other part: 'There is special providence in the fall of a sparrow.' What does he mean here? Anyone?"

The class is silent. Papers rustle, chairs scrape against the rubber-tiled floor. Justin, too, is uncomfortable, uncertain of the truth of the answer: Does one do nothing? Should one simply put one's life in the hands of destiny? Fate? God? Should he have suppressed his fears when Sally turned away from him in bed?

"Anyone?" he asks. "Anyone? 'There is special providence in the fall of a sparrow.' Do any of you go to church? Doesn't seem to me any of you has been in a church lately." He fakes sarcasm, for he is riddled with doubt, a training in rational thinking that will not allow him to give in easily: Should he have left it up to Him to sort out his problems with Sally? "Are we atheists here?" he asks his students.

"Ahh, Professor." Several of the women protest.

"Never been to a funeral?" he asks.

"Professor, you not serious?"

"Never sang at a funeral?"

Some of the younger women begin to giggle.

"Is there a special gospel song you sing at a funeral?"

A thin woman with ropes of veins running down her arms,

which, though it is winter, are bare to her elbows, raises her hand. "His eye is on the sparrow, and I know He watches me."

"Excellent. Excellent. Do you know that gospel song?" he asks the class.

But the thin woman does not wait for anyone else to answer. With her two hands lifted above her head, palms open wide, as if she is about to give witness in a church, she recites the entire song. "'Why should I feel discouraged, why should the shadows come, / Why should my heart be lonely.'"

Justin does not stop her; he cannot stop her. She will finish the song. "'I sing because I'm happy / I sing because I'm free.'"

Another student asks to be acknowledged. She stands up. "'Are not two sparrows sold for a farthing? and one of them shall not fall on the ground without your Father.' Matthew Ten, verse Twenty-nine."

The class is quiet. No one stirs. The young man in the back row lowers his head. *Yes, and one of them shall not fall on the ground without your Father.*

"Hamlet is confident that God will look after him," says the woman. "He will accept His will. He does not have to decide anything. He can leave his future in God's loving hands."

"'Let be.'" Justin reads Hamlet's conclusion.

Let be, but the stage directions that follow suggest the consequences: *A table prepared. [Enter] Trumpets, Drums, and Officers with cushions; King, Queen, [Osric,] and all the State, [with] foils, daggers, [and stoups of wine borne in]; and Laertes.*

One dagger, unbeknown to Hamlet, has been dipped in the unction of a montebank. There is poison at its tip; the wine, too, is poisoned. In the end all will die: Hamlet, the king, the queen, Laertes.

If this is what *Let be* will bring to Hamlet, what would *Let be* have brought to him if he had let the morning pass, as Sally had planned it to, he sitting at the kitchen table reading the newspaper, Sally with her back to him facing the stove while hot batter sizzled in the frying pan? It is a question Justin cannot answer. He can only say with certitude what did happen when he disturbed the morning, when he did not let be. And for a minute he feels pure envy for the faith that silenced his students. *Let be.* Yes, they tell him, their confidence in the miracle of Providence unshakeable, Hamlet did the right thing.

IT IS AFTER five when Justin gets home. Giselle meets him at the door. Her finger is pressed against her lips. "Shh," she whispers in his ear, "Shh. Mommy's been crying. I heard her in the bathroom. But she didn't hear me, Daddy. Shh."

"And where is Mommy now?" He picks her up and kisses her.

"She's sleeping. She told me to play quietly. See. I am playing quietly. Shh." Justin puts her down and takes off his coat. "How long's Mommy been sleeping?"

"She came out of the bathroom and her eyes were red, red, red."

"What did she say?"

"She said she was tired. She was going to take a nap."

"How long has she been taking a nap?"

"A long time. A long, long time." She takes his hand. "Tiptoe, Daddy. Don't wake her up." She is standing on her toes. She has a blue sock on one foot and a red one on the other. "Let's go in the kitchen. Quiet. Not a sound."

Everything is in a mess in the kitchen. Laundry is scattered on the floor, spilled out of the basket that is lying on its side. Towels and underwear that had been folded are undone, heaped in a pile. Justin sees the other side to the dirty red sock Giselle is wearing on top the pile of clean towels. He picks it up.

"My socks were dirty," Giselle says, taking off the other red sock. "I can't find the blue one." Justin takes a white pair from the basket and puts them on her.

There are three uncovered pots on unlit burners on the stove. Justin looks inside of them. They are empty. The covers are on the floor.

"Mommy says I can play with them," Giselle says when Justin picks them up. "She turned off the stove. Mommy told me not to touch it," she says.

"Mommy told you the right thing."

A bag of rice, a box of frozen peas, the salt and pepper containers are on the counter next to pieces of raw chicken on the cutting board. Near to the chicken is a carving knife. Justin's heart lurches. He grabs the knife quickly and puts it in the sink.

"You have to put away your toys," he tells Giselle.

"When I am finished playing, Daddy." Her toys are strewn under the table.

"And where's your lunch box?" Justin looks around the room. Sally's thermos is on the counter.

"Mommy didn't have time to clean it," she says and she runs to where her lunch box lies open, next to her backpack, in a corner of the room. The grapes Sally had packed for her that morning are squashed all over the top of the backpack.

"Tell you what, Giselle. Help Daddy clean up the kitchen and we'll go to McDonald's"

The little girl claps her hand. "Goody, goody." She knows this is a special treat. "Can we take Mommy?"

"Let's clean up first and then we'll see if Mommy wants to come."

Giselle puts her toys in the toy box, Justin removes the pots from the stove, he wraps up the raw chicken and puts it in the refrigerator. He cleans Giselle's lunch box, wipes the grape stains off her backpack and washes the dishes in the sink.

Sally is still sleeping when they go upstairs.

"We'll bring back something for her," he says to Giselle.

But Sally is not awake when they return.

Later, when he is giving Giselle a bath, she asks him, "Why is Mommy so sad? Why was she crying? Doesn't she like us?" She says this to him while she is combing her doll's hair. She does not look him. Her eyes remain fixed on her doll.

"No. Mommy loves us. Especially you, Giselle. Mommy is not feeling well. She will be all right tomorrow, you'll see."

"Will you take her to the doctor?"

"Yes," Justin promises. "I will make sure Mommy goes to

the doctor." He does not say he will take her there. He will not lie to his daughter.

SALLY WAKES UP at ten. She comes into the den.

"I'm sorry, Justin. Really I am. Is Giselle all right?" She is wearing a thick, pink bathrobe. Her face is pale; her lips are dry. She stands near the door pushing back her hair. Her hand moves back and forth slowly across her right temple. Her eyes are half-closed.

Justin leaves his desk and comes toward her. "Come." He takes her hand. "Come sit with me, Sally." She lets him lead her to the couch.

"I am feeling much better," she says. "I was just so tired. I couldn't keep my eyes open. I was starting to make dinner. I thought Giselle would be okay. I turned off the stove. I knew you would be home soon."

"It's okay, Sally. Giselle was just fine." He does not tell her about the knife.

"I was so tired," she says again. "I needed a nap."

"I took Giselle to McDonald's," he says.

"You?"

"Desperate times call for desperate measures."

"Did I really leave things in that big a mess?"

"I was exaggerating," he says. "I just took the easy way out. You know how much she likes McDonald's."

"I slept so long," she says.

"You needed the rest."

"Was Giselle worried?"

"I told her you would be better tomorrow. I gave her a bath. I read her a story. She even came in your room and kissed you good night."

Sally removes her hand from under his. Justin is not surprised. It was a matter of time. He had felt the stiffening of her muscles under his hand.

"So, so, Sally," he says. He folds his arms over his chest. He feels the emptiness there acutely, the space where he longs for her to be. His fingers clutch his armpits. "Things are not getting better for you, are they?"

"My therapist says it will take time."

He is aware that he has not yet asked about her therapist. "Did he say I am making things worse for you?"

"He says he sees your point."

"And you are still finding it hard to stay here with me, Sally?"

"He says he's sees my point, too."

"Does he think that your point is better than my point?"

"I don't want to leave Giselle," she says.

"Then don't leave her, Sally."

"You want to force me to leave her."

"I want you to stay. Here. Stay with us here."

"You don't understand."

"Get me to understand. I want to understand you, Sally."

"I've told you everything already. There's nothing more to tell. I've told you I feel useless. I feel there's no meaning to my life."

"And what will give meaning to your life, Sally? Will leaving this house give meaning to your life?"

"I don't know," she says.

"So if you don't know, stay. Stay, Sally."

"I only know I have to find myself. I have to find Sally."

"I will give you space." It is fear that leads him to these words he ridicules.

"I don't know," she says again.

He puts his arm around her. "Stay. Find yourself here."

She lets him draw her closer to him but she still does not respond. She does not embrace him; she does not resist him.

"You can go out for as long as you like after work," he murmurs in her hair.

"I don't know," she says.

"For a weekend." His heart is pounding. "Go away for a weekend. That's it, Sally. Take a break. A weekend in Bermuda."

"Bermuda?" She sits up.

"A week if you want. Call in sick. Tell the therapist to write a letter for you."

"And then everyone at work will think I'm mentally ill," she whines, a childish whine, a make-believe whine. She does not mean this, he can tell.

"Ask him to have a doctor write the letter," he says. "An internist. An internist will do it." He is speaking quickly, excitedly now. He wants to infect her with his excitement. *Why hadn't he thought of this before? A weekend in Bermuda will appeal to her.*

"And Giselle?" she asks.

"Don't worry about Giselle. I will take care of Giselle." He kisses the top of her head.

"There is so much to do."

"I can do it."

"And what will you tell her?"

"I will tell her that her mother has gone to visit the place where we went on our honeymoon before she was born. We were happy there, weren't we, Sally?"

"Yes," she says. "We were happy there."

He takes a chance. "Do you love me, Sally?"

"Yes," she says.

"So stay, Sally. Stay."

LET BE, says Hamlet.

Let be. No more accusations. No more questions. In the end, did Hamlet not achieve his goal? Did he not set things right again? Claudius dies. The king's murder is avenged. He will not think of the other consequences: that Hamlet, too, dies—that in the end blood is everywhere. He thinks, *Let be and Sally will stay.*

SEVENTEEN

In the morning he remembers that in two weeks he has to present a paper at a national conference in Atlanta. He said Bermuda on impulse, without forethought. He presented it as an offering to staunch her uncertainty, the steady repetition of *I don't know* that frightened him. But he knows now, impulse or not, it is a good idea. He wants her to go. The separation will give her time to think—him time for her to cool down, to reconsider. To find herself. But he also knows that it is possible, if she takes his advice, she could leave the week he is expected in Atlanta.

The chance that he could find himself in such a predicament does not disturb him, as it should. He will not be able to go to Atlanta, of course. He will have to stay home with Giselle. He will have to let the conference director know. But it does not bother him that he may not be able to present his paper. Literacy rates in the inner city is not his area of expertise. His area of expertise, if he can still call it that, is British Renaissance literature. But for all his high-mindedness about the laxity of tenured professors, the lack of respect they show for their students by not keeping up with the research in their field, he has not written a single paper on a single Renaissance writer since his arrival at the college.

More and more what he finds himself doing in his den at night is grading papers. He could not have imagined that this would have been such a daunting and demanding task. Before he can get to the substance of what his students are trying to say, before he can unravel the logic of their arguments, he has to wade through a morass of comma faults, run-on sentences, fragments, tense inconsistencies, subject-verb agreement errors, pronoun reference errors, dangling and misplaced modifiers, faulty parallelism—a plethora of syntactical challenges. It takes him at least half an hour to correct one paper, many times more than that, and there are at least thirty students in each of the classes he teaches, four classes in the fall and three in the spring.

He insists that his students write an essay a week. It is no less than what his teachers in Trinidad had required of him. Writing leads to better writing is his mantra. He believes, regardless of the fancy theories—the current pedagogical approaches to teaching composition making the rounds in colleges like his—that writing, his careful correction of what his students have written, and rewriting, is the only way his students will learn. It is a conviction that has cost him a career.

Anna has been forthright about her disinterest in writing

academic papers. “They have no relevance to what I do,” she said. “Professors write those academic articles just to make themselves feel important. Nobody reads them but graduate students who are obliged to. No, I don’t pretend that my students come from middle-class homes, that they went to the best high schools, that they have great SAT scores. I meet them where they are.”

“And take them where, Anna?”

“Where I know they can be.”

“And is that the same as where they are capable of going?”

But he is the one who has been the hypocrite with his arguments about the need for research when he himself has done no serious study since he left his previous job. No, apart from the problem of finding time after he has graded his students’ papers, there is the problem of finding like-minded scholars. You need such a community to sustain your enthusiasm for work which you know beforehand may never be read except, as Anna has said, by a handful of scholars. No one here, where he is, is interested in what he has to say. The one other Renaissance scholar at the college, a historian, has caved in. He saw the writing on the wall, he said. He retrained himself and became an expert in computers. Now he lectures on search engines and Web sites. Now he is in demand.

Justin acknowledges that he has come to be thought of as an expert on literacy in the inner city by a series of accidents that began with his guilt for misunderstanding his father, for not appreciating the importance of his work to those who needed him.

"What does it matter if the whole world loves you when your son does not?" he asked his father when he returned to Trinidad.

He loved him, his father insisted. He was proud of him. Seven distinctions? No one in his family had made seven distinctions in the O level Cambridge exams. None of the children of his friends.

"Love is not words," he told his father. "Love is doing, showing. Being there for the ones you love. Words are cheap. You were not here. You do not know me. You have no rights."

"I am your father."

"You have no right to call yourself my father. My aunt is my father. She was there for me. She woke up early to make me breakfast. She spoke to my teachers. You have no right to be proud of me."

When his father's heart burst open—a massive heart attack, the doctor said—Justin told himself that it was the contradictions in his father's life that had killed him. But he had killed him, too. If he had forgiven him, his father would have found the peace that would have permitted his heart to slow down, that would have allowed it to beat for a few more years.

A son cannot take responsibility for his father's death and go on. Justin was no exception. He continued to blame his father through graduate school and in the years he taught in New England. He would be all his father was not. He disassociated himself from the Africana Studies department that courted him at Harvard. He chose the Classics. He was not unaware that the

Classics were his father's first love, but his father had betrayed the poets who had taught him. He had allowed his poetry to serve a single, political purpose, as if it had no relevance except to those who found it useful. His father had allowed himself to be defined.

Now, Justin wonders if he himself is not allowing the same to happen to him. He has stopped going to conferences on Renaissance literature. It embarrasses him that he has not kept up with the research. When he goes to the annual meeting of the Modern Language Association, his name is listed under headings for either college composition or the core curriculum. Because his college is in Central Brooklyn and his students are black, he is expected to deliver treatises on the peculiar learning styles of black students. It is a topic he finds revolting and racist. Poverty and racism, he contends, are the culprits, not the student's race. But there are many who have carved thriving careers for themselves with their theories about learning styles based on race. In Trinidad, at the time he was there, black students competed in O level and A level Cambridge exams and many times scored higher grades than Asians and whites.

Yet Justin has allowed himself to be drawn into the conversation. He cannot manage a paper on theories about illiteracy, but he has promised to write one on the relevance of Shakespeare to inner-city students. Applied Shakespeare, he notes wryly. His area of expertise tangentially.

He cannot complain. It is he who has chosen to teach in this college. A teenager who stumbled on his father's lines, a teenager who could not read, that is what has brought him here.

He will have no regrets. Whatever the losses, his work is more meaningful here. He cannot be called a leech. No one can doubt he has paid for his scholarship a hundred times. Yet he does not have his heart in writing the paper. If Sally goes to Bermuda the week he is expected in Atlanta, it will not matter.

SALLY FEELS BETTER the next morning and decides to return to work. She tells Justin that when she meets with her therapist in the afternoon, she will discuss his idea about Bermuda.

"Why don't you go to a movie with Anna after dinner?" he says, hopeful now. Her mood has changed. The lethargy that bogged her down has lifted. It is early, not yet six, but he has followed her into the kitchen and while she refolds the clothes in the laundry basket, he turns on the fire under the kettle for her tea. Mystical Mornings. He takes it out of the canister willingly. "I'll stay with Giselle. It'll do you good to go out."

She'll see, Sally says. She'll talk to Anna.

On his way to the college, Justin stops at the hospital. They have moved Mark to another room, out of the crisis center. He is sitting on a side chair, next to his bed, when Justin walks in. He jumps up immediately. Justin reaches out to him and they hug, male style. Each grasps the other's right hand and brings it to his chest. They move in close, shoulder to shoulder, they make a fist with their left hands, they strike each other's back. The embrace, if it can be called that, lasts no more than seconds and then they part.

"Sit, Professor. Take a load off." Mark offers Justin his chair.

Mark is not the only patient in the room. Through the thin canvas screen that surrounds his bed, Justin can see the prone outline of another man. Mark follows his eyes. "He's zonked out," he says. He points to his head. "They got him drugged up. Don't know a thing."

Mark is in the psychiatric wing of the hospital. It is a cheerless place. The walls of his room are a graying white, his bed frame a dismal dark metal, the rubber tiles a lackluster beige, the baseboards a gloomy green. Justin wishes he brought him flowers. Mark cannot get better, he thinks, if he stays in this place much longer.

"How's it going?" Justin sits but he does not take off his coat.

"Fine, Professor, fine. Everything's going good, real good." Mark perches himself on the edge of the bed. "I'm feeling strong. Good. Doctor says I should be out tomorrow."

"Tomorrow?" Justin forces a smile. "That's great, Mark."

"Going to stay at my mom's."

"That's really great. A great plan," Justin says.

Mark tightens the cloth belt around his thin, blue cotton bathrobe. He is wearing pajamas beneath them. Striped gray ones. He bites his lip. "To tell the truth," he says, "I had no choice."

"But it'll be good to be at Mom's," Justin says, determined to keep the conversation upbeat.

"Only way the doctor will let me out of here," Mark says.

"Your mom will be glad to have you back home." Justin

knows he is lying. He knows it will not be easy for Mark. Mark's mother counted on Mark, her eldest, the one who escaped the seemingly inevitable, the one in college, the one who was supposed to be a model for his siblings. He knows Mark will be tormented by the disappointment he will certainly see in her eyes. "It'll be temporary, Mark," he says.

"Mom doesn't have the space. Two brothers, three little sisters, no father. But she's my mom." Mark's face lights up. "Says I can stay as long as I'm her son."

The effort he makes to sound confident and hopeful tugs at Justin's heart. He stands up and takes off his coat. He wants to put his arms around Mark. He wants to comfort him. This is not the self-assured young man in black leather jacket and tight, black jeans who just a few days ago was challenging him about Morrison. This is a child, a vulnerable, fragile child. But Justin changes his mind and sits back down again. He does not know how Mark will react if he folds him in his arms. He does not know how *he* will react. He puts his coat on his lap. He crosses his hands. He lays them on his knees. "It won't be forever, Mark," he says.

"No, not forever. I have to go for counseling and I can come back to college. In three weeks the doctor will reassess if I can live on my own."

"That's not such a bad deal."

"And Mom needs the help. There's a lot that needs fixing in her apartment. And I miss the kids."

"Things have a way of working out." *Sally's platitude.* Mark is reassured.

"Yes," he says. "Things have a way. The love thing didn't work out, but, hey, those are the breaks."

"She hasn't come to see you?" Justin bends toward Mark; his voice is strained with hope.

"She sent her girlfriend. A righteous white woman." Mark cracks his knuckles. His eyes skirt the floor. "She thinks you're to blame," he says.

It takes Justin less than a second to know whom Mark means. He sits back. He does not ask, Who thinks I am to blame? He waits for Mark to name her. But Mark is silent; he offers nothing more.

"Does your girlfriend go to the college?" Justin measures the question carefully.

"Ex." Mark corrects him.

"Does she?"

"Used to. Matter of fact, that's where she met her lover."

"At the college?"

Mark shrugs his shoulders. "Would offer you something to drink, Professor, but . . ."

"Was she a tutor?"

"No, not a tutor."

"Another student?" Justin asks, though he is sure, one hundred percent sure. There are no white women students at their college.

"A white woman?" Mark raises his voice, pretending surprise. It is as close as he gets to naming her.

Justin uncrosses his hands, he fiddles with the lapels of his coat, he does not speak. But soon it is clear that if he is to get confirmation, he will have to be direct. "Why won't you tell me it is Professor Clumly, Mark?"

Mark shifts his body on the bed and turns away.

"I know it's Professor Clumly," Justin says. "You don't have to hide it from me."

"I could call the nurse to get us some water." Mark turns around to face him again.

"Did you think I would take her side?" Justin ignores his offer.

Mark lowers his head.

"Did you?"

"I know you used to date her."

"A long time ago, Mark."

"And you knew she was a lesbo, Prof?"

"No," says Justin. "No, I didn't know she was gay when I dated her."

"I didn't want you to feel like a chump."

"I don't feel like a chump," Justin says.

"I feel like a chump for going out with a lesbo."

"Don't be so hard on yourself."

"I thought she was the one, my soul mate. I thought a lesbo was my soul mate."

"I think you should say *gay*, Mark."

"What?"

"*Gay* not *lesbo*. That's how they want to be called."

"I don't care how they want to be called."

No, he cannot give him a lecture on political correctness

now. He had let such remarks go unchallenged before. He permitted them with his silence.

"Were you trying to tell me about Sandra, Mark? That morning you came in my office, was that what you were trying to tell me?"

"I had my suspicions then," Mark says, "but I wasn't sure."

"I'm sorry, Mark." It is not an apology. Justin is sympathizing with him.

"You think I made her a lesbo, Prof?"

Mark blamed Sethe's husband. He said that it was Halle's failure to help Sethe, it was his abandonment of her, that led her to do the unthinkable.

"No," Justin says. "It is not your fault. You didn't make her gay, Mark, no more," he adds, "than Halle made Sethe kill Beloved."

Mark considers this. He does not contest it. "You must have thought what I said about Sethe was crazy."

"I should have known you had something else on your mind."

"Professor Clumly seduced Sandra," Mark says.

"She couldn't have seduced her if Sandra weren't gay," Justin says.

"We were having some problems, you know," Mark says.

"Everyone has problems."

"But I wasn't easy to live with, either," Mark says.

"Who is?"

"Sandra was working full time and bringing home most of

the bread. She started getting bossy. Wanting to tell me how I should spend my money. Telling me I shouldn't buy a TV."

"What size, Mark?" The question is incongruous, but Justin grabs this chance he sees to relieve some of the pain that is squeezing the breath out of Mark. Squeezing the breath out of him. "I know how the brothers like it," he says.

A wan smile begins to form across Mark's lips and then gets brighter. He raises his hand, palm wide open. "Supersize," he says.

Justin meets his open palm. They slap high fives, palm upon palm. "Big screen, huh, Mark?"

"Big time."

"Now, you have to say Sandra had a point."

"Yeah. She had a point." But Mark is no longer smiling.

When Justin gets ready to leave, Mark tells him that he didn't pay attention to a word Professor Clumly said to him. "Don't even think for a second I believe you have anything to do with what happened to me. You're the best, Professor. If I turn out to be any kind of worthwhile person, it will be because of you. You're the best."

And though Justin knows Mark means this with all his heart, that Mark wishes to dispel any traces of guilt that he may feel for what has happened to him, that he wants him to know that he does not in any way hold him responsible, his words do not have the effect they should. Justin leaves the hospital feeling sadder than when he came, a nagging sense of discomfort making it difficult for him to find any joy in the compliment Mark has given. *It is Mark who is the best, Mark who will one day write books that will disturb the consciences of the world.* Justin wishes he had told him that.

HE DRIVES DIRECTLY to the college and heads straight for Helen Clumly's office. The door is open. She is sitting at her desk grading papers.

"How long did you think it would have taken me to find out?"

"Shouldn't you close the door?"

He disregards the question. "How long did you think you could keep up this game?"

She gets up, walks around her desk, passes close to him but careful not to brush against him, and closes the door. "It was not a game," she says. "Someone almost died."

"Yes, and you wanted to put the blame on me when you knew all along it was you."

"Sandra doesn't think so. She thinks you are to blame."

"I just saw Mark. He said you were having an affair with Sandra. Don't you know, Ms. Feminist, Ms. Women's Rights, Ms. Defender of Women, that it is an abuse of power to sleep with one of your students?"

"Was. She *was* one of my students."

"Is that why she left the college?"

"Now don't be ridiculous, Justin."

"Am I? Am I being ridiculous? You lied about having an affair with her."

"I didn't lie. I just didn't tell you."

"So what else didn't you tell me? That there was no complaint? That the only complaint was in your head?"

"I protected you," she says.

"*You* protected *me*? How could you make a complaint against me when you were having an affair with a student? How long, Helen? How long was it going on?"

Helen sits down. With the tips of her fingers she slides the papers in front of her across her desk. "I was attracted to her when she was a student but the affair did not begin until after she left the college."

"Until you forced her to leave you mean."

"I had nothing to do with her leaving. She was tired of school. She wanted to work, to buy things, while she was young. And then one day she came to my office."

"Just like that? Out of the blue?"

"Mark sent her to collect his term paper. He had missed class."

"So you knew she was living with Mark?"

"Yes," she says.

"I will never understand this." Justin slumps down in the armchair in Helen's office. His shoulders sag and his jacket rises ridiculously above them. "This is too much. Too much," he says.

"What is? That two people love each other?"

"You dated me, Helen. Sandra was living with Mark."

"You are so naïve. Why do you think we stopped seeing each other?"

"We had different interests," he says. He sinks deeper into the armchair.

"Mine was women."

He thought it was feminism. He had become tired of the incessant arguments, the constant accusations, the articles she insisted he read: Women get less pay than their male counterparts. The pro-life movement is a smoke screen for men who want to control women's bodies. The Kennedy date rape case was about the Good Old Boys' Club in action. Men stick together, she said, because they all have skeletons in their closets.

Now he is thinking of her skeletons. "Why did you go out with me?"

"I wasn't sure," she says.

"You weren't sure of what?"

"Whether I was gay or not."

He is dumbfounded. "Didn't you always know?"

"Did you always know you were heterosexual?"

"I didn't have to think about it. I liked women."

"I didn't think about it, either. I didn't think about whether I liked men or women. I was expected to like men, so I dated them."

"Sandra was your first?"

"I don't have to answer that."

"Why, Helen? Why did you want to blame me?"

"Sandra said—"

"I know what you said Sandra said, but you are the professor here. You are more intelligent than that. You knew it had to be absurd for Mark to try to kill himself simply over something I said or something he read."

"I hadn't intended for it to get this far. I didn't know she was going to leave him."

"You didn't want the responsibility, is that it, Helen?" He does not camouflage his scorn. "You didn't want the commitment, right?"

"She wanted to move in with me. She told that to Mark. But she told him too soon. I wasn't ready." Her voice has a whining quality to it. "I mean, I couldn't jeopardize my career. All my work. If people found out . . ."

"You didn't want her to move in with you because you wanted to protect your career?" Justin looks at her in amazement.

"You don't know how difficult it is for women to get to the top."

"The feminists wouldn't care if you're gay. I would think they'd like you more."

"They wouldn't like the scandal about Mark and Sandra. That Sandra was my student."

"That Mark *was* your student when you were sleeping with Sandra," Justin says.

"I didn't think Sandra was ready. She got so upset when I told her. She began to cry. I thought she was having a breakdown."

"And what about Mark? Did you care about Mark?"

"You have to believe me, Justin. I didn't intend for any of this to happen."

"But you caused it all the same. You see, Helen, men don't have the monopoly on selfishness and abuse."

"Are you going to report it?" A vein pops out of her forehead. It is thick and blue.

"I think there are things you need to do. You need to find a way to help Sandra."

And you? Do you have to find a way to help Sally? Light as a wisp of cotton the thought rises and then floats out of his head. He gets up.

"I think you need to do some real soul-searching about who you are, Helen," he says. "I think you need to rethink your theories about the abuse of power. Even if Sandra was no longer your student, Mark was. You need to figure out if you weren't still in a position of having power over her. I am sure Sandra wanted Mark to succeed. You had the power to pass or fail him, the power over his grade. I can't understand why you were not able to see that. I can't understand why you were so ready to transfer your guilt to me. But there is a lot I can't understand."

"If it means anything to you, I was ashamed. When I left your office that day, I was ashamed of myself."

Justin has his hands on the doorknob.

"So will you report it?" she asks again.

He does not answer her.

Seconds later he is halfway down the corridor when he hears the brisk patter of feet behind him. He turns. It is Helen.

"You know," she says, pausing to catch her breath, "it was within Sandra's rights to leave Mark."

He stands back against the wall to let two professors pass by. Helen does not seem to notice them. She does not seem to care that they are in a public space, in the faculty corridor.

"She is her own person. She has a right to choose her own life," she says.

"Ideology before people. That's the way it is with people like you, isn't it? It doesn't matter who is sacrificed. Well, people come first, Helen." He lowers his voice. He does so for her sake. "Sandra knew she was attracted to you. She should have told Mark before you began your affair."

"And you think that would have made a difference?"

"He would have felt hurt, rejected, but not betrayed. It's the traitors who are on the ninth circle of hell," he says.

"That is a truly nasty thing for you to say."

He has gone too far and he is apologetic, but he has last words for her. "A person can't just think of his own happiness," he says. "Not if there are others to consider. I bet if you scratch the surface of any middle-class kid on drugs, you're likely to find a self-absorbed parent, a mother, a father at the top of their careers. Some celebrity."

It is not merely a hunch. Justin believes this. Which is why, though Sally may not be fully convinced to stay in their marriage, to raise their daughter with him, under the same roof, he has no doubt about the correctness of what he has asked her to do.

He repeats his conviction to Helen. "A person can't just think of his own happiness," he says.

But is he thinking only of his? Has he put his happiness before Sally's?

SALLY IS ON the phone to Anna when he gets home.

"She said *that*. Oh, Anna!"

"I don't believe you."

"What a fool!" She bursts out laughing.

He comes into the kitchen. Sally sees him. "I have to go," she says and puts down the phone. Traces of laughter still linger on her face.

"You seem to be in a good mood," he says.

"That Anna! She can always make me laugh."

He will not say the thought that comes to his mind: *And I cannot make you laugh? I make you sad?*

"I'm making chicken for dinner."

"Where's Giselle?" he asks.

"Upstairs."

"You seem to be really feeling better."

"I told my therapist what you said. He thought a week in Bermuda was a great idea."

"Good. Then that's settled."

She smiles. "Chicken okay?"

"You don't have to cook. Aren't you going to the movies with Anna?"

"Anna is out. She had somewhere to go."

"But didn't you say that was Anna on the phone?"

"Yes. She called from Manhattan."

"She called you while she's on a date?"

"It isn't a date. She is with a friend. She called to give me a joke. Nothing you'd appreciate." She opens the refrigerator and takes out a head of lettuce. "Do you want salad?"

"Not really," he says.

She puts it back in the refrigerator.

"Is it a girlfriend?"

"What?"

"Is Anna's date a girlfriend?"

"Why do you insist on calling it a date?"

"Well, is it a girlfriend?"

"I don't know. Why do you ask?"

I ask because I won't be fooled this time. I won't be naïve.

But Justin manages to control himself through dinner. They talk about Sally's trip to Bermuda.

Will Daddy go with you? Giselle wants to know. Sally says no. Mommy's going by herself. Mommy wants to remember the good time she had with Daddy on their honeymoon.

Even to a four-year-old child this does not make sense. Then why doesn't Daddy go with you? she asks. Sally has no answer, so Justin volunteers. Because Mommy is tired, he says.

Oh, says Giselle. She remembers yesterday when Mommy went to bed early and didn't even get up to say good night.

Mommy needs the rest, she declares in her imitation of a grown-up voice.

"Yes," Justin assures her. "Mommy needs the rest."

EIGHTEEN

He telephones Anna the next day. He wants to meet for lunch. She does not seem surprised. Is it about Sally? she asks. Yes, it's about Sally, Justin tells her.

They decide to meet in a restaurant near the college. It is a sunny morning, one of those days that seem to mock the griminess of the streets in the inner city. The sky is clear, a luminous blue. The few clouds that hover beneath it are bright white and transparent, thin and light like fresh-washed gauze. They float by like gossamer. A golden sun has warmed up everything: the snow, so it has turned to filthy slush, the garbage so it stinks, the air so it is leaden with the smells of people shuttered up in stuffy apartments, body odor insulated against the cold under layers of clothes worn all winter.

Everywhere people are dressed in black or almost black: young male students in black hooded parkas and black pants, female students in tight black jeans and black leather jackets. They walk by briskly to the sounds of island laughter, for most of them are new immigrants from the Islands, their lilting speech bouncing against the Southern drawl and Northern assertiveness of the African Americans. In between them, shuffling for space on the narrow pavement, are men who have lost hope: the unemployed, the ones battling drugs, the infirm. Their clothes are a collage of dark colors, torn and stained.

None of the women one usually sees early in the morning rushing to work with a string of school children behind them, their faces set in stony defiance of statistics that would denigrate them, are here at this late hour. Only the old, pushing their walkers, their knit hats askew, socks rolled down over thick, worn out stockings.

The sun misses nothing. It illuminates everything: the longing for home in tired eyes. The bewilderment. The disappointment. Regret for the loss of turquoise waters, the sun and the green, chasing after the American Dream.

There are no restaurants nearby where one can sit to eat a meal, only carryout, the vendors behind barred gates like prisoners, so Justin has chosen a church restaurant six blocks away for his meeting with Anna. He frog-leaps over puddles and melting snow. More than twice he narrowly escapes sliding on the patches of ice that have formed on the pavements where the snow melted from the constant stream of pedestrians and froze again.

Anna is there already, waiting for him in her coat. "For

heaven's sake, why doesn't someone complain to the Sanitation Department or to the mayor?" she asks when Justin apologizes for being late, explaining that the icy pavements slowed him down.

"Do you think the mayor cares? No one here voted for him. He cleans the places where people voted for him."

"Well, the past presidential election should tell future mayors a thing or two. Bush may be president, but he almost wasn't. The number of black people who came out to vote this time has to be a wake-up call for him, for any politician. Wasn't it something like ninety percent of black people voted in the last election?" She unbuttons her coat.

"Something like that," Justin says.

"The landlords of these buildings should be made to clear the sidewalks. A person could easily break a hip on the ice. I don't know how those old ladies manage. What about your college, Justin? Don't they have clout there? Can't they get the Sanitation Department to get off their don't-care-a-damn duffs and clean the streets and pick up the garbage?"

For the first time Justin notices that Anna is not unattractive. She is wearing a brown wool dress. When she takes off her coat, the static in the air makes it cling to her body. Before she shakes it out, Justin observes that her stomach is quite flat, her waist defined, and her breasts larger than he thought.

She is wearing lipstick. He can't remember ever seeing her in makeup. Whatever she has done to her eyes, they seem alluring. This is the word that comes to his mind. *Alluring. Alluring Asian eyes.* The thought sends a shiver of fear down his spine.

"I haven't ever seen you so dressed up," he says.

"I had an important meeting this morning."

Justin knows it cannot be anything to do with her work at the college.

"With the president of the Botanic Garden," she adds, responding to the question that has formed on his forehead.

"I hope I didn't force you to have to leave before you wanted to."

"No, we were done. This is convenient. I had only a few blocks to walk."

The restaurant is run by three large women in their fifties. They are no-nonsense businesswomen who know their clientele. They offer three choices on their menu: fried fish, fried chicken, pork chops smothered in gravy. The sides are the same: candied yams, collard greens, potato salad, corn on the cob. Peach cobbler is the only dessert. As soon as he and Anna sit down, one of them comes over. They have taken a table near the corner. Justin has led Anna there on purpose. He will need privacy for the questions he has for her.

"So what are you having?" Anna asks. The woman has just recited the menu. Justin orders the fish.

"I'll have the chicken," Anna says. They agree to share sides. They will have everything except the corn. "It'll get caught in my teeth," Anna says.

All the tables in the restaurant are covered with clear plastic on top of a checkered red-and-white cotton tablecloth. On the wall, next to the table where Anna and Justin are sitting, is a framed photograph of Billie Holiday. The church ladies have hung a picture of the Sacred Heart and a large plaster-cast crucifix on the wall facing the street, but on the other walls they have put their favorite singers: Ray Charles, Ella Fitzgerald, James Brown, Aretha Franklin, Nina Simone.

"Sally called me this morning to tell me that Giselle is all excited about the seeds we're growing. She said that before she left for the sitter's, Giselle noticed that they are sprouting something green. That's what she said. 'Something green, Mommy.' Like it was something from outer space." Anna laughs.

"Sally called you this morning?"

"Yes. From work."

"She didn't tell me that Giselle said that." Justin struggles to suppress his resentment.

"I guess you'd already left for the college."

"No. I was home when they left."

"Then you weren't in the room. It's *our* project, you know."

"Our?"

"Sally's, Giselle's, and mine."

"Sally is my wife and Giselle is my daughter, Anna."

"Yes," she says dryly. "You said as much to me already. And?"

"And any project they have is also my project."

"Nobody excluded you."

Justin clears his throat. He wants to put the conversation back on an even keel. This is not the fight he wants to have with her. "So what was your important meeting with the president of the Botanic Garden?" he asks, and yet he finds himself egging her on. "Not thinking of switching jobs, are you, Anna?"

"I like my job just fine, Justin."

"Because I'm sure the president has to be impressed with all you know about gardening."

The church lady brings their food. She gives the fish to Anna and the chicken to Justin, and when they tell her they had ordered just the opposite, she begins a long story about a man who looks exactly like Justin and always orders fried chicken. "All the Southern men around here love my fried chicken," she says.

Anna laughs. "This is not a Southern man," she says.

"Well, he sure looks like one to me."

She leaves and Anna says, "See, Justin, she took you for an American. You know what they say. All black people . . ." She leaves the rest of the sentence hanging.

He knows she is getting back at him for his innuendo about Chinese food a few days ago. She was none too pleased either with his quip about her interest in gardening. But he lets her have the upper hand. There will be time enough to let her know what he thinks of her.

They eat. They talk. Light banter. If Anna is curious about his reason for inviting her to lunch, she gives no indication. She comments about the food. She says she wishes she could make fried chicken the way the church ladies do. Hers is always too dry, she says, or undercooked.

Justin complains of the many papers he has to correct. Anna says it's the worst part of teaching. Justin restrains himself, but not entirely. It's not the worst part, he says, but yes, the hardest part.

They talk about the cuts the mayor has proposed. Anna says

that just when the immigrants who come to the City University are no longer white, the politicians charge tuition. It is an offering to Justin. She is being nice. Generations of European immigrants have had the advantage of going to college free of charge, she says, but the poor Caribbean immigrants have to scrimp and save.

The church lady brings their dessert. They are talking now about marriage, not Justin's and Sally's marriage, about the marriage of a colleague of Anna's whom Justin knows, a marriage that is on the brink of tottering. The subject is close enough, and after his second forkful of the cobbler, Justin decides to begin. "I was thinking, Anna," he says, "that Sally needs time for herself. Lately, it seems to me, you and she—"

Anna stops him "Look, Justin," she says, "I know we don't get along. I know you don't care for me, but I wanted to have lunch with you today. I was glad you called. I wanted to tell you that I was wrong about you. I had no right speaking to you the way I did the other night. Sally told me."

In spite of his best intentions, Justin finds himself becoming irritated again. "Sally told you?" He puts down his fork.

"That you said she should go to Bermuda for a week. I think that is a very good thing to do. I think that was really thoughtful of you."

"Thoughtful?"

"I think that was really kind of you?"

"Kind? I am always thoughtful and kind to my wife, Anna."

"I know. I wasn't saying—"

"Then what were you saying?"

"Sally has been so depressed lately. I was saying a trip to Bermuda will be good for her. That's all. It will give her a break."

"A break from what, Anna?"

"I'm not fighting with you, Justin. I may not have the right words, but I just want to tell you that I'm glad Sally is feeling better. It was great to hear her laughing on the phone with me last night over my silly joke."

It is the wrong image to put in his mind. It is Sally's laughter that set him off. But they have come to the end of their lunch and now is the time to let her know that he is on to her. He knows her dirty secret. "What is it you want with Sally, Anna?"

The expression on Anna's face changes. The softness vanishes, replaced by a simmering indignation, not yet anger. "What is it I want? Sally is my friend, my best friend."

"I am Sally's best friend."

"I mean after you, of course." Anna smiles, a forced smile that unnerves him.

His jaw tightens. "I know what you are doing, Anna."

"Doing?"

"Working your way into getting Giselle to like you."

"What do you mean? I've known Giselle from the time she was born. Of course she likes Aunt Anna. I take her for ice cream. Okay." She raises her hands in a gesture of surrender. "Okay, I know you don't want me to do that, but I should've thought you'd want her to like her Aunt Anna."

"Not if her Aunt Anna has plans for her mother."

"Plans?"

"To seduce her mother."

"Seduce?"

"You know very well what I mean."

Had he not been blindsided by Helen, Justin would have thought he was in the middle of a tawdry melodrama, something one sees on a soap opera in the early afternoon. And, indeed, it is in the early afternoon that he is having this conversation with Anna. He would have laughed at the character who had spoken his words, regarded them as the simpering ravings of a foolish, weak, insecure, paranoid man. But this is no laughing matter for Justin. He is serious, dead serious, and Anna can see that he is.

She leans over to him, her eyes hard as nails, and whispers: "I like men, Justin. I fuck men. It may not seem to you I fuck at all, but I do. Men. Men who are a hundred times more handsome and smarter than you."

Justin sits back shocked by the language she has used, by the reference she has made to her sex life, by the intensity of her emotion. He has no repartee, nothing he can think of this second to say in his defense.

"I could never figure out how a woman so beautiful as Sally could be married to a stick-in-the-mud shit like you," Anna is saying. She picks up her fork and points it at him. "You are Sally's problem. You criticize her for the books she reads, the programs she watches on TV. You make her feel stupid."

Justin reaches for the glass in front of him. Anna does not let him speak. "That is how you want Sally. You want her to be your little wife who has your dinner ready for you when you come home. You want her to be the mother to your daughter who feeds her, dresses her, plays little games with her. You want her to be a teacher of little elementary school children. But you don't want her to think. You don't want her to write. Because, Justin." She is looking intently at him now, forcing him to face her. "Because she may discover that she does not need you to make her happy. She may find out she can be happy without you. That she can write again without you." She puts down the fork and gets up. "Sally was a good poet, goddamn it." Her voice is strained; it comes through clenched teeth. "I don't know how you can sleep at night, Justin, knowing that she's wasting all that talent."

She leaves without giving Justin a chance to respond, but he comforts himself. He says to himself, to her back advancing toward the coat rack near the front door, "But I don't know that, Anna. I don't know for sure that Sally is a good poet, that she is wasting her talent." All he has read are four poems. All he knows is that they terrified him. And what he believes is that a poet, a real poet, would let neither his terror nor hers silence her.

NINETEEN

Later that afternoon he sees Banks at the college. Mark's back in school, Banks tells him.

He is still thinking of his lunchtime conversation with Anna. Stick-in-the-mud shit is what she called him. "Then I should be hearing from him soon," he says.

"He looks great," Banks says. "That's the advantage of youth. No question about it. You get over stuff real fast."

"I think it'll be a while for Mark," Justin says.

"Don't know about that. Looks like he's back in the swim."

Banks walks with him down the corridor. They are on the side of the building where the classrooms are. It is Wednesday. Faculty like to teach on Wednesdays. All the doors are shut, and though the corridor is empty, it is noisy. It is the kind of noise Justin likes to hear—the sounds of students thinking, seeping out from under closed classroom doors. But today these sounds do not lift Justin's spirits.

"Bet you wish you were home right now," Banks says, stopping in front of a bulletin board in the corridor. He twists his head in the direction of an ad for a vacation in the Caribbean. A blonde wife and an equally handsome bronzed husband are windsurfing on a bright blue sea. From a white sandy beach, the children wave to them—a blonde boy, and an equally golden-haired girl.

"That, there, is not where I come from," Justin says.

Banks misses his point. "Perhaps it's not Trinidad, but it's the Caribbean and I wouldn't mind being there."

"So go at Easter break."

"Wouldn't know which one to take."

"The wives?" Justin asks.

"They both want to come."

"Well, they get along like a house on fire."

Banks frowns. "You making fun of me, man?"

"That's what you told me." He does not want to be mean, but it is hard to feel kindly either, not when he has just been accused of causing his wife's unhappiness. If what Anna said is true, then he deserves the name she called him. Banks makes an easy target. Less painful than aiming at himself.

He turns to walk away but Banks stops him. "They're threatening to leave me, man," he says. "They're ganging up on me. They want me to choose."

Justin knows he wants his sympathy. Banks can barely mask the pleading in his voice. But Justin has no sympathy left to give. Thoughts of Anna, his uncertainty about his marriage, make it impossible for him to give Banks the attention he seems to be begging to get. "That's how it is in the free world, Banks," he says. He shrugs. "Women want more."

Those last words expose him. Banks detects his fear. "Sally, too? I told you you should've asked about those letters. That's some heavy shit, man."

Justin feigns indifference again though Banks gets under his skin. "Hey," he says and throws up his arms.

"I don't know what to do. Things are getting worse at home." Banks remains mired in his problems.

"Decide."

"I can't choose."

Justin steels himself. He wants to separate Banks's troubles with his wives from his. Their situations are not the same. He has one wife, not two. He is going to make things better in his home, not worse. "This Afrocentricity is a bitch, isn't it?" he says, not masking his sarcasm.

But Banks is too absorbed with his Solomonic dilemma to pay attention to him.

IN THE EVENING, after dinner, he talks to Sally.

"Have you decided when you will go to Bermuda?" he asks.

They are sitting in the living room. They are reading. Usually at this time, he is in his den grading papers and she is in the bedroom looking at her tapes of the talk shows. But something has changed between them. A yet unarticulated intimacy has eased them, if not to its ultimate expression, at least to the point where, unconsciously, they seek each other's presence. He has not said any of the words Anna probably would think he should say, but he wants to try. He wants Sally to be happy and he thinks she senses his sincerity.

She looks up from her book. It is not one of those books that are stacked on her night table, offering airy solutions and false promises to the desperately hopeful. He recognizes the dust-cover with its black background, its title in red, a stamped letter wrapped into a scroll and pointed downward in the middle as if it were a dagger. He had brought it home and left it accidentally on the kitchen table. He is glad she has picked it up. Anna is entirely wrong. He does not want a simple wife, a mere mother for his daughter. He does not want a wife who does not think, who does not read books that challenge her.

"I've been wondering if a week isn't too long," she says. "Anna disagrees. She thinks I should go for a week, but I'm not sure."

It upsets him that she has sought Anna's advice, but he is reminded simultaneously of his folly, his stupidity. His desperation. Hadn't he told Banks and Mark that a person cannot be seduced into becoming a homosexual?

"Why is a week too long?" he asks.

"To tell you the truth," she says, "it's not just the length of time."

"Then what?"

"It's the place, too."

"Bermuda is terrific. You loved it."

"You were there," she says. Her eyes drop to the book on her lap as she says this. "That is why I loved it."

It is the second time in only a few days that she has told him she loves him, and he had to ask the first time. Now she volunteers and they are both made shy by her admission.

"Well, I think you should think it over some more," he says.

She returns to her reading and he is angry with himself. He has let the moment pass. There is so much he could have said to her. He could have said, for example, *That is why I will not go there without you, too.* Or, perhaps, perhaps, he could have seized the moment, put an end to the formality still skirting the edges of their conversations, and said, *I love you, too, Sally.* Instead, he has spoken like a counselor, an advisor, a friend. Anna.

Now he wants to begin again, to engage her again. "Do you like it?" he asks, titling his head toward the book.

"This novel?" She uses her finger to hold her place.

"What do you think of it?"

"Have you read it?" she asks him.

"No, I just got it."

"Do you mind if I read it first?"

"No. No, not at all."

"It's about a black man passing. I think the author wants us to feel sorry for him, but I don't see why. Not for the way he hurt his family. To me, he took the easy way out of his problems. But I guess this book was not written for us. I suppose the writer wanted white people to feel sorry for all that black people have to go through, even the ones that pass." She opens the book but before going back to it, she says, "What I would truly like to read is a book where the writer is not feeling sorry for us, but is admiring us for something we have done. This writer does that, but he says it at the end of the book and that is too late for me. It sounds gratuitous."

He has said something like this to Banks. He has said that the emphasis on victimization has obscured all they have achieved, all that could have been achieved if the Europeans had come to trade instead of to enslave. And suddenly he remembers a woman with flowing dreadlocks. Banks had introduced him to her not long after they chanced to meet one evening as he was leaving a restaurant with Helen Clumly on his arm. The woman Banks wanted him to date instead of Helen Clumly was a collector of African art. He remembers her standing in reverent silence in front of a carving of an African warrior.

"It dates back to a time when Europeans were still making scratches in caves," she told him. Then she gave him a lesson in art history.

Their relationship did not last. Why? he wonders now. Was it because he did not like to be challenged by a woman who knew more than he did? Helen Clumly had given him her reason for ending their relationship, but was this *his* reason for breaking up with her? Was she too smart for him? He complained that Sally had turned to reading psychobabble, but he did not encourage her to read other books; he taunted her. When he saw her sliding, he did not help her.

Sally does not wait for his response. She murmurs that she is almost at the end of the book and settles back into the armchair.

It is clear she does not want to be disturbed. But later, before he falls asleep, Justin takes encouragement from this small thing: She is reading a book he plans to read. There is hope. It will not be long, he thinks, before they return to those days, only eight months ago, when they read and talked late into the night, sometimes until dawn.

THE NEXT NIGHT, as she prepares for bed, Sally says to him that she has heard of an ashram upstate. Perhaps it wouldn't be such a bad idea to go there for the weekend.

"When do you have to present that paper in Atlanta?" she asks him.

He lies. "In three weeks," he says.

"Then I can go next weekend."

She picks the weekend of the conference. He does not mind. He is not anxious to go. He does not want to be a problem.

"Anna says I will like it. She's been there."

She is sitting on the bed, taking off her slippers. He closes the book he is reading and turns off the light on his side. He has not left their bed since that night he dreamed of his father. He walked toward Sally. She whispered his name. He kissed her. And every night afterward he has slept here, with her, but they have not made love.

"I wouldn't have thought ashrams were Anna's style," he says.

"Anna says she loves the silence. She goes there to communicate with nature. She takes Wordsworth with her."

Not until now, not until Sally mentions Wordsworth, does it occur to Justin that there could be a connection between Anna's interest in horticulture and the classes she teaches. Could he have been so wrong about her? Twice? When she told him she took her classes on trips to the Botanic Garden, he scoffed silently at her self-indulgence, her lack of conscience. He thought then that not only had she done no research since she got tenure, not only had she switched her interests so completely away from her academic discipline, but she was willing to compromise her students, to cheat them of the literature they should be learning.

"She says she gets closer to Wordsworth's poetry when she is there," Sally says. She lifts the covers and gets into the bed. "She says she understands the poems better."

Make the work accessible and the students will own it. It was his defense to the Great Books committee. *Let the students discover the relevance.* Justin berates himself for his arrogance.

"Anna thinks the ashram would be perfect for me. She says it'll give me the chance to think about all the things that have been on my mind lately."

"Will she go with you?" he asks. He has given up the idea that Anna is gay, but he cannot overcome his jealousy of their friendship.

"Why would you ask such a question?" Sally turns her head toward him. "She just recommended it. Besides, it's a place you need to go to alone, Anna says."

Does Sally confide in Anna more than she confides in him? Has she told Anna about the man she once loved? Has she told her about the poems she wrote for him?

He had dismissed Lloyd Banks in the corridor, but perhaps he was right. He should have asked. When she burned the poems, he should have talked to her then about Jack, found out if her love for him was lasting. If his memory still burns in her heart. If she still thinks of him, *now.*

He begins with an apology he should have made days ago. "I've said some insensitive things to you, Sally," he says.

"About Anna?"

It bothers him that she should think he means Anna, that Anna is the first thought that comes to her mind. "No," he says, "not only about Anna."

"She said you had a fight." She sits up and props up the pillows behind her back.

"A misunderstanding. I was wrong and she told me so."

"She said she had just come out of her meeting with the president of the Botanic Garden when she ran into you. She said you lit into her with your usual accusation about her using her research days for gardening."

"Is that all she said?"

"Yes. Was there more? Did you quarrel about something else also?"

"No," he says. Anna had covered up for him. He will cover up for her, too. "I was stupid not to realize that what she was doing was related to her classes. She was arranging tours for her students on the nature poets," he says.

"You are so hard on Anna."

She is about to slip back under the covers when he tries again. He wants to know if she has settled for him. He has accused her of this. He has said to Banks she married him on the rebound, but he does not want to believe it.

"I want to apologize for what I said about your relationship with Jack," he says.

"That is in the past. I told you so."

"But we never really discussed it."

"I think we did."

What he should say next is that he wants to apologize for calling her passionate love for Jack an illusion, but he takes the escape she offers him. What he does say is what is most on his mind. "I never asked you why you burned those poems."

"I wanted to put them behind me."

"But why did you *burn* them, Sally?"

She hears the emphasis on burn. "Burn them?" she asks.

"As opposed to tearing them up or throwing them in the garbage."

"You ask that as if there is some special significance in my burning them."

"Don't you think burning them is significant?" he asks. *Fire is a symbol for passion. The symbol for passionate love.* He does not have such confidence that he can say this to her. He does not trust himself with her answer.

"Jack was a criminal," she says. "I had burned the others. Reporters were going through my garbage. If I had a shredder, I would have shredded them. Who knows if some ambitious investigator was still following me? I didn't want to leave more trails to me than were there already. Reporters were going through my garbage. I burned them."

The explanation is logical.

"It's impossible to read ashes," she says, and puts an end to the discussion.

TWENTY

The day Sally leaves, the crocuses come out. The sun that had made Brooklyn so ugly just days ago is now forgiving. It melts the last of the snow still left after the rain the night before. It heats up the earth and crocuses sprout in odd places: between stone and rubble, dead limbs that have fallen off bare trees, metal that has rusted in backyards. From the centers of green leaves clumped in bouquets close to the ground, delicate pink, blue, violet, white, and purple flowers push their way out. Overnight it seems there are buds on trees. This morning, as Justin puts Sally's suitcase in the trunk of his car, he notices them for the first time.

"They've been there for weeks," Sally says when he points them out to her. "The tulips will be here soon." In the fall, she had put tulip bulbs in the large cement planters on the pavement, in front of their brownstone house.

Giselle, too, is aware of the coming of spring. "Aunt Anna says we can plant my seeds in just a few more days, Daddy," she says.

"When the ground thaws," Sally tells her gently. "It's much too early. The soil is still cold and hard."

IT IS FRIDAY. Sally has taken a professional day off from work. She reminds Justin that very recently she used a sick day when she and Giselle had colds. She does not want to raise a red flag by using another one. They agree she has not lied: a three-day weekend at the ashram will be good for her personally as well as professionally. She will be a better teacher, they both say, when she feels less stressed.

The ashram has arranged for a bus to pick up its guests and Justin drives Sally to the meeting place. They kiss each other good-bye. There are no tears. Giselle is dry-eyed. "Mommy'll be back before you know it," Sally tells her. "You'll have Daddy all to yourself." The prospect pleases Giselle.

When they get home, Justin calls his mother. He and Giselle can visit if she is not too busy, he tells her. She is not busy, she says. Never for her son or her granddaughter.

The landscape along the Southern State Parkway is different this time. Three weeks ago when he drove to his mother's, the snow was stretched far and wide on the banks of the parkway. Here and there some patches of white still remain, but mostly the ground is covered with a sort of brownish grass, and bordering it, in front of the pine trees, what Justin took for bramble bush the last time he passed here is awash with yellow. Forsythia. A blaze of light surprises him at every turn on the parkway.

"March is coming out like a lamb this year," his mother says when she greets them. "Too bad for the Niña, the Pinta, and the Santa Maria."

Giselle frowns. "Oh, Nana," she says, "don't say it's too bad for Columbus's boats."

Her grandmother bends down and Giselle wraps her arms around her neck. "My, my, what a big girl you are." She returns Giselle's hug and pecks Justin on the cheek. "Nana didn't mean anything by that," she says. She turns to Justin. "She *is* bright. Just like you were. And she looks every bit like you, too. Do you know you look just like your daddy, pretty girl?"

"I look like my Mommy, too, Nana," Giselle says.

"That you do, but you have your Daddy's eyes."

"And Daddy says I'm going to be tall," she says.

"Well, I hope not as tall as your Daddy. He's real tall."

"I'll be in-between tall," says Giselle. "In between Mommy and Daddy. Not too tall and not too short. Just right."

"What a smart child." Her grandmother helps her out of her coat. "And what a beautiful dress you have on."

"We went to take Mommy to the bus and Mommy said I could wear it. It's not my Sunday dress, you know, Nana. It is my second to Sunday best dress, but Mommy said I could wear it because today she went away on the bus."

Justin and his mother exchange glances but say nothing.

"Do you like it, Nana?" Giselle twirls around in front of her. It is a pretty dress. A red and green plaid with a white collar laced at the edge and black velvet trimming around the waist. She is wearing matching red ribbons in her hair.

"She likes dresses," Justin explains when his mother asks if her legs don't get cold.

"When I go outside, I wear pants over my pantyhose. But we didn't go outside today. Not outside, outside. We were in the car."

Her grandmother laughs. "Pantyhose! She's so grown-up."

They walk into the kitchen. "Will you stay for a while?" she asks Justin.

"A couple hours," he says.

"Good. I'll make lunch."

"I don't want you to make a fuss."

"A fuss? It's a pleasure. And young lady, do you want to see the toys Nana has for you in her room?" She grasps Giselle's hand and takes her upstairs. When she comes back down, Justin is pouring water from the kettle into a mug.

"I'm making tea. Do you want some, Mother?"

"No, I've had enough for the morning. It makes me jumpy."

"It's the caffeine. Why don't you drink decaffeinated?"

"Because it doesn't taste like tea. Lord knows what it tastes like, but it's not tea."

Justin reaches into the refrigerator for the evaporated milk. His mother will not use regular milk in her tea either, another habit from Trinidad she cannot break.

"You keep toys upstairs?" he asks her.

"You know I always keep a few for Giselle. I bought her a doll last week. I meant to call you to come for it."

"And why didn't you?"

"Oh, you know. You and Sally. I didn't want to disturb . . ."

"You worry too much, Mother," he says and pulls out a chair. "Come sit with me."

She sits down opposite to him at the kitchen table. "That little girl of yours is so precious, Justin," she says. "I can see why it has to be hard for you to let Sally take her."

Jason bristles. She would remember. He will not let Sally take Giselle away from him, he said to her the last time he was here.

"I think things are getting better for Sally and me," he says.

"She's come around to seeing things your way?"

He tries to keep his voice calm. "Sally and I have been talking," he says. "Like you suggested. We are trying to work things out."

"So what's this that Giselle was saying about Sally taking a bus?"

"She went away for the weekend. To an ashram."

"An ashram?"

"A kind of retreat. You don't talk, you do yoga, you meditate."

"And why didn't you go with her? I could have kept Giselle."

"It's something Sally needed to do by herself."

"When you get married you don't do things by yourself, Justin," she says.

"There are things Sally has to work out alone and things I have to work out alone. We are not doing things separately to be away from each other. That's not why Sally's away. We are doing them separately so we can be together."

She sighs. "The new generation," she says.

"It makes sense for us."

She puts her hands on the table and pushes back her chair. "Good," she says. She gets up.

"Sally wanted to go alone," he says.

She is already next to the stove. "I was worried that you two would start fighting over Giselle." She does not turn around to face him. "That poor child will suffer if you two do that. She's so happy now."

"And we want her to be happy all the time," Justin says.

"Good," she says again.

They are silent now. An awkwardness comes between them, the ancient dance between mother and son. When he needed her, he became a boy, but he does not want to be reminded. He has found his footing again. He can work out this problem in his marriage.

"Sally and I are doing fine, Mother." His tone is conciliatory when he says this.

She smiles. "Pelau is okay for lunch?"

It's a digression, but he lets her to take it. "That would be great if it won't be too much trouble."

"No trouble. Anyhow I bet you don't get much of a chance to eat pelau at home."

He responds cautiously. "Sally's never gotten the taste for pelau," he says.

"She doesn't like chicken and rice?"

"You know what I mean, Mother."

She takes a can of pigeon peas from the cupboard. "You may both be black," she says, "but you come from two different places. The culture is different."

"I've gotten to like collard greens," he says defensively.

"Good." She speaks over the whirring of the electric can opener.

"I like candied yams, too."

She seems not to hear him. "I finally figured out how to thaw frozen meat in a hurry," she says. She opens the freezer. "Do you know how, Justin?"

He shrugs.

"I put it just as it is in cold water. It thaws out in a hour."

He is still wrestling with the need to defend his marriage, but he stirs his tea and waits patiently while she puts a bag of frozen chicken parts in a pot and fills it with water, all the while talking nonstop about the perils of bacteria. "If you leave meat to thaw on the kitchen counter, it can thaw unevenly and then before you know it, bacteria," she says.

He makes assenting sounds; he sips his tea, but when at last she returns to the chair beside him, he stops her. "Do you really think we are so different from Americans?"

As if (as he thought) the subject of Sally has never left her mind, she says, "You mean you and Sally? Yes. That could be a problem."

He drains his mug and puts it down firmly on the table. "Anna said to me that the difference between us and Americans is that they are optimistic and we are pessimistic."

Is this the reason he has come to see her, a nagging doubt that was there years before Anna said it, a fear that the source of his quarrels with Sally is this difference in how they see the world? Is this why the clichés Sally has begun to use, the teas she drinks as panaceas, the talk shows with their Pollyanna solutions to the most debilitating problems, are so unbearable for him?

"Anna? Sally's friend?" his mother asks.

"Yes, Anna. Giselle's godmother," he says.

"Well, if she means that we don't go around seeing everything through rose-colored glasses, I guess she's right."

"She says, to quote her, it's because we come from a world of disappointment and hardship."

"That, too. But I sometimes think that Americans see the world all rosy because they've never had a war here. Oh, I know about Pearl Harbor, but I'm talking about the continent: New York, Massachusetts, California, Wisconsin, Mississippi, places like that."

"We've never had a war either, Mother."

"You think so because your memory is short. What did Anna say? Hardship? Yes, we know about hardship. Our history was built on hardship. First the Spaniards wiped out the Carib Indians. Then the English brought us as slaves from

Africa. You want to talk about babies burned alive? You can't imagine the horrors." When she says this, she shakes her head and presses her lips tightly together. Justin is not certain—for he has never heard his mother utter a profanity—but it seems to him she mutters, *Damn bastards,* before she speaks again.

"Our history was built on wars, and worse than wars. And all those bloods run in your veins, Justin." She points her finger at him. "You have African, Carib, French, Spanish, and English in you: the slave and the slave master. Just like me."

She is giving him a lesson in history he already knows. He has a typical Trinidadian face, he is constantly told, but it is the face of the torturer as well as the tortured, of the oppressor as well as of the oppressed, of the exploiter as well as the exploited, of the conqueror as well as the conquered.

"You're different when you have that kind of history inside you," his mother is saying. "America is a young country. Most people here act like adolescents. They want to have fun and be happy. If you talk to them about death, they shun you. You are depressed, they say. You are pessimistic."

"Yes," he says. He agrees. To most Americans death is an obscene word.

"Still, you have to say that in this country hard work pays," his mother says. "You work hard here and you can get a dollar, and if you get a dollar, you can buy a house."

"Anna says that working hard is all immigrants think about."

"What else is there?"

"I think she wants to say we don't know how to have fun."

"We face the fact we are going to die," she says. "That is the difference. We know life is not meant to be easy."

It is what Justin also believes. He believes that he can achieve whatever he sets his sights on, but only through hard work, only through struggle. It is a triumph over the inevitability of gravity, though a transitory one.

Sally had threatened to surrender. When trouble rose between them, she thought of Anna. A new place, a new page to start over again. He thinks of the trenches. Of waging his battles there and winning.

He finishes his tea and goes over to the sink to put down his mug. "Do you ever look at those talk shows on TV, Mother?" he asks her.

"You watch those shows? A Harvard Ph.D.?"

"No, but Sally does. It amazes me how they simplify the most complex situations, how they pretend the most difficult problems can be solved in a heartbeat."

"Those shows do some good, Justin. I can't say they're all bad."

He comes to sit next to her again. "I think," he says, "they're symptomatic of that difference I was trying to explain to Anna. But I suppose optimism is ingrained in the character of America. You'd have to count us out, of course. Black people I mean. But the whole idea of America is based on people fleeing from persecution, running from a bad situation hoping to find a better one. The Pilgrims. Immigrants."

"Don't forget that's what we are, Justin."

They have boxed themselves in a contradiction. His mother glances in the direction of the staircase. "I wonder if Giselle is hungry," she says.

Before she can call out to her, Justin says, "But we don't go around wearing rose-colored glasses."

"Yes," she says.

"We are optimistic about the rewards of hard work."

"I suppose."

She calls Giselle and Giselle answers immediately. She comes bounding down the steps toward them. "Nana, I love it. I love it. Thank you, Nana." She is clutching the doll her grandmother bought.

His mother turns her attention to her. "So what shall we call her?"

Justin leaves them huddled over the doll and walks into the living room.

Nothing much has changed since he used to come here on semester breaks from Harvard. His mother has modernized the kitchen, but she has left the rest of the house just as it was when she lived here with his father. The furniture in the living room is as unattractive as he remembered it, but it has sentimental value to her and she refuses to change it. The sofa is upholstered in blue crushed velvet and the two armchairs next to it are covered in a plush white fabric with a busy floral pattern that matches the blue in the sofa. The coffee table is made of pressed wood painted dark gold. It has scalloped edges and curved, ornate legs. The only contemporary-looking piece of furniture in the room is the plain white bookcase. The books there tell his father's story: the Greek tragedies and comedies, volume after volume of Shakespeare's plays, the Neo-Classics, the Romantics. African American writers are on the second shelf, West Indian writers on the top, the great Trinidadian intellectual CLR James placed prominently in the middle. V. S. Naipaul is given a special place, too, for Naipaul had not yet regretted his origins when Justin's father was alive. Walcott is not there, but his father had not known of Derek Walcott, who was just beginning to get recognition for the poetry that would earn him a Nobel Prize. From the row of anthologies that contain his father's poems, Justin picks one. He is reading a long poem when his mother comes into the room.

"I've given Giselle a sandwich and she's taking a nap with her doll. You don't mind a late lunch, do you?"

"I'm fine, Mother. I'm not hungry."

She glances at the book in his hands. "Your father's poetry?"

"Yes," he says.

She sinks into one of the armchairs. "Why do you stay here, Justin?"

The question catches him by surprise. "In America?"

"Yes. In America."

"I stay here because I am married to Sally and Sally is an American."

"But before you were married, when you finished at Harvard, why didn't you return?"

"I guess I lost touch with my friends back home," he says. "Like you did."

"Ah," she says.

"And you were here." He is standing close to her. He shuts the anthology with his father's poems and holds it against his chest.

"Yes," she says.

He is unsure of this strange mood that seems to be settling on her. Her eyes have drifted back to the book in his hand. She is staring dreamily at it. "It's true, Mother," he says. "I stayed because you were here."

"But you didn't want to come back with your father and me when we came for you." She turns away.

"Dad died," he says.

"I didn't."

He sits in the armchair next to her. The book rests on his lap. "We both agreed, Mother, that it turned out better for me, right? I mean the scholarship and all that. It was better that I stayed, right?"

She sighs. "There is something else we can learn from those talk shows on TV. Americans don't keep secrets as much as we West Indians do. We hide our dirty laundry."

He braces himself. "And isn't that a smart thing to do?"

"Dirty laundry stinks after a while," she says.

He knows there is more to come.

She bites her lower lip. "You never asked about me. You never asked if it was easy for me. I don't mean after your father died. I had a job then, a real job as a nurse. I had American credentials. The hospitals hired me. I am talking about before. Before, when your father was alive."

Before, when his father was alive, she was happy. *Sophie Anderson and James Peters: Ah, there was a marriage made in heaven.* Wasn't that what everyone said?

"Your father had a life beyond me. I had nothing beyond him," she is saying.

Did everyone also know there was another woman, an American girlfriend?

"Dad loved you," he says.

"Oh, I know he loved me," she says, "but he didn't understand what I needed. He was a celebrity. People loved him. I had to work. Poetry didn't put food on the table, you know."

Justin knows. "Dad was grateful," he says. He knows it was her money that paid for their house.

"Don't get me wrong. I didn't mind being the one to bring home the money. I never reproached him for that. But he thought I was happy being a caretaker for that rich old man. He thought it was the same as nursing. But it was baby-sitting; that's what it was. It wasn't nursing. He didn't know how unhappy I was."

Justin is taken aback by this admission. He does not know how to respond.

"Being a wife is not enough for a woman," she says before he can find his voice. "Not even being a mother." She leans forward and surprises him again. "That's also true for Sally."

She knew. That was why she had not asked him what Sally meant when she said she wanted more. Still, she had clicked her tongue and murmured disparagingly, *These modern women.*

"In moderation, Justin," she says. "That's how we can have it all, a career and still be a wife and mother."

SHE HAS NOT been inconsistent. On his way back home, Justin acknowledges this. A year ago when a female student complained about his insensitivity, accusing him of being a macho man, a chauvinist pig, a woman hater who had no place in a college where there were women, she had taken his side and said the same thing: in moderation. Everything in moderation. That's how women can have it all.

The student had been absent for four weeks. When she finally showed up, it was not to class, but to his office. She came with a toddler straddled on her hip, a boy not more than three tugging her skirt, and his sister, perhaps a year older, lagging behind, her thumb in her mouth, her eyes rounded dark with sorrow.

Justin remembers that while she was reciting her litany of troubles, the multitude of reasons that had made it impossible for her to come to class, he was looking at her daughter. Giselle was all he could think of.

Go home, he said to the student. Take care of your children.

Don't you know that what you do with them when they are young will affect them all their lives? You have to prioritize.

Later that night when he puts Giselle to bed, he thinks, Sally has prioritized. She is a good mother; she is a good wife.

But he is also forced to admit: Sally is not a happy mother. Sally is not a happy wife.

TWENTY-ONE

Banks calls Saturday night. Justin has already put Giselle to bed and is reading in the den.

"Where've you been? I've been trying to reach you all day."

"I took Giselle to the museum, then we went to the park, then there was a birthday party. I forgot to buy a gift, and so then—"

Banks does not let him finish. "Have you heard the latest?"

"What?" Justin is tired, whipped from a day keeping up with Giselle. He is not ready for a long conversation with Banks.

"Helen Clumly," Banks says.

Justin perks up immediately. "Helen? What about Helen?"

"Rumor has it that she's got an offer she can't refuse."

"A book deal? A fellowship?"

"Some say book deal, some say fellowship. I only know for certain she's left the college."

Good, Justin thinks.

"In the middle of the semester. In the middle of the freaking semester." Banks is shouting.

"Now?"

"She's gone. She cleaned out her office yesterday."

"Just like that?"

"That's the problem with these white faculty. They don't have the commitment. She just dropped everything, her classes, everything. Her students will be in an uproar come Monday."

"Some," Justin says.

"Some students?"

"Some of the white faculty," Justin says. "Only some of the white faculty don't have the commitment. And, for that matter, neither do some of the black faculty."

"Freaking bullshit. There you go again, Justin, with your everybody's-the-same bullcrap."

"It must have been a real big offer," Justin says, wanting to end his ranting.

Banks chastises him some more and when he cools down he says, "Well, there are people who are saying there was no offer at all. It's a big sham."

"Then why would she leave?"

"That's the big mystery on campus. Of course, the feminists are blaming you."

"Me?"

"They say you were having an affair with her. Everybody knows you two were an item."

"Used to be," Justin says.

"Couple of people heard you arguing in the faculty corridor the other day. They say she was shouting and you were whispering all intimate like, as if you had something to hide."

She had something to hide. "I'm not having an affair with her or with anybody else. You know that, Lloyd."

"I know that, but you can't convince the femininos. The phones are ringing. They have you down on two counts: one, for cheating on your wife, and two, for messing over Helen."

"And what count do they have Helen down on?"

"Can't say. She just left a note saying she was quitting. Nobody's been able to reach her, I hear. She's cut off her telephone and she doesn't answer her doorbell."

Justin feels vindicated. He feels at peace. The world has righted itself. Justice has been meted out. The punishment has fit the crime. Helen Clumly was not fired, of course, but not having a job is what she deserves. When he gets off the phone with Banks, he is filled with such a sense of satisfaction that he allows himself to think kindly of her: in the end she had a conscience. In the end, she did what was right.

He picks up his book and settles back down in his chair. He reads one page but cannot finish another. His mind drifts. He is thinking again of Helen, thinking how readily she surrendered the values he thought were so important to her. (More than once they discussed it: the professor is not merely conveyor of knowledge, but she is role model. She has an obligation at least to try to embody the values she espouses.) Could it be that Helen was able to delude herself into blaming him for Mark's attempted suicide because her career was so important to her?

He tries to refocus again, but the words on the page blur, they merge into each other.

Her career mattered to her, his mother said. Being a nurse mattered to her. He had thought it was his father. He had thought her job was no more to her than a paycheck, and later, an occupation that filled the emptiness when his father was gone.

It was so unlike her, this confession, but she pointed to his father for her unhappiness, and, if not directly, to him by implication for Sally's dissatisfaction.

He puts down his book and picks up the phone. It was her life's work Sally said she wanted, and he responded with a sneer.

He dials Anna's number.

"It's the stick-in-the-mud shit who's married to Sally," he says when Anna answers.

She laughs, and he knows she has forgiven him. "At least the stick-in-the-mud shit had the sense to encourage her to go to the ashram."

"It was your idea," he says, then hesitates and offers a more substantial olive branch. "You probably saved my marriage."

"Not so fast, Tonto. It takes more than an ashram to save a marriage."

"I know. That's why I am calling you."

"Me?"

"Do you know anything about that small press where Sally was working?"

"Defunct. Closed down. Kaput."

"Was she writing poetry when she was there?"

"What are you getting at, Justin?"

"Well, was she?"

"Yes," she says.

"Look, Anna, I know all about the poetry Sally was writing when she was living with Jack."

"You are wrong, you know. She did not marry you on the rebound."

His back stiffens.

"She knows you think that," Anna says.

"What did she tell you?" It is an effort to make sound leave his throat.

"She should have taken more time for herself. To recover. It was big blow she took from Jack."

"So she said what I thought."

"She didn't say that. I am saying that."

"Space," Justin says. "She said she needed space for herself." *That is what Sally told him.*

"I don't think people necessarily have to be in love when they marry," Anna says. "The best marriages are those where two people fall in love with each other during the marriage."

His heart lurches.

"I have learned a thing or two from my parents' marriage," she says. "Westerners scoff at arranged marriages. They think Asian husbands and wives don't love each other. They think Africans don't fall in love because someone arranges the marriage, but people fall in love with their partners if they are kind to them. My parents are happy. They love each other."

"So Sally is not in love with me?" Justin manages to ask the question.

"You are the one who can help her."

"She sees a therapist. But I suppose you know that." Why hadn't he asked Sally to tell him what she discussed with her therapist? The closest he had come was the night he felt her slipping away to that oblivion that swallowed up her mother. Was he afraid that if he asked she would say, *The therapist said it was too soon. I was still in love with Jack?*

"The therapist does not love her," Anna says.

"She seems to think he can help her."

"He has. He has helped her understand why she gets depressed."

"It's only recently," he says. "In the last few months. She was not depressed before."

"There," Anna says. "I told her that. I told her it's a phase."

"A phase?"

"Sally will get over it as soon as she starts doing something that is meaningful to her."

He does not say, *Our marriage should be meaningful to her.* He says: "Like writing again?"

"She had started. She was trying," Anna says.

He swallows the knot in his throat. "When?" he asks.

"About a year ago. I think she wrote for five, maybe six . . . She stopped completely about seven months ago."

A month after Giselle's half birthday.

"She wanted to surprise you," Anna is saying. "You would have liked the poems she was writing."

"So you have seen them?"

"I wasn't supposed to tell you."

No, he won't be so foolish to say, I am Sally's husband. What do you mean you are not supposed to tell me? If anyone is *supposed* to know, it is I, her husband.

"I think it's important for me to read them," he says.

"She loves you, Justin. In answer to the question you asked, Sally is in love with you."

He is silent.

"I can't say I like the things you do, or the foolish, overblown image you have of yourself," she says, "but that apparently doesn't bother Sally."

"I wouldn't be so sure," he says.

"She loves you," Anna says again.

"Like a wife in an arranged marriage?" he asks.

"I would have left you months ago. Especially after you threatened to take my child. Sally isn't stupid. She knew she could have left you and taken Giselle with her. The law would have been on her side."

It is not necessarily true. He could have gotten joint custody, but he cannot deny she could have left him and taken Giselle in spite of his threats. She could have made him a part-time father. He cannot deny that he had not forced her to stay. "Will you give me the poems?" he asks again.

"I'm not sure," Anna says. "I don't know if Sally would approve."

"You said she wanted to give them to me."

"That was before. You know, before you and she . . ."

"You said I am the one to help her."

"Yes," Anna says.

"I want her to help her. I want her to be happy."

He senses her turning over his answer in her mind, weighing it, judging him. "When you read the poems, you'll see how good she is," she says at last.

"So can I have them?"

"I suppose I could give you the ones she had planned to show you."

"Can you fax them?"

"Now?"

"Sally comes back tomorrow."

"Can't you wait?"

"No," he says.

"I suppose . . ."

"So, now?" he asks.

"I want you to know, Justin," she says, "I did not tell Sally to leave you."

"Now, Anna?"

"I'll fax them," she says.

"You're a good friend to Sally, Anna."

"I would have left you, but all I said to Sally was that my apartment was open to her."

It is an apology. Or Justin takes it as such, for he believes, he is convinced, Anna's invitation, however well meant, had made it easier for Sally. Without that, without a place to go, somewhere for Giselle, Sally would not have said, as she said that evening when he came home with tulips and the intention to save his marriage, *I think the best thing for me to do is to move out, don't you think?*

"It's okay, Anna," he says. "It's in the past. Put it out of your mind."

SHE FAXES TEN. He reads each one three times, changes for bed and then picks them up again. It is past midnight when he puts them down. They are poems of loss, of betrayal, of hidden selves. Of selves longing to be revealed. They are not poems about him, about their relationship. If at first, when he began to read them, he was disappointed to find that they are not, he is not now. They are poems of great power and beauty. They leave him speechless.

One poem, though, troubles him. It is not Sally's, but Anna has faxed it along with the others. At the bottom of it is an inscription: *To Sally from Dennis Nurkse.* Either Anna has not realized that she has sent it, or Sally had placed it there between her poems and wants it to be read with hers. A married man, a planter of fruit trees, reflects on his love for his orchard: *I loved them best in winter / when I could see them all in one glance / no longer hidden by wind or each other, / as I could never see that woman / from start to finish.*

The poem is dated at a time before they were married, before they ever met, when she was still with Jack. It is not a love poem written to her. Justin does not think this Dennis was her lover. A friend who cared for her, he thinks. So why then did she keep his poem with hers? Because it pointed to Jack accusingly? But if so, does it also point to him? He asks himself the two questions the poem demands: Is it the wife's fault that her husband cannot see her from start to finish? Or do the fruit trees he loves so much block his vision?

Then he remembers the night of Giselle's half birthday. A clod. That was what he was not to have understood the depth of her expression of love for him. Was it too late? Had he so blocked her vision she no longer saw herself in him?

LET BE. Afterward the stage is bloody. No, Justin says to himself when he turns off the light next to his bed. He will act. He will do something. He will not have a bloody stage.

TWENTY-TWO

First he has to get the boxes. This means he has to be at the supermarket early, before they unpack the groceries.

Anna calls at seven. She has forgotten to tell him that Sally asked her to take Giselle to the movies. That's perfect for him, he says. He needs a couple of hours. He will drop Giselle by her apartment after breakfast.

"Did you read the poems?" she asks.

"Yes," he says.

"What do you think?"

"They are extraordinary," he says. "I am at a loss for words."

"You?"

"They are powerful. I didn't know she was that good."

"I told you. I tried to tell her, too."

Was he so absorbed with his failure as a novelist, wallowing like a gluttonous pig in self-pity, that he could not see what a poet she was? Is.

* * *

HE WAKES GISELLE. She is irritable. "I want my Mommy," she says.

"Mommy'll be back tonight," he tells her.

"I want Mommy *now*."

"Come, Giselle. Get up for Daddy."

She gets off the bed. "When tonight?" she asks him. She is rubbing her eyes.

"After we're finished with the things we have to do."

"Like what things?"

"Come and be a big girl for Daddy. Daddy has to go to the grocery store early this morning."

"Why?"

"To get boxes."

"Why?"

"To pack my books."

"Why?"

"I'm moving around some furniture," he says.

"I want to help. Can I help you, Daddy? Can I?"

He tells her Aunt Anna is taking her to the movies. She can help when she comes back.

Her face brightens slightly. "When?" she asks.

"After breakfast. I'm going to drop you at her apartment."

"But I want Aunt Anna to come *here*. I want her to see the plants." She is whining. "They have leaves on them. I want Aunt Anna to see them *now*."

"Aunt Anna can see them when she brings you back from the movies."

"But I want her to see them *now*."

This peevishness, Justin knows, is there because she is missing her mother. "We'll go out for breakfast," he says.

"For pancakes?"

"Yes," he says. "After we pick up the boxes."

JIM GRANT IS sitting on his stoop when Justin comes out with Giselle. "Told you," he says. "Matter of time and the snow be gone."

Justin laughs. "Jim Grant, the prophet," he says.

"My daddy's taking me out for breakfast," Giselle announces. "Then after that, I'm going to the movies with Aunt Anna."

Jim Grant pats her head. "Getting to be a big girl."

"But before we go out for breakfast, my daddy's taking me to the store to get boxes. My daddy's moving furniture today."

Jim Grant raises his eyebrows at Justin. "Moving?"

"Not a chance."

"Good. Neighborhood's changing fast. Hardly see one of us these days on the block."

They get there on time for the boxes and are almost too early for the restaurant. It's Sunday and they serve brunch, but not until ten. It's nine-thirty when Justin and Giselle arrive, but the owners know them. He, Sally, and Giselle are frequent customers.

"Where's Sally?" The wife unlocks the door.

"Taking a little vacation," Justin says.

"What I wouldn't do for one of those," she says and rolls her eyes.

The ceiling at the restaurant is covered with drawings made on paper placement mats like the ones in front of them on the table. There is a container filled with different colored crayons there, too. Giselle reaches into it and pulls out five crayons. She draws a house and colors it red and blue. In the house she draws a brown man in black pants and a black shirt, and a brown woman in a yellow dress. It is the picture she often draws. This time, however, she adds another figure, a smaller version of the woman in yellow. She puts this tiny figure between the drawing of the man and the drawing of the woman.

"You, Mommy, and me," she says.

Justin smiles at her, but he is saddened. Not long ago she reprimanded him for asking why she had not drawn herself into the picture of Sally and him. Has he made her feel insecure? "Always," he tells her.

After breakfast, Justin drives her to Anna's house. She makes the same announcement to Anna that she made to Jim Grant, but with a slight difference.

"We got boxes because Daddy's moving," she says.

"Oh?" Anna looks at him quizzically.

"Furniture," he says. "I'm moving furniture."

Anna does not interrogate him.

HE HAS PACKED one box when the phone rings. It is Mark.

"Want company?"

"Sure," he says. "Come."

But before he is halfway through packing the second box, the doorbell rings.

"You must have been nearby."

"On the pay phone at the corner," Mark admits sheepishly.

"You look great." Justin means it. Mark has shaved off his hair. Gone are the dyed blond tight curls that reminded Justin of a toga-clad attendant to Caesar, albeit a black one. Bereft of hair to frame his face, Mark's features are more pronounced: his wide brow and abrupt chin, his proud nose that flares slightly at the end, his perfectly shaped full lips. But his eyes are sad. Justin thinks, as sad as they were when he last saw him at the hospital.

"I feel good," Mark says. He smiles, but Justin detects he does so with difficulty. He takes off his coat. He seems smaller, his shoulders not as wide.

"You lost weight?" Justin asks.

"A pound or two. Plan to put it back on in a couple of days."

"You can start now. Hungry?"

"Famished," Mark says.

Justin pats him on the back. "Scrambled eggs okay? Or omelet?"

Mark says omelet and Justin leads the way to the kitchen. He takes cheese, tomatoes, and eggs from the refrigerator. He gives the cheese to Mark.

Mark takes a knife out of the butcher block on the counter. "You have it perfect here, Prof," he says.

"I bought at the right time. When you graduate and start earning money, you can buy a place, too."

"I didn't mean that." Mark begins to cut the cheese.

"Then what?"

"Not that you don't have a great place. I mean look at this big kitchen." He turns around. "The flowers in the pots on the window sill, the garden outside. Don't get me started about the living room and dining room." He points the knife to the orange Le Creuset pots hanging from the ceiling. "I wouldn't dare to put my pots there, but these . . . French, right?"

"Mrs. Peters's the decorator." But Mark knows this. He has been here before. Sally has given him the tour.

"You have a beautiful house, Prof," he says.

"But that was not what you wanted to tell me, was it, Mark?"

"I would give anything to have a family like yours," he says.

Justin avoids his eyes. "You'll have a family one day, too, Mark."

"You have a beautiful wife and a beautiful child. The perfect marriage."

"No marriage is perfect."

"I'd want mine to be as good as yours."

"It will be," Justin says. He resists the temptation to say *I hope it will be better than mine.* His marriage is good. He plans to make it better. "Do you want to put something else in your omelet?"

"Like what?"

"Check the refrigerator."

"What do you have in here?" Mark has his hands on the door of the refrigerator. "I'm the omelet meister, you know."

Justin grins. "Take what you want."

Mark opens the refrigerator, stops, turns. His eyes look pained, his mouth stiff at the corners.

"What?" Justin asks.

"I heard the rumor, Prof."

"Oh, that." Justin's face relaxes. For a second he thought something more had happened to Mark.

"I was at the college on Friday," Mark says.

"Professor Banks told me you've been back since Wednesday."

"I came by your office but you weren't there," he says. He lowers his voice. "I don't believe what they're saying about you."

Justin takes a bowl from the cupboard and throws the tomatoes he has just cubed in it. "Don't worry, Mark," he says. "It doesn't bother me."

"They're just jealous because you have the perfect family," Mark says.

"I don't listen to that trash," Justin says and reaches for the eggs.

"Most of them have nobody," Mark says.

"Let's forget it, okay? I think there's some leftover chicken in there." He cocks his head in the direction of the refrigerator. "It should be good in your omelet."

Mark searches the refrigerator and pulls out a dish covered with clear plastic wrap. "Are you sure we can use this?" he asks.

"Absolutely," Justin says. He cracks open four eggs. He has had too much to eat at the restaurant but he will sit with Mark.

"Does Mrs. Peters know?"

"Huh?"

"About the rumor they're spreading," Mark says.

"No," Justin says. "But it won't matter to her, either. She knows the truth." *He will tell her later. She knows he is not having an affair. That is not their problem.*

"I wouldn't want Mrs. Peters to be upset," Mark says.

"She won't be."

Mark has put the chicken on the counter but he has not yet unwrapped it.

"Are you going to use that, yes or no?" Justin asks.

Mark seems not to have heard the question. "I wanted you to know, Prof," he says, "I know it's all a pack of lies."

The sincerity in his voice makes Justin uncomfortable. "There are some people who live for gossip," he says. "I ignore them." But his hand falters as he beats the eggs and he has troubling maintaining the brisk pace he started.

"I came to tell you that I know they are lying," Mark says.

Justin clears his throat. "That was good of you," he says.

"And to see how you're doing."

Finally, at last, shame washes over Justin. He puts down the egg whisk. "You must think I am an insensitive good-for-nothing, Mark."

Mark looks at him, puzzled.

"I should be the one asking you how you are doing."

"No," Mark says quickly. "You came to see me in the hospital."

But Justin knows that is not enough. It does not exonerate him. Banks told him that Mark had returned to the college, yet he had not gone in search of him. Sally, Giselle, his own troubles with finding a way to make them a family again had so absorbed him, he had not stopped to think, to bother to find out, if Mark needed him. Mark had lost the woman he loved, his soul mate. He had had a brush with death, but he is here, at his house, because of a rumor he thought could hurt him, the same Mark that days before tried to protect him from discovering that a woman he dated in the distant past was a lesbian.

Is this what professors do? They profess but do not believe? They have no obligation to be, only to say? He has spoken to Mark about shame and responsibility, about human decency, about the need in a civilized society for people to care for one another, but he has spoken about these things through the prism of literature, through characters in books. Banks had called these worlds make-believe and he defended their relevance. But does that relevance apply only to the students and not to the teachers? It is Mark who is decent here, who puts aside his own troubles to worry about his.

"Have you seen Sandra?" The question comes too late.

"We're talking."

"Good, good," he says. "Thinking of getting back together?" His need at that moment to have things right for Mark, to see again that spark that no longer shines from his eyes, propels him to this fantasy.

"No. Not a chance. She's gay for sure. Friends. That's all we are now." Mark grins. "Want to hear a joke, Prof?"

Justin returns his smile.

"You should see us. We are real pitiful. There is Sandra crying over Professor Clumly and there I am crying over Sandra."

It is not a pretty picture. "You'll get over it, Mark," he says. "You'll see. I guarantee that soon you'll have someone."

"Like you do, Prof?"

He decides to tell him, to air his dirty laundry. "Sally was thinking of leaving me," he says. "I don't have the perfect marriage." Yet if he were truly honest, if the truth is what he really wants to face with Mark, he would have said *is*. Sally *is* thinking of leaving me.

"Nothing works anymore, does it, Professor? I mean, everybody's getting divorced these days. Nobody stays together."

"It's a different world, Mark. We think we have so many more options. The grass is greener, but we end up snagging ourselves in all the choices we think we have. Can you guess how many types of toilet paper you get to choose from? We have exchanged the big things to be snarled in a quagmire of little things, a dizzying array of petty choices that can squish us. But all the while the big things are being taken away from us. Nobody knows who his neighbor is anymore. Fewer and fewer children live with both their biological parents. And we happily tell ourselves stepparents are just as good. The more the merrier. Children get to have two mothers and two fathers instead of one of each. I wonder who we think we're fooling? Not the children, I can tell you. Not the lonely men and women out there who would do anything for a history beyond a year or two with someone they love. Dig deep, Mark, not wide. That is what I plan to do."

He believes what he says, and, in this instance, he is practicing what he believes. The more will not be the merrier for Giselle. She will have one mother, one father. He will have a history beyond the five years he has already had with Sally.

"Yes," Mark says. "That's what I will do. Dig deep, not wide."

A new intimacy is sealed between them, yet all through breakfast, while Mark devours the omelet they have made together and Justin sits next to him sipping orange juice, a question hovers over the stories they swap, still unasked, threatening to put a lie to the honesty from which this new friendship was forged. They are standing near the front door when Justin finally gets the courage to ask it.

"Why did you do it, Mark? Why did you try to kill yourself?"

"Depression. I was overwhelmed. I couldn't see any reason for living."

"But why that way?" Justin comes closer to Mark. "Was it the poems, Mark? Was that it?"

"I had been reading them. But no, it was not the poems."

"Then what I said about Plath?"

"I can't remember what was going through my mind. I was in a fog. I was looking for a way out."

"And then you remembered what I said. Is that what happened, Mark?"

"I don't know. A lot of people do it that way. I was in the kitchen. I saw the oven."

He puts his arm across Mark's shoulders. "I'm sorry," he says. It is an apology this time; it is not an expression of sympathy. "Truly I am, Mark." He wants to say more. He wants to say he should not have been so irresponsible. "I should have said something. Explained. I should not have said it that way. I was not thinking."

"You didn't do anything wrong."

"I told you . . ."

"Chaa, Professor."

"I should have been more careful."

"Don't say that. Don't say that." Mark returns his embrace. He puts both arms, not one, around Justin's shoulders, and draws him close to his chest.

Justin's throat constricts; the tears do not surface, but after Mark leaves, he berates himself. He is guilty, in spite of his protests to Helen Clumly. He must bear some responsibility. He is the mentor; Mark is his student. How lightly he had considered his pain, how little significance he had given to it, dismissing the furrows that rose on Mark's brow, the anxiety in his voice, as no more than melodramatic expressions of the pangs of an adolescent infatuation.

He should have taken the time to tell him that the way Plath ended her life was tragic, an immeasurable loss of a future that promised so much.

But Mark has taught him. With his selfless assumption of responsibility for Sandra, he has exposed his teacher's self-centeredness.

He was not wrong to tell Mark he had not caused Sandra to

be a lesbian, but he could have listened more carefully. When Mark blamed Halle for Sethe's unspeakable act, the murder of her infant, he could have paid attention. He could have heard his point about the rightness of Sethe's rejection of her husband's excuse: Halle was not there to help her.

Is it enough for a man to say he has troubles of his own, pain of his own, that *Things get to him*? Shouldn't a husband be responsible for the safety and happiness of his wife and children?

"God," Sally's mother said before they were married, "will make you responsible for my Sally's happiness."

He had vowed for better or for worse. He had promised to honor and cherish. Sally is responsible for finding her life's work, but he, her husband, ought to help her. He should cherish her.

God's sprinkling of stardust, as Ursula Henry had called it—His grace—falls on Justin then, so Justin will think years later. For his confidence soars after this admission, after this acceptance of the part he played in Mark's descent, in Sally's unhappiness. And though he will admit there was nothing he could have done to earn it, it is, nevertheless, now that he receives this gift of an unshakeable certainty in what he is about to do. He will not look back.

He must act, he tells himself again. He knows what he must do to stop the unraveling of his marriage.

TWENTY-THREE

He has four hours: two before Anna returns with Giselle, two before it is time for him to meet Sally at the bus station.

When Mark leaves, he increases his pace. He picks up four, then five, books at a time and piles them in the crook of his arm. He bends down and deposits them in the boxes on the floor and straightens up again. His back aches from the bending and the reaching, for he has to stretch his arm to get to the ones on the top shelves, near the ceiling.

He could have asked Mark to help him, but he wants to do this alone. This is his responsibility. This is something he has partially caused. He had offered to share his den with Sally, but he had done nothing to prove he meant it. Maybe, perhaps, perhaps if Sally had a room that was hers where she could think, dream, she would not have lost hope.

The den is the same as it was when they married and Sally

moved in. The desk he used in his office, at his former college in New England, is here, in the corner, at an angle that gives him the advantage of the windows and the door that leads to the rest of the house. It is a small desk, mahogany, with brass fixtures. There are books and student papers on it. They crowd the desk, but do not make it untidy.

The space in front of the desk, where he works, is covered with a brown leather-bound mat that Sally had given him one Christmas. The matching container, filled with pencils and pens, is at the left of the mat, his computer to the right. There is no space on this desk for Sally's things. There is no space in this room for Sally's things.

The Oriental rug on the floor came from his old apartment, the gray-and-white striped sofa was in his old living room, the pictures on the wall have sentimental value to him alone: an old photograph of his parents, a picture of his aunt, two of him, one with his schoolmaster at St. Mary's when he won the scholarship to Harvard, the other when he graduated from Harvard. There is a framed watercolor on one wall. It is a painting of the sea, Maracas at dawn in Trinidad, the eastern end, where the fishermen pull in their seines before the beach becomes cluttered with bathers and their paraphernalia: boom boxes, umbrellas, plastic chairs, pots of food served from the trunks of cars, liquor that makes the laughter raucous.

If Sally wanted to use this room, where would she sit? On the chair at his desk that is locked to his height? On the cushion softened to his weight? Where would she work? Among the clutter on his desk, and when she cleared it, in the space that seemed to have his name on it? And her books? Where would she put them? On the bookshelves already crammed with his?

Only his books are here: the ones he used at Harvard, the ones he taught in New England, the ones he teaches in Brooklyn, the ones he was given as presents, the ones he is currently reading. These are the books he is packing, though he has not yet considered where he will put them. He has cleared three shelves and filled two boxes when where finally occurs to him. He will put some on the bookshelves in the living room, some in his office at the college, and some, because there are too many, he will leave here, in the den, on the top shelves, where they are not as accessible. He unpacks the books and re-sorts them.

He is replacing the last of them on the top shelf when Anna rings the doorbell. He does not hear her. She rings again, three more times. He still does not hear her. She bangs on the door. She shouts. "Justin!" Giselle shouts. "Daddy!"

He is thinking of Sally. Of what he will say to convince her. *Stay,* but he does not want to force her. *Stay,* but he wants her to do so willingly.

A book falls out of his hand and tumbles down the height of the room. The thud it makes merges with the banging on the door. When the book settles, the noises separate. In seconds he is at the front door.

"Lord, I thought you'd gone deaf, or had gone out somewhere," Anna says.

Giselle jumps into his arms.

"She was getting nervous," Anna says. "She was worried you had moved with your furniture."

"Oh, Giselle, Daddy's never, ever moving from you." He kisses his daughter.

"Told you, Aunt Anna."

Anna shrugs and makes a feeble attempt to explain she had suggested no such thing.

"I know." Justin shakes his head. "Children."

"I was sure you were home, Daddy. Extra, positively, very sure." She remembers these words from the ending of a story he read to her.

"Did you like the movie?"

They walk into the living room, Anna following closely behind them. "There were monsters," she says, and makes a face.

He looks at Anna. "She wanted to see it," she says.

"My friend Carol said her Mommy took her," Giselle says. "But I didn't like it. Not at all."

"Why didn't you leave?" he asks Anna. "She'll have nightmares."

"She wanted to stay."

"I had to see it all," Giselle says. "Carol will call me a crybaby."

"You are not a crybaby." Justin hugs her and puts her down. "You are a big girl."

"I'm sorry, Justin," Anna says.

But he is chastened now. He, too, should have been more responsible for the charges in his care.

"I took her for pizza," Anna says.

"Good. So you're not hungry, Giselle? You can wait 'til we have dinner with Mommy?"

"Told you Mommy's coming today," Giselle says to Anna.

Anna laughs. "And I told you that, too." She tugs her braids. "She's looking forward to seeing Sally," she says to Justin. "When she wasn't talking about the furniture you're moving, she was talking about Sally coming home tonight."

"I'll eat with Mommy," Giselle says to Justin, and she pulls Anna's hand. "Come see the plants, Aunt Anna. They got real big."

Anna passes close to Justin. "Making some changes?" she asks Justin.

It is evident she has noticed the new row of books on the top shelf of the bookshelves in the living room where there were photographs.

"For the better," he says.

After Anna leaves, Justin continues to reorganize the bookshelves in the den. Giselle helps. She gets excited when he tells her it's a surprise for Mommy. Can she keep a secret? he asks her. She will not say a word, she says. Then it will be your secret and mine, he tells her. But when will he tell her mother? she asks. Late at night, he says. Can she keep a secret until morning? Cross her heart and hope to die, she says.

When he is finished rearranging the bookshelves, he begins to work on the pictures. He takes down the photographs of his parents and his aunt, and the painting of the beach at Maracas. He will hang the photographs and the painting in the hallway, outside the bedroom, but only after he has shown Sally the changes he has made in the den.

He removes the print of jazz musicians in New Orleans from the bathroom wall. It is a cheap copy that most certainly has no value, but it belonged to Sally's mother. Sally wanted it hung on their bedroom wall. He opposed her.

The space it leaves is obvious and he realizes immediately it will be obvious too to Sally. He wants to talk to her first. He wants to explain before she misunderstands his intentions. He replaces the print on the hook, adjusts it to its original position, and, satisfied, bounds down the steps to the dining room, Giselle following closely behind him. He picks up the framed photographs of Sally, at her graduation at Spelman, from the credenza, and bounds back up the stairs again.

He is breathing heavily when he gets to the den. His heart is racing. He presses his finger into the pulse at his wrist. Giselle looks up at him, worried. "Just need to sit a moment," he tells her. But first he arranges the three photographs of Sally carefully on the desk.

This is right. This feels right. The fear in Giselle's eyes when she flew into his arms had unsettled him. If he finds the right words, if he says the right things, Giselle will know—he and Sally will make her secure in knowing—they will always be here for her.

He slumps down on the couch and Giselle snuggles next to him. He is not a young man. He is approaching fifty. His father's age, he reminds himself.

Later, on the way to pick up Sally, he stops at the soul food restaurant. He has not had time to cook, but he does not want to eat surrounded by strangers. For tonight he means to make a change. For tonight—the thought comes to him in the simplicity of a platitude he despises—he and Sally will begin the first day of the rest of their lives.

Sally is the fourth person to come out of the bus. She smiles and waves at them. He waits for her in the car. Giselle is jumping up and down in the backseat. When Sally slides in next to him, Giselle throws her arms around her neck.

"Not so tight," Sally tells her and turns to kiss her.

"Glad you're back," Justin says.

"Me, too."

"I missed you, Mommy." Giselle kisses her again. "Daddy missed you, too."

"I missed you all," Sally says. She looks rested. The darkness under her eyes has faded. The furrows on her forehead have disappeared.

Giselle is bubbling over with news. She tells Sally that her grandmother said it was too bad for the Niña, the Pinta, and the Santa Maria. "Nana didn't know that is the names of Columbus's boats, Mommy," she says. "I had to tell her."

Sally knows the old joke her mother-in-law plays with Justin. "You had a good time at Nana's?"

"She gave me a doll. A pretty, pretty doll."

"Oh, Nana spoils you, Giselle."

"I'll show you when we get home, Mommy."

"What else did you and Daddy do?"

Giselle winks at her father. Sally misses the secret signal between them.

"Anna took her to the movies," Justin says quickly. "And I took her for pancakes."

"Pancakes? So that's what you two do when I'm not here."

Giselle giggles. "But Daddy bought you soul food," she says.

"Sorry. I didn't cook," Justin says, but he knows Sally will not miss this attempt to please her. Soul food, though he eats it, is not his favorite food.

"A treat for me, too," she says.

Justin smiles. "That ashram seems to have done you some good. You look great," he says.

"It's peaceful there," Sally says.

"And what did *you* do?"

"At the ashram? Sleep, eat, walk, yoga, meditate, sleep and eat some more." Then, as if in an afterthought, she adds, "Oh, yes, I did some writing."

"Poetry?"

"No. No, nothing like that. In my journal," she says. "I wrote in my journal."

WHEN THEY ARRIVE at the house, he unlocks the front door and walks quickly ahead of them to the kitchen. He switches on the light. It is sufficient to illuminate their way through the living room, but not enough to expose the books he has placed on the top of the bookshelf, or the empty space on the credenza where he has removed Sally's photographs. He knows, like Anna, Sally notices everything.

Giselle helps him unintentionally. She hurries Sally to the back of the house. She wants to show her how much the plants have grown. Aunt Anna, she says, told her she must have been a really, really good girl because plants don't grow that fast.

Later that night, after they have their dinner, Sally gives Giselle her bath and Justin reads a bedtime story to her. Sally sits on the rocking chair while Justin reads, and when Giselle begins to nod off, she gets up. She is unpacking her suitcase when Justin comes into the bedroom.

"How was Giselle?" she asks. "Did she give you any problems while I was away?"

"No. Not at all. She was an angel."

"An angel?"

"Well, to be honest, I wasn't unhappy when Anna came this morning to take her to the movies."

Sally smiles knowingly. "Giselle can be a handful," she says. "Anna is really good with her."

Justin agrees.

"You two getting along better?"

"Trying," he says.

She continues to unpack her things. He wants her to tell him more about the writing she did at the ashram, but he is unsure how to begin. "I'm glad you got the chance to write," he says.

"Yes," she says. She is moving back and forth in the room, from her suitcase to the drawers in the armoire. "I think I know exactly what I'm going to do in the weeks that are left before school lets out for the summer."

He is puzzled. "School?" he asks.

"I got a chance to work on my lesson plans at the ashram."

"But you also wrote in your journal, right?"

"That's what I wrote in my journal," she says.

"Lesson plans?"

"Well, thoughts I had in the day about projects I could make for my students. Ideas for trips. That sort of thing."

"I thought . . . ," he says. He begins again. "I hoped when you were there, you would write. Poems, I mean."

She is carrying a folded sweater to the drawer. She stops and turns toward him. "There were a lot of people in that ashram just like me, Justin, all agitated about life's meaning, life's work. But the truth is we were just afraid." She wraps her arms around the sweater and pulls it tightly to her chest.

Justin thinks of a life preserver. It could be that she is holding on to, a woman treading water.

"You know that old fear of getting old, dying," she says. "Confronting your mortality. It's so common at my age. I can't see why we are surprised by it." She loosens her arms and puts the sweater in the drawer.

"And are you afraid, Sally?"

She had her back to him when he asked the question (she was bending down to put away the sweater), but he is certain she grimaced. He is sure her shoulders lifted and stiffened. The movement was barely perceptible, but it was perceptible to him.

"Afraid?" she asks. There is a slight fluttering in her voice, but it disappears altogether and hardens when she asks the question again. "Afraid of what?"

"Of getting old. Dying. Is that what was happening to you?" He says *was* for he senses she wants him to think it is in the past, whatever it was that had troubled her. It is over now. She has resolved it.

"I *was* afraid," she says. "Forty comes so suddenly. Suddenly you find yourself thinking that there is not much time left. You must use the time you have carefully, do the things that are important. You think of all you should do, could do, should have done."

"And have you thought of those things?"

"At the ashram I got a chance to think of them and I realized I had it all. Giselle, my marriage."

She does not look at him. She does not say his name. She says Giselle's name. She says *my marriage*, as if it were an entity apart from him, apart from her.

He wants to tell her he has changed; they can start again. He knows he could lose her if they do not work this through.

"Before I was forty I never once thought of the person I could have been had I never left Trinidad," he says. "Then cracks began to appear in the stories I told myself. I felt like you did when I was forty. Sometimes, even now, I am haunted by the person I might have been had I not stayed here."

She frowns. "I do not have your regrets," she says.

"Oh, no, I don't have regrets." He speaks quickly. It is not his intent to hurt her. "If I had not stayed, I would not have met you. And that," he adds, catching her eye, "would have been the biggest regret of all."

She softens. "I know you miss it sometimes," she says.

"Not as much anymore. I am living exactly where I want to be. In this house. In Brooklyn, with you, with Giselle."

"Still, it must be hard for you."

He takes the chance now. He wants a real wife, a real partner, a friend, a lover. "Are you living exactly where you want to be, Sally? Are you doing exactly what you want to do?"

"I want to be a teacher," she says. "I want to be a wife, a mother."

"A few days ago you said that was not enough."

"That was before I went to the ashram."

"And one weekend has made such a difference?"

"I thought this was what you wanted," she says.

"I want you to be happy. I want you to do what makes you happy."

She takes off her skirt and then her blouse. She puts on her bathrobe. She does not speak.

"I was wrong," he says, "to suggest, to say—"

She stops him. "No. You were right. I have everything."

He cringes.

"At the ashram I met a lot of women who would die for what I have."

The words are exactly, almost to the letter, the words he said to her that day when he claimed she had no cause to be dissatisfied with her life. No cause to be dissatisfied with him.

"Is that what I said?" He knows it is.

"Most of the women there were raising children by themselves. They had to depend on relatives or friends. Some had been abused. Some had nowhere to live. I have this, this house." She spreads out her arms. "I have a lot. Meditation calmed me. I was restless. Now I'm calm. Now I know all those things I said were just my fear of growing old speaking." She walks into the bathroom. When she comes out, she is ready for bed. There is no chance for him to tell her now, to show her what he has done to the den.

She kisses him, but not on the lips. He touches her breasts and she moves his hand away. She is gentle, but she is firm. "Not now," she says. "It's been a long day."

TWENTY-FOUR

But it is not only her fear of growing old. She will not convince him of that. When she woke up that morning, the skin below her eyes jet black from lack of sleep, she said it was space. Space for Sally was what she wanted. It took another argument for her to define it. *I want to write poetry. I want to be a poet.*

Why does writing poetry frighten her?

It was jealousy, he acknowledges, that made him take that leap to Jack, his fear that though it was he she married, Jack was the man she loved. That it was those floodgates she did not want reopened. That she had grown tired of scouring street walls night after night, in search of graffiti. So she compromised. So she settled for him.

But Anna says Sally loves him. And isn't Anna right? Eight months ago, on Giselle's half birthday, Sally said she saw her face in his. It had taken her a lifetime, but she had found her love at last. He was her soul mate. He, Justin. He was that and more. So it cannot be Jack. If Jack, it cannot be all Jack, not after those sweet words.

Forty? That, too, is not the answer. Whatever it is that has lulled her into this state of—he struggles to find the word—compliance (an ugly word that causes him to grimace), it will not last and he does not want her this way.

He asks for grace. No words. He is not a praying man, not even a true believer. An apostate. For when he was a boy he used to pray, but nothing happened. His parents did not return, not when he needed them. Nine years later, it was too late. Still, deep in his heart a prayer comes: *Tell me why, Lord. Let me find the answer.*

He knows the cost to Oedipus: this hubris, this disbelief, this reliance on reason, this insistence that it is limitless, that the human will is invincible. How many times has he pointed this out to his students? How many times has he said to them that reason, intelligence, or will alone cannot give us answers to the mysteries of human existence, cannot lead us to the truth?

And he remembers something else: a plane trip, the grinding noise that filled the cabin when the plane ascended. He was seated at the window. He could see the flaps on the wings shuddering, unable to close. It struck him then that though we had achieved what Daedalus could only dream of, we had arrived no further: We were still at the mercy of God. He could strike us down, or save us if He wished.

So he will take his own teaching. He will submit. He will let reason yield to that which it does not, cannot, comprehend.

On her deathbed, Sally's mother told him it could happen—grace—the bestowing of a gift on the nonbeliever.

Let me put away my jealousy, Lord.

Then it happens. Out of nowhere, a number enters his head. *Four.* It comes to him, a soft tingling in his ear, a feather fanning his chin. Not a sound. He will not remember it as a sound. A revelation, a tiny epiphany. Not one that jars him, that forces his eyes to open, for not all is revealed. It is a clue he receives, a hint of the truth. A gift, but he must find his way.

Four. He turns and pulls the covers to his neck. *Four.* He flicks his hand through the nothingness around his ear.

TWENTY-FIVE

It is Sally's face Justin sees first the next morning. It is dark. Gray. Tears are pooling in the corners of her eyes.

Justin! Her lips form a word. His name. He rubs his eyes.

Justin, I know you can hear me.

She is in her bathrobe. Her hands are on her hips.

Justin! she shouts again.

The bathrobe is open. Her fingers at her hips pull it further apart. Her nightie shimmers, a mesmerizing blue, and beneath it, brown breasts rise.

"How could you?"

Desire grips him. His eyes drop downward to the roundness of her belly, her navel sunk in the well he adores.

"How could you?" She is asking the question again.

He shakes himself alert. When he looks at her again, her lower lip is shaking. "How could I what?" He throws off the layers of sheet, comforter, blanket piled on top of him and swings his legs over the side of the bed.

"Do such a thing," she says.

He is still not fully awake. He glances at the clock on the dresser. "It is five o'clock," he says.

"What I want to know," she says, "is why. Why have you removed my things?"

"Removed?" The word reaches his tongue and the fog clears in his head. It will be now, this morning, they will have their talk, not later, after work, after dinner, when Giselle is in bed. "Have you been downstairs?" he asks her.

"Yes, I have been downstairs."

"I can explain," he says.

She does not let him. "Why have you touched my photographs? I never touch anything of yours. Those were my personal photographs. Photographs of *my* family, of *my* mother, *my* father, *my* brother."

"Sally. Sally, listen." He stands up.

"Isn't it enough you have a whole room to yourself? Must you control the other rooms, too?" The tears simmering in the canal of her lower eyelid are not tears of grief or pain or mere anger, but tears of indignation. They do not fall down. "You had to remove my books, too. My father's books. They were mine, Justin, not yours. But, no, the great professor had to remove them. The great professor needs more space for his grand collection. No, the den alone wouldn't do. Four bookcases that reach the ceiling won't do. They are not enough for the Nobel laureate."

He knows nothing he can say now, while she is in this state, will calm her. He puts on his robe and then reaches for her hand. "Stop. Stop, Sally," he says. She pulls away. He reaches again and holds her firmly. He tightens his grip. He lowers his voice. "Stop," he says.

She swings her free arm around her waist and clutches the small of her back.

"I can explain, Sally."

She purses her lips.

"Come," he says. "Come with me, Sally." His hand encircles her wrist. "Come." He says so gently.

"Where?" But she does not fight him.

"Come, and afterwards you may say whatever you want to me."

They are standing close to each other now. He can, if he wants to, kiss her on her mouth, but it is a real kiss he wants. He believes, he is sure, that when she sees the changes he has made, she will want to kiss him back.

"Come." He leads her to the den. He opens the door.

She sees her photographs immediately. "What? Why?" She breaks free from him and walks over to the desk.

"I didn't adjust the chair," he says, but she is not listening. "I didn't know the height you'd like."

She picks up a photograph, the one of her mother. "Why, Justin?" Her fingers trace lightly over it.

"I want you to begin to write again."

She down puts the photograph and looks around. "Your books?" She gestures to the empty bookshelves.

"Space for yours," he says. "I've already put some of them there."

She presses her hand against her mouth.

"Not a journal," Justin says. "Not lesson plans. I want you to write poetry."

The canals at the bottom of her eyelids flood.

"You are a poet," Justin says.

She shakes her head. Tears fall down her cheeks. She does not dry them. Justin puts his arm around her shoulders. "Sit," he says. He sits with her, but her body is rigid next to him on the couch.

"Why?" Her hands are clasped tightly in her lap.

"Anna let me read the poems you gave her," he says.

"Anna had no right," she says.

"I asked to see them."

"She shouldn't have given them to you," she says.

"Anna is your friend," he says.

"I can't." She moves away from him, to the center of the couch. His arm falls limply to his side. "Anna was wrong," she says.

"You can," he says. "You should. Anna believes it, too. You should write again."

"It's too late," she says. Her voice quivers.

"You are an incredible poet. I was a fool not to see that."

"I can't." The tears fall heavily on the neck of her nightie. The fabric, thin, transparent, sticks to her skin, three brown wet splotches in the midst of a diaphanous blue.

Justin gets up and brings back a box of tissues. He wipes

her face. He blots the top of her nightie. "You can, Sally. You must," he says. He does not try to embrace her. He waits. *He will wait.*

"I told you. I told you, Justin. I can't. I can't deal with the grays."

Why? It is the question he must answer.

"Gray is all we have," he says. For now, this is all he knows.

"I want the black and the white," she says. The tears have stopped. "I want life to be simple. Life is easier when it's simple. It's better when it's simple."

"You don't believe that, Sally."

"Grays get me confused. Grays get me in trouble."

"Not grays, Sally. Seeing only black and white will get you in trouble. It has gotten the world in trouble. But the truth is we are imperfect beings. We are flawed, and no one is absolutely beautiful or absolutely ugly, absolutely good or absolutely bad, absolutely right or absolutely wrong. There are no right choices, only better ones."

He is conscious, as he speaks, of seeming to lecture, and he does not want to lecture, not to her. He is in his house, his home, not in his classroom. He is speaking to Sally, his wife, not to his students.

She sits up. "And yet you want to tell me what is best for me and Giselle."

It is too late. The tone he used, the manner, was of man certain of himself, an opinionated man, an academic, who in spite of what he has just said, thinks and speaks in absolutes.

"You want to tell me that what is best for Giselle is for you and me to live together. You tell me *that* is the right choice."

"No," he says, making an effort to shift his tone, to speak with the voice of a husband, lovingly, with concern for her. "I think it is the better choice."

"I don't know how you can be so sure," she says.

Do. Act, he told himself. But it is not working.

"Are you still thinking of leaving me, Sally?" He is trying to keep his fear in check, but the words sound strained, artificial. Melodramatic.

"Giselle loves you so much," she says.

"She loves you, too. Yesterday, when she woke up, the first thing she did was to ask for you. Anna says she talked about you all day."

She looks down on her hands. "It's these grays," she says. "I hate these grays."

"I should not have insisted. I should not have said what I said." He is filled with remorse. "I saw how unhappy Giselle was that day you were crying in the bathroom."

"I didn't want her to know," she says.

"She wasn't fooled. She knew you were unhappy. I told her you were tired, but she knew something was wrong." He berates himself for his stupidity, his insensitivity. "I know it will not be good for Giselle if you are unhappy staying here, Sally. I want you to be happy here."

Her eyes remain cast down on her hands.

"That is why I put your things in the den," he says. "I

want you to stay, Sally. I want you to write, here, in this den. It's yours, Sally."

"No."

"I've fixed it for you. You can put your books here when you are ready."

"No. It's your office."

"You can write here."

"No." But she looks up at him. "And what about you?" she asks. "Where will you work?"

"I have my office."

"And your papers? Where will you grade your papers?"

"I can work in the kitchen. There's a big table in the kitchen. Close the door, Sally, and write."

"Write what?"

"Write what you feel."

"It got me in trouble," she says.

He takes a deep breath. "Passion is not an illusion. I was wrong to tell you that."

"It *was* an illusion."

"The man you created was the illusion. What you felt was not an illusion." He breathes deeply again, down to a place it seems he has never been. It is not a sigh he emits. Nothing like a sigh. There is no sadness lurking in the air that pours out of him. If he could name it, he would say it is joy. It is a feeling, he would say, of reckless relief that propels this breath forward, out from his chest. "Four," he says.

"Four?"

He, too, can make no sense of the number, the dream he had (was it a dream?).

"Four?" she asks again.

He connects it to the present. "Giselle is four," he says.

The last time she said she loved him, the last time she said it from her heart, they were celebrating Giselle's half birthday. Then the long spiral downward began. On Giselle's fourth birthday, for the very first time, she turned away from him in their bed.

"Yes," she says, puzzled at a statement so obvious to them both. Her eyebrows merge.

It was a clue. He can see that now. But a clue leading to what? Suddenly he remembers an argument he had with Lloyd Banks: You like to be in control too much, Banks had said. Loosen up. Go with the flow. The jockey won't win the race if he holds on to the reins too hard, even if Secretariat is under him.

He loosens up. "You were four when your father died," he says. More words come. "Giselle had just turned four when you began looking at those shows and reading those books." He understands.

She never forgot that night in Alabama. The men in white hoods, her father's blood curling into the dry dirt, red, then brown like manure. Her therapist was wrong. This loss she suffered, this hurt that has come back now and paralyzed her mind so that she will not, cannot, find her way through the grays of poetry, was not caused by Jack. It was caused by something more than Jack, something that had happened much, much earlier than Jack: her father's murder. It was that that had left its mark on her.

"I think those are the grays that frightened you, Sally. That time when your father died and your mother had a breakdown."

"No," she says.

"You felt abandoned."

"No," she repeats.

"You said your father was reckless and when you changed your mind about that, you said you admired him. He had the courage of his convictions, you said. But you never acknowledged what he had done to you."

"My father loved me," she says quietly.

"Yes, Sally. But you were only four years old. You were a little child. To your little child's mind, he had left you."

"Not intentionally," she says.

"No, not intentionally. But that is how it felt to you when you were four, Sally. You felt he had left you intentionally. That is what you were afraid to admit. You preferred to hide in your room."

"I did not hide in my room."

"You didn't want to come out because you were afraid to be loved, to be hurt again."

"I loved to read. That's why I stayed in my room. I told you that."

"If you spoke your feelings, if you admitted that you felt your father had abandoned you, left you alone to fend for yourself, you would have to condemn him, you would have to admit he was not a good father to you. You could not face that, Sally. You needed to have a father you could love, you could admire, even if that father was not physically there."

"You're wrong. I didn't think of those times too often," she says.

"How could you love a father who had abandoned you?"

"You're wrong," she says again.

"Jack Benson helped you not think of those times too often," he says.

"Jack?"

"That's why you stayed with him."

"Jack was an evil man."

"But he said he loved you and you believed him."

"Jack was a bad man."

"I think when you burned his letters *(Let me read the ashes, Lord.)*, you were not only burning his memories, but the memories he helped you forget."

"When I was with Jack," she says, "I thought Tony was happy. I thought he was getting better. Jack was talking to him. I thought Jack was helping him."

"You needed to believe that, Sally. You wanted your brother to be happy. But I think all along you knew Jack was not the man he pretended to be."

"Tony was trying. I know he was trying, but Jack was so evil."

"You created the man you wanted, you needed, in the poems you wrote. You could not afford to be abandoned twice, once by your father and then by Jack, but that man in your poems was not the man you lived with. The man you lived with and that other man were two different persons."

She is quiet, breathing softly next to him. *He too could not afford to be abandoned twice.* He tells her so now. "When my father died, I felt he had abandoned me."

"He had a heart attack," she murmurs.

"Yes, and I was much older than you were when your father died, yet I blamed my father for dying. If he had loved me enough he would have lived for me. It was an irrational thought, but that was how I felt."

She looks away from him.

"I created an illusion, too, Sally. When my parents went away I pretended I was strong, but the truth is that many nights I cried myself to sleep. I swore I wouldn't let anyone hurt me like that again. I clamped down. Look how old I was when I got married. I would not commit to anyone, could not, until you, Sally. But I loved you so much it didn't matter that I was afraid you could leave me, too, that you loved Jack more than you would ever love me."

It is taking him courage to admit this. But this courage that comes to him now is not of his making. Even as he speaks, he thinks of himself not as himself, but as some other person who has invaded his brain, put words in his mouth: a puppeteer with his puppet, a ventriloquist with his doll.

"That is not true," Sally is saying. "I don't know if I ever loved Jack. I don't know if the Jack I knew ever existed."

"It doesn't matter. You have a right to love Jack as much as you want. I just want you to love me, too."

"I stayed with Jack because he was there."

He knows what she means. "I used to think that my parents didn't have to live in the same house I did. Just in the same country. That would have been enough for me."

"But I didn't love Jack," she says.

"He helped you."

"Not in the right way," she says.

"Not in the right way," he concedes.

She bites her lip. Her eyes are teary when she releases it. "Dad had a choice," she says.

"Yes," he says.

"And he made the right choice."

"Yes," he says.

"He didn't want to leave me."

"No, Sally, he didn't want to leave you."

A quiet grows between them, a calm that seems to envelop them. They have made peace; they are friends again.

"Everything came back so suddenly," she says. "I thought I was okay again. I had you, Giselle, the kids in my school. The books were helping, the shows on TV. But they were not enough to hold back the memories."

"We can't burn memories. We don't heal; we continue."

"I can't continue if I am weighed down by baggage."

It is the fundamental difference between them: her belief in the American myth of the Do Over; his resignation to the impossibility of the tabula rasa.

"We are who we were," he tells her, "and who we will be."

He does not convince her.

"It is what it means to be human," he says. "It is why we

need each other. It is why I need you. It is why you need to write."

She cannot accept all that he says. Not totally. "I am not sure," she begins.

So he tries again. He wants his marriage to work, and not just because of Giselle. He loves her. And there is more: he wants no more memories he has to bury, no more losses, no more history he has to repress. Trinidad is enough.

"I will never abandon you, Sally," he says. Tentatively, because he does not know if she will move away from him again and his arm will drop foolishly to his side, he embraces her.

She stays. She lets his arm remain where it is, hugging her shoulders.

"You are safe with me, Sally," he says. "Don't be afraid. If we face the grays together, we both won't be so afraid."

She comes closer to him.

"I want to know you, Sally," he says. "Unburden yourself of those memories in your poetry. Write so we can know you—Giselle and I."

She smiles and he seizes upon her change of mood.

"Giselle has your gift," he tells her.

"Giselle?"

He tells her that when he read his favorite passage from Shakespeare to Giselle, she asked, *Twangling like birds?*

Her smile widens. "Twangling like birds?"

"She has a natural ear for poetry."

He had said Giselle was his spitting image, but it is from Sally she inherits this talent.

"You have to teach her," he says. "But not like me. Teach her by doing."

She slips her hand in his. "I won't abandon you, either," she says.

He folds his fingers over her hand. "Do you still see yourself in me?" He dares to ask the question now.

"You resemble me," she says.

Eight months ago when he thought that that was what she meant, she said no. She said she meant more than that. "I see *me*," she said. "When I look at you, it is *me* I see."

It is enough for him. For now, it is enough that she says she resembles him. She loves him—he has no doubt—but he will have to be patient. It will take time for her to surrender to that dizzying abyss, to that place where self merges into other self, where two are fused into one. He will have to earn her confidence. She will have to learn to live with her past.

"Stay, Sally," he says.

"Yes." She lays her head on his chest and closes her eyes. "In an hour," she says, "we must wake up Giselle."

We.

Grace.